IN THE CLAWS
OF AN ANGEL

IN THE CLAWS
OF AN ANGEL

Jean-Paul Robert

English translation: Michael Bayliss

*(Original title: **Dans les griffes d'un ange**)*

About the author

Author of crime novels based upon historical events, Jean-Paul Robert has always stood firm in his commitment to narrate and use history without compromising or betraying said history. A principle always followed in his writing, be they novels, testimonials or historical monographs.

Jean-Paul Robert managed the international business aspects for a large industrial conglomerate. In this capacity, he discovered the diversity of outlooks and cultures. Presently retired, he devotes himself to his writing but without neglecting volunteer work and his love of sport, be it cycling, jogging or golf.

His writings and novels have garnered two awards : Short Story Prize in the Spring of 2015, Short Edition, and 'Prix de l'Ile' in 2016.

About the translator

Michael Bayliss read French and Latin at Royal Holloway College, University of London, and gained a Master of Arts degree from Birkbeck College, London, specialising in the works of François Rabelais. He also holds the degree of Master of Science in Organisational Behaviour from Birkbeck College. He has been a schoolmaster, an officer in the Royal Navy, a senior education officer in Kent and deputy Director of Education for a local authority in London, retiring in 2001.

For many years, Michael has also pursued activities as a freelance translator. He Is a keen francophile, a member of the Société d'Histoire Chinon Vienne & Loire (formerly Les Amis du Vieux Chinon) and the Association des Amis de Rabelais et de La Devinière, and was inducted in the 'Caves Painctes' of Chinon as a Chevalier of the Confrérie des Bons Entonneurs Rabelaisiens. Having himself stayed at the Château de La Vauguyon and translated the history on its website, he is well acquainted with all the places and institutions described in this book.

To David & Cyril, my two sons

To my wife Danièle

To Jeanne, my aunt and first proof reader, too soon departed

To you, my friends and readers

CHAPTER 1

SAVIGNY-LE-TEMPLE: ARCHIVES OF THE MINISTRY OF FINANCE

The building stood in a prominent position, surrounded by lawns. It proudly flaunted its modernistic design which, essentially, was an ostentatious and optimistic statement made by a civil service that was very sure of itself and of its future. It was five storeys high and consisted of eight blocks linked by long columns of windowed stairways. The sides of this edifice were covered with cylindrical decorative elements which, viewed from three-quarters on, gave the inescapable impression that it been put together with giant Lego bricks. A central tower of glass and metal over the entrance made the whole structure look perfectly symmetrical. At this early morning hour, the doors were at last being opened to let in those few researchers who wanted to consult the precious documents stored within it.

The complex had an air of serene calmness about it, due perhaps to its elaborate external decoration. The smiling faces in the reception area ensured that this ambience was maintained inside the building.

An ambience that was reassuring, but deceptive. At that very moment, some distance away from the plush waiting room reserved for visitors, principal archivist Pascal Aupetit had just cut short his telephone conversation and made an angry gesture, holding back the stream of invective that was on the tip of his tongue. He missed the old-style dial phones which allowed you to slam down the handset on its base and induce premature deafness in the caller.

He thrust his phone into his pocket, wondered whether to show his disapproval by starting the day with a stroll over to the coffee machine, paused for a few moments, then sat down at his desk and stared hard at the classification folder as if trying to hypnotise it or make it rise in the air.

The screen of the computer next to him, which hadn't been switched on in months, watched him with a deadened eye.

The archivist had ginger hair tending to grey in an extraordinary mixture of colours which, together with his general air of world-weariness and the white overall coat he always had on, made him look more like a run-down laboratory assistant than an alert civil servant in the Finance Ministry. However, his put-upon appearance was contradicted by the liveliness of his eyes, in perpetual motion, and by carefully toned muscles that were scarcely noticeable under his overall.

He got up slowly, pushing the folder away from him. It was almost as useless an aid as the computer that had been wished on him by one of the section managers. He had no need for complicated equipment like that to find files in HIS archive room, the one he'd been in charge of for the best part of his career! His memory rarely failed him, and he returned the compliment by taking pride in it. In all circumstances. Or nearly all…

Forgetting his coffee for a moment, Aupetit walked along the faultlessly-arranged rows of shelving on rails that occupied the huge room. He stopped when he came to the marker he'd been looking for, then slowly turned a chrome steel hand wheel, causing the twenty or so storage cabinets on his right to move out effortlessly into the space he'd just created.

He picked up the two filing boxes marked *May-June 1940* and slid them over to his trolley.

"Not too heavy," he muttered, "and the ones after this will be even lighter."

Between the 'phoney war', the catastrophe, the Armistice and the aftermath, so many documents had disappeared or been destroyed by bombs or in fires that only a small part of them remained. These had often been filed away as a job lot, without any attempt at classification. The priority after the war had been to rebuild, to salve the wounds of a society that had been torn apart and had lost everything. Nobody cared about archives…

Pascal had the disagreeable impression that he was now reliving this same lack of interest, ever since senior management had decided to computerise all the records, transforming memories of the past into incomprehensible electronic data. From that point on, the same unchanging scenario had been played out almost every day: he'd spend some time ranting on the phone, then do as he'd been instructed, waiting for the masters of the digital world to come and take away some of his old files. Today was the second batch. At this rate, he wouldn't be able to last out until retirement...

His dislike of computers had started with the invasion of the scanner and the destruction of the world in which he'd built up his professional career. He had progressed after that to reject anything imposed on him by directives and decisions, recalling only the negative aspects. He'd once been an enthusiastic innovator but had now become devious and conservative, trapped in a vicious spiral of bitterness and resentment.

He wheeled his loaded trolley to the office where he recorded the files that were being taken out.

In the present circumstances, Aupetit confined himself to a daily routine that he was continually trying to simplify: a cursory glance over the batch of documents, then a brief check of the bundles and their dates. What was the point in putting any more effort into something that he knew in advance would be a waste of time?

He nevertheless paused when he came to a sheaf of papers stapled together, some of them badly folded and out of alignment. Conscientious by habit, he automatically picked them up to put them together properly.

"The war was a catastrophe even for the paperwork," he murmured, as he took the sheaf apart.

The thinness of the document encouraged him to take a rapid glance at its contents, but he stopped at the second page, taken aback, and then continued reading with considerably more attention. The two sheets that followed made him increasingly intrigued.

"I don't believe it," he muttered at regular intervals.

He hadn't finished reading when he was interrupted by the sound of the lift announcing the imminent arrival of the scanner technicians. He hesitated, wondering what to do, then stuffed the document into a drawer in his desk.

He'd give it to them later. And besides, those creatures from another planet didn't give a damn about what was actually in the files!

A few irritated comments were made each time a signature was placed on the form for taking out a document, then he was left alone once more. He fervently resumed his interrupted reading. Nobody cared what he did all day in any case.

When he'd finished, he got up slowly and thoughtfully. He began to walk up and down the room, muttering. Over the course of time, he'd got into the habit of talking to himself: it was his way of reflecting on things while giving himself the illusion he was sharing his thoughts.

This document was fairly ancient and had apparently been of no interest to anyone for the last sixty or seventy years, but should he keep the information to himself?

In the absence of his section manager, he had no option but to go the departmental director, Laure Pellegrin, which did not help matters. Rumour had it that she owed her position more to whom she knew than what she knew – a statement always accompanied by a knowing smile or a wink. Aupetit merely noted that the Director carried her forty years very well and that she had an engaging appearance, but she could exhibit all the warmth of an iceberg whenever she deigned to penetrate his lair. How should he approach her?

His working day was coming to an end when he at last decided to pick up the phone.

Laure Pellegrin saw him very quickly and welcomed him with a cordial smile, the one her detractors said she kept in reserve for union representatives when she'd decided not to agree to anything. Aupetit's mouth was dry as he outlined as well as he could the contents of the document he'd just discovered: it was an account of a strange event that had taken place in June 1940, at the time when ministerial services were being moved out to southern Touraine – where they'd remained for just one year, before being transferred yet again, in total disorder, to Bordeaux.

His departmental head was interested at first, but eventually started to give increased attention to the waiting files that lined her office.

"Is that all?" she asked, just as Aupetit was about to finish. "Don't you think this is all very dated, and it's rather late to bother about it now?"

"Quite possibly, but I wanted to make sure you knew about it. Perhaps we should check…"

She interrupted and pointed a fingernail at him, red and

slender like a gunshot in a cartoon strip:

"Perhaps, as you say. But I hope you're not expecting me to go trawling through your archives just to verify whatever it may be. That's your job, not mine. It's for you to bring me the relevant documents. If they exist."

"Yes, I understand. But don't you want to read this short report?"

He offered her the document he'd taken out of the filing box.

"OK," she sighed. "Leave it there, I'll have a look at it when I've got time to waste."

Once the archivist had left, fuming, to go back to his workplace, Laure grabbed the sheaf of papers and began reading.

Half an hour later, and ten minutes before the authorised office closing time, Pascal Aupetit left the building, carrying his usual sports bag. He was divorced and as solitary at home as he was at work. He was a regular user of running machines and body-building equipment at the sports centre near where he lived, and he'd made a few friends there, some of whom were of questionable reputation. But what did that matter when all they ever talked about was athletic performance, dietary regimes or the comparative advantages of different kinds of apparatus?

CHAPTER 2

CHINON, ONE SATURDAY SIX MONTHS LATER

The force of the slap made the old man's head shake. He was semiconscious, held up bodily by a younger man. He could scarcely groan. His eyes were open, gazing at nothing.

"Wake up, granddad."

The one who had given the slap uttered these few short words in a loud voice that echoed under the vaulted ceiling. He shone the beam of his head lamp anxiously towards his victim.

"He's not going to drop dead on us, is he?" asked the square-jawed, fair-haired man who was holding him.

"We just need him to remain conscious until the drug takes effect, and then we shall be more or less OK."

"If he hadn't been knocking it back so much we shouldn't be here" replied the other man in irritation.

"That's enough, Karl, don't keep on about it. He…"

Their conversation was cut short by the old man making a sudden movement of his shoulders, followed by a hiccup. Seeing a mound of debris near them, they put their suffering victim on it and lay him on his side.

The older of the two hoodlums sat down on a nearby block of stone and extracted a bottle from his rucksack. He opened it without moving his eyes away from his captive, took a swig and passed it to his accomplice. They remained like that for another ten minutes or so, impatient, talking about why they'd come here and pausing only to make periodic checks on the pupils of their victim's eyes.

From time to time, one of them would sweep the surrounding area with the beam from his lamp, revealing a universe of rock falls and roughly shaped stones exuding moisture. Darkness, cold and silence were the masters who ruled this underground world, undisturbed by the presence of the intruders. These ancient galleries, carved out by long-departed quarry workers and themselves long abandoned, seemed very unwelcoming. The two gangsters didn't appear to be bothered.

When they felt the old man was in a state to allow it, they picked him up under the armpits and continued on their way. He was trembling wretchedly with exhaustion. Or fear. Or perhaps both. His feet scraped along the ground, adding an eerie accompaniment to the rasping sounds he emitted from time to time. The two other men paid no attention to his pleadings or to the pain and fatigue that distorted his face.

As they walked along, their lamps revealed thin stalactites fixed to the ceiling, projecting long shadows into the distance like the many fingers of a deformed hand moving in rhythm with their steps.

They stopped in front of an opening to a side gallery. A pile of rubble that had fallen from the vaulted roof blocked three quarters of the entrance, leaving only a dark, narrow corridor.

"This way?" asked the guy who slapped.

"I don't remember," the old man stammered. "I was very young then. It was so long ago."

The other two looked at each other hesitantly.

"Are we going in there?" asked Karl, the fair-haired man, after a few moments.

"Yes," growled the other, taking a step forward. "We can't overlook any possibility. And seeing the state he's in, we haven't got much time."

They entered the tunnel, their progress hindered by the irregular floor of shifting stones and the narrowness of the passage. Karl stopped walking, bodily lifting up the exhausted old man in front of him.

"Shit!" said his companion, after a few seconds.

A few dozen metres further on, more rock falls had closed off the passage. He studied it for some time, shining his lamp into every crevice before doing the same with the ceiling.

"It doesn't go any further," he confirmed. "Look at the size of the stalactites and the way the stones are welded together by the calcium deposits – this corridor must have been blocked off for over a hundred years. More time wasted."

"Do we go back?"

"No, we smash into the wall. What do you think? Of course we go back."

They'd been walking for over four hours through these wet, slippery galleries, which were sometimes wide avenues, sometimes as narrow as a mountain path. Agitated and nervous, they'd explored every recess and every passage, looking for the slightest hint, watching to see whether any glimmer of memory would light up in the old man's face. Without any result.

The slap-giver stopped again to consult his map. This was simply a check, as he knew they were retracing their steps back to the main gallery where they'd come in. Their exploration was almost at an end. Despite all their efforts and all the risks they'd taken, success still eluded them. Too much time had passed, too many people had disappeared, too many memories had faded since…

"We're screwed?" Karl muttered in frustration.

"Looks like it."

"I think he's been buggering us about from the start. Either he really doesn't remember anything at all, or else he didn't want to show us where it was. I hope tomorrow…"

A groan interrupted this exchange. He was still holding up

the unfortunate man, who now weighed more heavily on his two supports. He was exhausted, his legs were trembling and he could no longer stand up.

"He won't last much longer," said Karl, passing a hand through his untidy hair. "Do we leave him here?"

"We can't, it's too risky."

"But we can't take him out of here looking like that, particularly at this time of day. It would be better to stick him somewhere in this bloody labyrinth, until we can come back for him."

"Out of the question. Even if we did hide him, it would be sod's law that somebody might come across him before we'd left the area. And we're likely to be kicking our heels round here for some time yet."

"So what do we do now?"

"We've still got enough time to get back to the vehicle and change the old man's clothes. Afterwards, you can help me take him to a place I've already got in mind. With a little cunning, we can perform miracles."

"And what about our hair, fingerprints, DNA traces?"

"That's OK. Leave me to sort that out, I know what to do."

CHAPTER 3

That Saturday evening, a festive air prevailed in the Caves Painctes, the 'Painted Cellars' that were the temple of that illustrious wine brotherhood, the Confrérie des Entonneurs Rabelaisiens[1], now invaded by a noisy throng attending one of the seasonal grand chapters. Commandant Dufournet and Lieutenant Georges, dressed in their best uniforms, were standing in the space reserved for VIP guests, watching the crowd and saying hello from time to time to a face they recognised. Next to them were members of the Council of the Entonneurs, resplendent in their official robes and lined up as if on parade in front of a large expanse of wall in the reception hall.

The voice of the Grand Chambellan, greatly amplified by the loudspeakers, rang out under the vaulted roof to announce the commencement of the proceedings.

"Trumpets, sound!"

He underlined the command with a generous wave of his hand, a gesture conveying a certain authority and majesty that he was to repeat many times. Firmly ensconced to face

---

[1] The Entonneurs Rabelaisiens, a Humanist Brotherhood, intends at once to perpetuate the teachings of its spiritual master François Rabelais, a humanist and truculent writer on the joys of living, and also to celebrate the virtues of the Chinon wine.

the auditorium, grasping his ceremonial book in his hand, he was as immovable as a marble statue amidst the flashes of the cameras.

As he gave the order, the laughter and chattering stopped and all eyes were fixed on the five musicians who had installed themselves a little further on, at the top of an imposing flight of stairs. They were resplendent in royal blue uniforms in the style of the ancient troubadours and, looking down on the crowd of guests, they put their trumpets to their lips and made the ancient stones of the vaulted space reverberate.

It was the first time that Georges had witnessed this spectacle, and he was very impressed. He took in every detail, starting with the Entonneurs' official dress consisting of a heavy red robe with an ermine-edged cape, the redness enhanced by the yellow-orange lighting and the warm colour of the *tuffeau* stone. The ensemble was finished off with a square cap edged with gold, and the ceremonial collar.

That evening's chapter, the 'Chapitre de la Fleur', celebrated as it did every year the promise of fine bunches of grapes to come. Provided, of course, that the summer weather was favourable. Filled with soft Touraine sunshine, those bunches would once again produce the red nectar praised five centuries earlier by the most famous son of the region, François Rabelais.

Several trumpet calls and speeches later, after the *vin d'honneur* and the *canapés* had been consumed amid laughter and conversation, the *beau monde* at last made their way into the main cavern where the ceremony and the gala dinner were to take place. Standing motionless on either side of the great stone staircase, the Entonneurs provided a prestigious guard of honour for their visitors.

The cavern could accommodate more than four hundred guests. It was set out with round tables covered in white tablecloths, decorated with flowers and enhanced by carefully installed lighting. It was a spectacle in itself. The huge stage, also carved out of the *tuffeau*, always attracted attention with its vivid colours, medallions and the large semi-circular ceremonial table. Some thirty new postulants for the title of Chevalier of the confrérie were about to pledge their allegiance in loud, clear voices in front of an audience seated ready to dine but watching the proceedings with interest. On the main table were some very large wine glasses worthy of the giant Gargantua, which occasioned worried looks from certain people, perhaps envious of others who were… more daring.

Silence was imposed as the Grand Maître appeared on the stage with his retinue. He began with the calling of the future Chevaliers. Suddenly attentive, the guests concentrated on the ceremony, watching to see who from their table would go up onto the stage. One of the Entonneurs tied a bib in the colours of the Confrérie round the neck of each recipient, while another filled the huge glasses in front of them with a few measures of wine. And then came the swearing of oaths of fealty and the anticipated moment when the novices would begin to taste the mouth-filling beverage. Every table, every group, had eyes solely for their members on the stage, nudging one another and exchanging pleasantries as the camera flashes went off.

"Philippe!"

The anguished cry of an Entonneur who had remained at the back of the hall, lost in the hubbub of this joyful spectacle, attracted attention only from the nearest guests. They saw the man bending over one of his confrères who was lying on the ground.

"Help me, there's something wrong with him" he shouted again, looking round in a distraught manner.

Two guests from a neighbouring table rushed up to him.

"Loosen his clothing," said one of them. "He'll be able to breathe more easily."

"Is there a doctor here?" another guest enquired, speaking to the room in general.

The commotion and movement around the afflicted man began to attract attention, causing several other guests to get up as well.

"Francs beuveurs, à vous salut!" proclaimed the Grand Maître as he dubbed each of the new Chevaliers. He turned round at that point to face the far end of the cavern and was surprised to see one of the Entonneurs rush up onto the stage and grab the microphone under the reproving gaze of the members of the Grand Council.

"The Doyen d'âge, our Oldest Member, has just suffered a slight attack. Nothing serious, but if there are any doctors present could they please go to the back of the hall. And let the ceremony continue," he added in a manner that he wished could have sounded more light-hearted.

The state in which he saw his elderly friend worried him more than he let show. At that age, any sudden illness must be treated seriously, but neither did he wish to spoil the evening for the four hundred guests. Some of them had come a long way, often from neighbouring countries, to take part in this exceptional event.

"I call Maître Jean Poinel, advocate, Chairman of the Bar Association in Liège", continued the Grand Chambellan, resuming the course of the ceremony. He nevertheless kept his eye fixed on the other end of the hall, near the passage that led to the toilets. A small group was standing huddled round the Doyen, who was still lying on the ground.

"His pulse is very weak, hardy detectable. You must call an ambulance and get him out of here so I can examine him properly", said one of the men, addressing Charles, the Entonneur who had first been seen bending over the Doyen.

"Are you a doctor?"

"No, I'm a ballet dancer. What do you think I am? This is an emergency, we can discuss the details later."

Three men immediately offered their services. The stricken man was lifted up without further ado and taken to the main building under Charles' direction.

CHAPTER 4

The festivities were in full swing, and a joyful farandole made up of the musicians and the vocal group of the confrérie was weaving its way between the tables to the sound of an accordion, brass instruments and timeless choruses in which all the guests joined.

The shimmering costumes, the laughing faces and the good humour were turning this into a magnificent evening. No-one took any notice of Charles as he went quickly over to the Grand Maître on the top table.

"The Doyen is dead!" he whispered in his ear; he was clearly in a very emotional state.

"No! He can't be!"

The Grand Maître's face turned grey, but he was reluctant to get up from the table in case this alarmed the guests. He once again assumed an impassive air. With all this noise going on, no-one could have overheard them.

"And there's another problem: the doctor has just called in the Gendarmerie."

"Is he mad? Why?"

"I've no idea, but the ambulance personnel agreed with him."

The Grand Maître stood up abruptly, causing surprise to

his neighbour at the table, excused himself with a wave of the hand and a strained smile and went over to the second VIP table.

"We'll get this sorted out very easily. Commandant Dufournet and his new deputy are here this evening. I'll speak to them."

A few moments later, the four men made their way towards the exit under the questioning gaze of the few guests who had noticed them walking round the room.

"Do you know what happened?" asked the Commandant, as soon as they were away from all the noise.

"No, no idea. I couldn't do anything, I just asked them to wait until I'd told the Grand Maître."

"Unnatural death?" asked Lieutenant Georges. "I can't see any other reason for involving the Gendarmerie."

"That's patently obvious," growled the Commandant.

"What makes you think there's anything unnatural about it?" asked Charles indignantly. "He was a couple of paces away from me when he fell and we were both near the tables at the back of the hall. I'd stayed near him because I thought he didn't look very well."

"That would explain why he was late. I didn't see him before the induction ceremony," added the Grand Maître.

"Is he married?"

"No, he's been widowed for over ten years. He lives on his own but we should have his daughter's telephone number on file. I'll go and check in a moment."

The two gendarmes maintained a cautious silence until they reached the main building.

"In here," said Charles, opening a folding door.

"Ah! The gendarmes," said the doctor, who was sitting next to a stretched-out body covered by a white sheet. He had a disconcerting appearance, dressed as he was in black trousers, a canary-yellow jacket and a navy blue bow tie worn with a white shirt. He immediately stood up, as if unsure how to present himself. Two paramedics did the same, looking worried.

"I should like to speak to you in confidence" said the doctor, looking at the two gendarmes without really knowing which of them he should be addressing. "This could be serious, and I wouldn't like to get it wrong."

"Gentlemen, could you give me a few minutes?" Dufournet enquired of the two Entonneurs, who retired unwillingly. "You two, stay outside and see that no-one comes in," he said to the ambulancemen.

Once the door was closed, he went over to the body lying under the sheet.

"I find this to be an unnatural death," said the doctor. "And that's putting it mildly."

"The man had a heart attack in public. But given his age, I don't see that…"

"Heart attack?" said the doctor. "Because of his age? I'm not so sure about that."

He lifted the sheet, letting the two gendarmes see the partly undressed body. Surprise immediately registered on their faces.

"Now do you begin to see?" the doctor insisted.

"Injuries and burn marks?"

"And recent ones!" commented Lieutenant Georges.

"Quite so. From this afternoon or this evening. But it gets worse: look at his jaw. In my opinion, he's suffered a fracture of the mandibular condyle.

"Caused by his fall?"

"That's very unlikely. The Entonneur standing next to him stated that he held on to him as he fell."

These exchanges between the three men were followed by a few moments of silence.

"Is the fracture very serious? Could it have caused his death?" asked the Lieutenant eventually.

"Death, no, but it's blocked the jaw and would have prevented the injured man from making any sound."

"You mean the Doyen was unable to call out or alert the people around him? Is that it?"

"Exactly."

"But he could have made gestures or written something down, for instance. He could have attracted attention from someone, and Charles was standing right next to him."

"Except that he was already dead, or at least on the point of dying!"

"I don't understand…"

"He has traces of injections in his left arm and his pupils are abnormally dilated. He was on his feet, but probably incapable of making any movement. Particularly if he was under the influence of a powerful narcotic drug."

"So he arrived here drugged and dying? With a broken jaw?" asked Commandant Dufournet incredulously.

"I cannot exclude that possibility."

"Do you realise what you're saying? If I accept what you've just told me, I'll have to take steps that will have a catastrophic effect on the evening, when nothing in this man's behaviour attracted any attention, and he couldn't have been assaulted in front of everybody here. I think all three of us of are convinced on that point."

"I asked you to come precisely because things are unclear. I'm only a doctor, but it's my duty to report any unnatural death. What happens afterwards…"
He was showing signs of mounting anger at the Commandant's hesitation.

"Georges, alert the scientific team and the police surgeon. And get two lads from your brigade over here," the Commandant continued, somewhat regretfully. "Have them cordon off the area where the victim fell while we wait for the forensic investigators to arrive. This is going to blight the atmosphere of the evening, but we don't really have any other option. Keep the area by the chairs clear as well, until we get better information."

"Given the number of people moving about all over the place, not to mention the ones who came across when he fell to the ground, I don't see what use that's going to be."

"I know, but it's the procedure!"

"And you're not supposed to move the body," the Lieutenant growled, walking away with his phone in his hand.

"And tell Pierre – I mean the Grand Maître," the Commandant corrected himself, "that he can go back to his guests."

"Is that all?"

"No. We shall have to bring the evening to a close, record the identity of everyone present and commandeer all the photos that were taken in the area from the start of events."

"What a circus. They're going to be really glad they invited us!"

Georges made no effort to conceal his bad temper. A wonderful evening that had barely begun was now ruined... He'd only recently been posted to Chinon, at his own request, and already he'd been caught up in an improbable investigation. And to think he'd chosen this town because it was peaceful, so he'd be able to spend a little more time with his wife and his two children!

All the same, the torture and murder of a ninety-year-old man during a gala dinner, in the middle of a dense crowd... it was totally insane!

CHAPTER 5

Although no announcement was made, the steps taken by the Entonneurs quickly caught the attention of the diners. The mood changed. There was no more music, laughter or shouting out. Conversations became increasingly subdued and serious at the tables near the spot where...

A number of the guests had already begun to leave the hall without waiting for coffee to be served. As they went out, they each gave a furtive glance towards the cordoned-off area, as if hoping it would supply the answers to their questions. Some were bold enough to ask one or other of the Entonneurs. As the latter knew as little about what had happened as their guests, all they could do was tell them the age of the victim or refer to his recent health problems.

The arrival of the forensic investigators in their overalls, gloves and masks immediately gave rise to a troubled silence and caused the departure of those remaining diners who had been determined to stay on. Members of the confrérie, their faces set in a grim smile, were still bothering to say goodbye to the last ones to go. They shook hands here or offered apologies there, but their hearts were no longer in it. The evening had been irretrievably blighted.

The Entonneurs were gathered together in a corner,

shocked by the situation. They had not even found the will to change out of their ceremonial robes, and the same went for the musicians, sprawling over the available seats. Sadness was now joined by exhaustion, which showed on all their faces.

Jacques, the officer in charge of the forensic team, was with the two gendarmes. He was extremely angry:

"If I've understood the situation correctly, people have been traipsing all over the scene, and the corpse has been interfered with and moved by a group of men but we don't know exactly who. Have you got any other good news for me?"

"There was no corpse at that point, it was an old man suffering from a health problem," said the doctor angrily.

"That's enough," interjected the Commandant. "No one is to blame, and certainly not you. Jacques is annoyed because he's come all the way from Tours to gather evidence that's going to be useless. I can understand his point of view, but nobody could have foreseen a situation like this."

Georges hesitated for a moment before deciding to intervene:

"I've sent a team over to the Doyen's home to see if his door's been forced and check that everything's in order. They'll stay there for the rest of the night. Given what you're going to find here, I assume you'll want to look for any leads at his house?"

Jacques looked strained and gritted his teeth. He made no

reply.

"You should go and see what your team are up to," said Dufournet, somewhat irritated.

"What for? Going over everything with a vacuum cleaner and counting the confetti?"

"OK, are we just going to stay here sniping at one another or can we try to get organised and decide what to do?" said Georges, standing up.

* * *

It was four o'clock in the morning, an hour that heralded disappointment and fatigue for the investigators, as well as those Entonneurs who were still present.

Commandant Dufournet went over to Lieutenant Georges, who was engaged in conversation with the forensic expert.

"I won't ask what the outcome of your investigation is, I can all too well imagine," he said to Jacques.

"Indeed, useless. We haven't been able to identify any location where the victim could have been detained and assaulted, either here or anywhere else in this complex. I hope we'll do better at his house. What about you?"

"Not wonderful either. None of the witness statements is any use in helping us establish when the Doyen arrived in the cavern, or how. Probably through the main entrance like everyone else, but there's nothing to prove it."

"We still have the photos taken by the guests", Georges reminded them. "They were firing off in all directions, so we should be able to get something from them: although it'll be a huge task. And I would remind you that the Doyen arrived late, so it's not surprising no-one noticed him come in."

"Have you managed to get all the photos?" asked the forensic officer. "Your chaps didn't miss any?"

"We've been quite successful there, other than with one or two people who didn't want to co-operate. We're only missing those where people had left before we arrived on the scene."

"Witnesses remember seeing the two Entonneurs before the Doyen collapsed," the Commandant continued, "but I still don't understand how this man, injured, burned and with a fractured jaw, could have made his way here unaided without saying anything and without being noticed. Even if he was drugged, it's still beyond belief. I hope the police surgeon can help us there."

"This isn't a medical matter, we really need a magician or a psychoanalyst," said Georges sarcastically, but without conviction. "And we're overlooking one point: if he was tortured somewhere else, why release him to public view, and in full ceremonial dress, rather than finishing him off and hiding the body?"

"Perhaps he escaped," Jacques replied, unconvincingly.

CHAPTER 6

SUNDAY

The walls were dripping with moisture, which oozed through the plaques of saltpetre that clung to them like suppurating scabs. The stones, eaten away by salt and the passage of time, still showed here and there traces of past centuries, recorded in great blotches of soot or old rusty nails driven in haphazardly according the needs of the former owners of the building.

The man wiped his brow. It wasn't so much the heat that made sweat appear like pearls on his face but tension and the ambient humidity. The screams of his victim didn't perturb him either. In any case, they were becoming fainter, swallowed up in a general inaudible gurgling sound. The victim was losing strength, but was still alert enough to resist the commands of his torturer. The latter was impassive: he was aware that in this cellar, under an empty house, his prey had no chance of being heard and knew it as well as he did.

"Why are you holding out on me?" he whispered softly. "You might as well tell me everything now, and I'll arrange for you to be found in your bed tomorrow morning, still alive. I don't even want to steal anything from you, I just want to know.... To know, that's all."

He got up so he could take off his mask and clear his nostrils. The stench was becoming unbearable, and the whiffs of grilled flesh mixed with the dank odour of the cellar were making him feel sick. He had to finish this off and get the information he still didn't have that was wanted by the gang leaders. He also had to find a dossier, if indeed there was one hidden somewhere in here.

He relit the gas burner, which immediately gave rise to desperate shrieks from his victim, struggling frantically despite being tied up.

"Why are you being so obstinate? I don't want to hurt you. I just want you to spit it all out and tell me what I want to know. You haven't seen my face. I'm wearing a mask, a wig and gloves, and if you tell me everything I'll be hundreds of kilometres from here by the time they come to free you tomorrow."

He waited a few moments, allowing his words to penetrate his victim's consciousness.

No reaction.

He sighed and approached him again.

"You leave me no choice. I'm warning you, it'll be worse this time. Did you ever hear about those old-time bandits called the 'pastern-warmers'? They used to burn their victims' feet with glowing embers from their own fireplaces to make them confess where they'd hidden their money. We've moved on since then. Better equipped, more efficient and causing less pollution, that's the modern world…"

Pleased with this speech, he paused to look at the poor quivering object lying in front of him, perhaps hoping to spare his suffering.

In vain.

"You'll see that it gets very hot. Better than a hot-water bottle," he said. "You must remember hot-water bottles. People used them to warm their feet in your day, eh? Or maybe heated bricks wrapped in newspaper? But they were too tepid to have any effect, in my opinion. I'll show you the difference, you'll be surprised..."

Cédric Lantois slowly brought the blowtorch nearer, watching for any sign of weakness and confession in his victim.

Despite what he did, he wasn't actually vicious by nature and could often display disarming naivety. He might have grown up to become a very nice, normal chap, had he not suffered the misfortune of being born with an excessive tendency to look for the easiest way of doing everything. This was certainly linked to his genetic make-up. Oh, nothing very serious, just a single gene coding for idleness, but that one gene had had such an effect on him, if truth be told, that it had severely tried the patience of both his teachers and his parents. Parents who'd despaired of him while they were still young and active, before wasting away in their retirement years. From his earliest childhood, he'd harboured one single obsession, which was to do as little as possible. He'd developed a remarkable sense of observation, linked with an astonishing capacity for avoiding blame on every occasion, getting other people to take the responsibility for what he'd done, as well as what he'd not done.

This predisposition had one drawback: Cédric had a natural inability to find a job on his own, coupled with the wonderful facility, whenever bad luck or over-eager friends found one for him, of making various excuses and losing it immediately. Since he nevertheless needed to live, he'd ended up undertaking a few – highly paid – services on behalf of people whose activities were not covered by official employment descriptors or the listings of the Chamber of Trade. When he was between 'jobs', Cédric often added to the advantage Nature had given him by staying in various lodgings provided by an officialdom that, while being severe with him, nevertheless supplied him with bed and board at an unbeatable price. He regarded these as unofficial annexes of the Employment Exchange, and they offered him professional opportunities that he couldn't have come across anywhere else. And that was how he had ended up taking on the role he was playing at this very moment, in a cellar in a provincial town that he barely knew.

It was thus Fate, although a rather aberrant Fate, that had made him what he now was: a parasite, a hired thug who didn't care what he did... provided no serious attempts were made on people's lives. After all, Cédric had his principles. He didn't really know where he got them from, but he had them nevertheless. He appeared to regard them as an inheritance, perhaps the only one his parents had left him.

He adjusted the flame of the little blowtorch.

Another scream rent the silence in the cellar, blocking out the gruesome sizzling of burnt flesh.

CHAPTER 7

The rain was still falling insistently, flooding the streets and gutters – cold rain, unworthy of the month of June. It was truly appalling weather.

Cédric went into the baker's shop he'd noticed a few hours earlier, his head covered by a large hood supposedly to protect him from the elements. Turning his back on the saleswoman, he pretended to be choosing a pastry from the window display, all the while observing the little square in front of him and the surrounding area. He took advantage of the bend in the street to watch the doorway of the house he'd just left, which was about a hundred metres away. He eventually decided on a *pain aux raisins*, paying for it with change extracted with great difficulty from his pocket because of his gloves, which he hadn't removed. He set off again, sure that he wasn't being followed, retraced his steps and again surveyed the neighbourhood. Still just as deserted. The usual passers-by were probably sitting by their firesides. It was ideal weather, a real godsend, he thought with a hidden smile.

The torturer went back to his vehicle which he'd left in a fairly empty car park about a kilometre away, a perfect spot with several ways of getting out. He was still feeling jumpy and kept his hands on top of the steering wheel for a few minutes, his arms stretched out and head lowered. It had gone well, perhaps too well. He went over in his mind everything that had happened, trying to identify any mistakes he might have made. Unable to think of any, he was at last reassured and began to relax.

It cost him some effort, accompanied by heartfelt swearing, to take off his soaked parka while still sitting at the wheel. Once he had started the engine, he bent over to pick up the mobile phone hidden under the passenger seat. He promptly inserted the battery concealed in the glove compartment, switched on the phone and placed it by the gear lever before driving out of the car park.

The bleep of an incoming text message made him jump. The second one just caused him to shrug his shoulders. These gadgets would make you paranoid. There was nothing here, nobody else around, and he was panicking just because of the phone!

Although he tried to adopt an assured manner, Cédric kept looking in his rear-view mirror as he drove on. He crossed a bridge and then followed a long straight road lined with plane trees, so he was able to check that he wasn't being followed. He continued his journey randomly along little country lanes before coming back to a hill overlooking the town, where he turned into an isolated side road. It was a perfect spot to set his satnav in peace and quiet, in accordance with the text messages he'd received a few minutes earlier. It was an unusual way of doing it: the first message simply gave latitude and longitude coordinates. Looking at the second one, he burst out laughing:

"You'll need to put things back by 20 minutes," he read out loud. Still as crafty as ever…

He subtracted 20 minutes of angle from the coordinates he'd just received. The position indicated by the satnav immediately changed by about 60 kilometres. You can never be too careful when you transact serious business over a mobile phone.

Lantois set off again, taking advantage of a lull in the rainstorm and being guided from then on by the directions given by the satnav. He drove past several fields and crossed the river before coming to a roundabout and taking a barely noticeable lane that led off it. He passed through a village and some fields and vineyards until the tarmac road he'd been following became a narrow ribbon channelled between high walls. A little further on, on his left, he saw what could be his rendezvous. The property was set high up: it too was surrounded by large walls, which prevented him from seeing the actual building. He stopped for a moment to read the name plaque: MEMENTO MORI. 'Remember that you are going to die.' That was very reassuring!

He was startled by the sudden wailing of a siren. Looking frantically in his mirror, he only had time to see flashing blue lights coming up very fast behind him. In a panic, he flung the car into gear and accelerated as hard as he could. Luckily, the road led downhill from that point with a lot of bends, letting him pick up speed rapidly and avoid being seen by his pursuers. He just needed somewhere to hide, a driveway, an open gate into a courtyard, anything, but quickly! Cédric wondered how he could have been spotted and followed without his being aware. If by bad luck the lane had already been blocked off at the bottom of the hill, he would have no other avenue of escape.

There was a succession of walls and closed gates on either side, making him feel he was caught up in a giant helter-skelter. No crossroads, nothing. This was a real nightmare. Fortunately, nothing was coming in the other direction to make him slow down or, worse, stop!

He was driving too fast on this wet, narrow and badly maintained road, and couldn't look in his rear-view mirror without taking a considerable risk. Listening to the siren, it seemed to him that his pursuers were falling behind, although he couldn't be sure of that. If he didn't lose ground himself, he still had a chance to outrun them. With a bit of luck. With lots of luck.

Cédric at last saw a junction with a narrow road on his right, about fifty metres ahead. It was at right angles to the one he was on and flanked by a wall protected by a large block of granite. Trying to turn into it at this speed would be suicidal. He hesitated, just long enough to see the end of the lane ahead. There was no road block. He recognised where he was: he was about to reach the main highway which, if he turned right, would take him back into the town. On the other hand, his only hope of safety meant turning left to get to a small parking area next to a retirement home he'd noticed that very morning, but that would be very perilous as he'd have to cross both traffic lanes without being able to see if anything was coming.

He cut across the two lanes with his foot to the floor. The car began to zig-zag owing to the aquaplaning effect, forcing him to steer and counter-steer before making a sharp turn to the left. With a great squeal of brakes, he arrived like a whirlwind in the car park he'd been so eager to reach. A few seconds later, a small Fire Service paramedic vehicle exited the lane and turned right towards the town.

An ambulance! All this blue funk because of an ambulance!

Cédric slumped in his seat, shut his eyes and remained motionless for a good ten minutes, the time he needed to clear his mind and regain his composure. From where he now found himself, he could see what appeared to be the place where he was expected.

It was a large building, possibly a manor house, positioned on a hill and concealed by the trees of its parkland so that all that could be seen were a few mossy walls and parts of the frontage. The closed shutters, lashed by the squalls of wind and rain, gave it a sinister appearance.

"That can't be it – the place looks deserted. It has to be further along, on the left," he muttered.

Having calmed down by now, the torturer set off back the way he'd come with all the wariness of a fox let out of a cage. He drove past his destination, made a U-turn after checking several times in his rear-view mirror that he wasn't being followed, and returned slowly. The gate into the grounds opened just as he reached it and immediately closed behind him.

The park seemed abandoned, with rampant weeds and the occasional bramble bush growing all over the paths and what had once been a French-style formal garden. From the look of it, he must surely be at the property he'd seen a short while ago. The gang leaders were concealing their presence very effectively.

Ignoring the entrance to an underground garage that he could see a little further on, Cédric parked his car next to another one that was already there, behind a screen of trees and a bamboo hedge.

Self-assured once more, and seeing there was no bell, he unhesitatingly pushed the door open. The hallway contained only some sparse, cheap furniture that looked as if it had come from a sale or a boot fair; there was nothing here in keeping with the ancient look of this old bourgeois mansion. Still no-one came. He looked around impatiently and was just about to go outside again to sound the car horn when a noise made him hesitate. Lantois stopped short, holding his breath. He had not expected to be welcomed by this beautiful mixed-race woman, all legs and breasts, who presented herself in front him with a radiant smile. He was shocked. A pleasant shock, but a shock all the same. She seemed amused by the effect she was having on him.

"I'm Angèle. Did everything go as planned?"
She had a slight accent, charming and vaguely Germanic, which surprised him.

"Er... yes," he stuttered, "and no-one saw me or followed me."

"I think they know that already," she confirmed, making a sign to him to follow her.

She didn't have to ask, he would have done so without any hesitation. Cédric had lived on his own since his last partner had decided to leave him after his third spell behind bars. He had a certain charm, a pleasant face, an athlete's build and an undoubted smoothness of manner which probably came from an inbred need to manipulate other people. He was a born seducer, but pretty women were nevertheless one of his weak points. They often ended up manipulating him in their turn before abandoning him.

Two men were waiting for him in the grand drawing room. The older of the two, his grey hair belied by an unwrinkled forehead, had a satisfied smile. Cédric thought he was probably about fifty years old. Although slightly overweight, he had the build of someone who might have been a boxer. The other man was younger and more muscular, with fair hair and a square jaw. He looked at Cédric with steel-hard eyes that contradicted the smile he was trying to give. Perhaps he was the first man's bodyguard. A hatchet man. Those were Cédric's first impressions, at any rate.

They didn't stand up or introduce themselves when he entered the room. They simply thanked Angèle, who immediately left. But not before giving a winsome smile to Cédric, who asked for nothing more.

"Give me your mobile phone," said the older man.

It was not a very cordial reception, no more welcoming than the park and this old pile…

Shame about the beautiful bird, but best not to get in too deep in this ant's nest. He'd get paid, and then he was out of here.

"I haven't got it on me. It's in the boot, switched off and with the battery taken out. I don't want those gadgets giving away my whereabouts."

"Search him," said the other man, looking at him with cold eyes.

So he was clearly the team leader, the one who made the decisions and who'd set up this job.

"He hasn't got one. I'll check in the car."

"Sit down and tell us what you've discovered," said the other man.

"Could I have a glass of something, a Scotch perhaps?" Lantois asked, to gain time. "It's a nice house, but there's no…."

"We'll see about that later," said his interrogator brusquely. "First, tell me what happened and what you've found out."

"It took time, a lot of time, to make him talk. I had to use every trick in the book…"

"Spare me the sordid details – they're of no interest to anyone but yourself. What did he say?" the man asked irritably, while his henchman appeared to be watching flies go past.

"He confirmed that he'd worked in the cellars where you told me, and he witnessed the transfer of the reserve funds in 1940. He was 14 at the time. He claims he secretly took a small part of the loot, just enough so that nobody would notice. All the rest seems to have been moved afterwards when the Germans came, as none of it's ever been found."

"Did he know when or how?"

"No. He told me that some other people, the ones who'd organised the heist, were arrested shortly afterwards by the occupying troops. They're all thought to have died, either in the forced labour camp in Berlin or in concentration camps. He didn't know any more, but he'd put together a dossier with a few of the documents from that time and sketches he'd made from memory together with a friend."

His two interrogators looked at each other in a knowing way.

"Maps?" continued the older man.

"Unusable drawings. It seems they couldn't find the spot again themselves."

"And the dossier?"

"It's not very thick. It's in my car."

"What have you got for brains? Cream cheese? We send you to get documents and you leave them in your car? Go and get them for me immediately. Karl, you go with him," he said, turning towards the henchman.

The latter got up without saying a word, fixing his

blue-steel eyes on Cédric who arose in turn, apologising.

The atmosphere seemed even heavier after he returned, still closely followed by Karl. Stress was insidiously getting through to him, making him lose his capacity for thought and the little control of the situation he still had left.

When he saw the dossier, his employer's face relaxed. He started leafing through it, abandoning his interrogation for the time being. His smile slowly disappeared as he went through the pages, raising the tension as well as Lantois' pulse rate.

"Fine, I'll look at that more closely later on," he said, closing the dossier. "Now tell me everything he said to you. And I do mean EVERYTHING, in the minutest detail," he insisted, staring at Cédric.

It was a look to raise goose flesh on the most hardened criminal.

The torturer did as he was told, not holding back, trying to recall every last point, sometimes even remembering the exact words used by his victim. He was almost exhausted by his efforts as he finished.

"Is that it? Nothing else?"

"No, I haven't forgotten anything."

Cédric had made an enormous effort to reply with as much assurance as possible. He felt he couldn't allow there to be a shadow of a doubt about what he'd just brought back from the mission he'd been entrusted with, but he was beginning to experience a growing fear.

"And finally?"

"Finally? Oh yes," he went on at once, "I gave him the sleeping drug and the anti-inflammatory one, and I made him swallow a drop of hooch. He won't remember a thing tomorrow."

The two men burst out laughing.

"Oh, he certainly won't remember anything tomorrow," said the henchman. "He'll be sleeping like a log for a very long time to come!"

He almost had tears in his eyes.

"You... you mean..." stammered Cédric. "But he can't be..."

"So you say."

"You got me to kill that wretched old man?"

"Cool it, laddie," said the one who seemed to be the leader of the group, in a menacing tone. "Do you want to wind up in the slammer again? What did you think? That you could just go into people's houses, torture them and then expect them not to remember you? Do you seriously believe we're going to put ourselves at risk just because you come over all squeamish? I suggest you calm down and think about the situation you're in. When everything's clear in your head, you'll be free to go and have the rest of your money. Meanwhile, make the most of your time here, but you won't be leaving yet. Understand?

Lantois hesitated.

"Understand?" the other man insisted.

"Yes."

He had no choice. He'd been caught in a trap, exploited,

used as something expendable.

He remembered what Angèle had said – they'd been cunning enough to track him and make sure he hadn't been followed. What would have happened to him if he HAD been spotted? He chose not to pursue that question. Perhaps they would have done something to help him, at least until they had the information and the documents… that thought reassured him a little, but also made him think of the other side of the coin: them first, him second.

In any case, from now on he was at their mercy, under house arrest and dependent on their goodwill. They certainly wouldn't let him go again until he'd agreed to carry out all their dirty work without asking questions.

He tried to keep his face impassive, and pretended to enjoy the Scotch that Karl was pouring for him, after filling the other two glasses. Was that to annoy him, or simply a lack of good manners?

They raised their glasses in unison, expecting him to do the same. He did not wait to be asked.

"To the success of our projects," declared the boss.

"To your health and your projects, gentlemen," he heard himself respond, before taking a swig of a very peaty whisky. Perhaps a Bowmore or a Talisker Storm, he said to himself automatically.

For a moment he savoured the warmth and force of the alcohol trickling down his throat, then he again raised his glass and looked at the other two:

"Now that I've carried out the first part of my task, may I know who I have the honour of working for?"

"You'll have to make do with our first names," growled the man who was more and more obviously the boss. "I'm Babar, or BA. That's easy enough to remember. You've already introduced yourself today," he added, after a short silence. "I won't present Karl: you made friends with him earlier."

Lantois raised his glass in the direction of the henchman. He gave a smile intended to improve relations, which seemed to have got off to a bad start, and took a second mouthful of whisky.

An assumed name, a false moniker. Perhaps two of them. What a way to start an open and frank partnership, when they knew everything about him in the utmost detail.

The relationship was a rather unequal one, bearing in mind that he was to all intents and purposes their prisoner. He was becoming uneasy but, thanks to the whisky, he smiled at the thought that the real Babar was an elephant who could fly, whereas the one opposite him was the type to cause devastation in a china shop. Even if he did have small ears.

"What's amusing you?" BA asked suddenly.

"Nothing much. I was just thinking to myself that you show a lot of humour when it comes to choosing code names. I lack the imagination. It's a pity."

"Well, there's no need for you to make any effort or rack your brains about that, you're going to stay plain Cédric Lantois."

Cédric noted that he was now being addressed using the familiar 'tu' instead of the more formal 'vous', indicating that his status was evolving – but towards that of a stooge rather than a partner!

A quarter of an hour later, the glasses were empty and he was shown up to his bedroom by Angèle, shadowed by Karl. He'd been under the spell of this young woman since he first arrived, and he'd scarcely noticed what she was wearing. He could only recall her slender figure, her breasts and her smile. He found her appearance wonderful, enhanced by brown hair cut to mid length, an oval face and pouting lips. She was in fact dressed in a very sober manner, in loose-fitting clothes as far as he could tell. Her black trousers and slightly indented white, short-sleeved blouse provided a contrast with her beautiful face.

His bedroom on the second floor was spartan, although there was a minuscule bathroom leading off it. The layout of the house meant that the room had a view from the side of the building he'd seen from the little car park down below in the town. Cédric noticed immediately that the windows were fully shuttered, reinforced by metal bars secured into the walls, and sealed off. Doubtless to prevent any light at all being visible from outside. He remembered that those of the drawing room had been left open, but that was on the other side of the house towards the rear of the park where nothing could be seen through the trees.

He hadn't failed to notice the CCTV cameras installed in the entrance hall and in the drawing room, as well as those monitoring the access drive. He'd thought about that from the time the gate had opened and closed for him. Monitoring the access, yes, but over what distance, and from where? Had they guided him in because they'd spotted his Mégane shortly beforehand in the lane outside?

"Give me your car keys," said Karl, holding out his left hand. "I have to put it in the basement and eradicate the tyre marks."

As he handed the keys over, Cédric joked that he ought to get rid of all four tyres as well.

"What makes you think we aren't going to do exactly that?" said the other man, scornfully.

"OK, you two pugnacious puppies," Angèle interposed, "if you would just calm down, I'd like to inform our guest that I'm not the general maid here and he'll have to make his own bed and take care of his own housekeeping."

"And do I have to cook my own meals?" he said playfully, giving her a wink.

"My dear sir, we have everything delivered that we require to survive here. The rations are just about acceptable, as you'll find out for yourself this evening. Unless you're too tired?" she added.

"And if you feel like going for a walk round the park without telling us first," Karl interjected, "you need to be aware that we've set traps, and the surveillance system is remarkably efficient. If I were in your shoes, I wouldn't do anything out of line. That is, unless you're not too bothered about what happens to you in the immediate future," he taunted.

"Understood."

Lantois was seized by doubt as he closed the bedroom door. Was he still alive because they needed him to undertake other hazardous jobs? Or because they hoped to extract further details from him under interrogation beyond those he'd given them that afternoon?

Afraid of being overheard or bugged even in his own bedroom, he held back from uttering the swearwords hovering on the tip of his tongue. He made no gesture, went into the bathroom, washed his face as calmly as he could and stretched out on the bed without taking his shoes off, even though they were soaking wet.

CHAPTER 8

Cédric Lantois awoke with a start from the siesta to which he'd succumbed. His conscience never troubled him to the point where it prevented him from sleeping the slumber of the just. Although his fellow criminals regarded him as a soulless monster, he saw himself instead as a victim of fate, obliged to ensure his own survival by any means available, including the most extreme. This tendency had evolved gradually since childhood, building up from petty pilfering to large-scale theft, and from the commission of minor crimes to those of a serious nature. Yes, he'd perpetrated a number of atrocities, including murder this time, but he'd given his victim a chance – it had been his fault for refusing to talk. And he felt no guilt about the substances he'd administered, as he'd believed they were simply intended to reduce the victim's suffering.

He took off his shoes, which were still wet through from the afternoon's rainstorm, and spent some time massaging his toes to warm them up. His spare clothes were in a bag in the boot of his car that Karl had parked in the basement garage, probably without checking what was in it. He'd no chance now of getting at the various items that he used as tools of his trade and which might have enabled him to escape.

His mind was wandering as he swept his gaze round the bedroom, trying to spot any hidden cameras. He hadn't really looked at the room when he'd arrived, being too disturbed by Babar and even more so by Karl. Karl was the arrogant, cocksure type that he detested most of all; Cédric had never been sure of anything in his life, and had spent most of his existence protecting himself and deflecting onto other people everything that looked as if it might be bad for him. He was always infuriated by the self-assurance emanating from these puffed-up, superior characters whenever he came across them in the course of his various activities. He felt such an inferiority complex in their presence that he could only hide it by provoking them, playing cock of the walk but also trying to manipulate them. But how could you manipulate a Pitbull terrier of that ilk?

The room was small and, besides the bed, had a dressing table with drawers that proved to be empty as he pulled them out, one by one. He ran his hands over the underside to feel if there was a microphone, or maybe even some potentially useful object that might have escaped the vigilance of his hosts. There was also a wardrobe that turned out to be as empty as it was filthy. He climbed onto the bed to check that there was nothing trailing across the top, but there was just a very thick layer of dust, old enough to contain some of the fallout from Chernobyl and possibly even the eruption of Krakatoa. The weight of the wardrobe dissuaded him from trying to examine the back of it.

An empty cupboard next to the wardrobe completed the furnishings. Cédric tapped on the sides of this. One of them, nearest the wardrobe, made a different sound. The cupboard was evidently placed between two bedrooms, separating them from each other.

"I've brought you your things," said Karl, knocking on the door. His unusually considerate manner set alarm bells ringing in Lantois' mind. Was the bodyguard's attitude changing for the better, or worsening as he feared?

Karl came in holding the bag and carefully studied the bedroom and bathroom, on the lookout for anything at all suspicious. Cédric's first thought was that even if he was being spied on by a camera, his adversary clearly had no access to it.

"Put it on the bed," Karl said, in a bored tone. "Open it in front of me, slowly. Don't make any sudden movements."

"What do you imagine is in it? Do you think I'm carrying guns in there? And you expect me to believe that you haven't already searched it?"

Karl's sarcastic smile left no shadow of a doubt: he had indeed gone through all Cédric's personal effects. He shrugged his shoulders to show he wasn't naive.

"You're taking the piss!" Cédric yelled, as soon as he'd opened the bag. "Have you seen the state you've left my things in?"

"I had to check what you were lugging around in there, one never knows. I've got a job to do."

"That didn't entitle you to tip it out in a heap and screw up all my shirts into a ball. Look at this, it's creased to hell."

Although Cédric was furious, he decided to play it low key and only responded verbally to his adversary's smug remarks.

"It's not even damp, I searched it indoors. I could have done it out in the rain to reduce the risk."

"I am amazed you didn't. You just didn't want to get wet yourself."

"Don't make so much fuss, I brought your bag up for you. I'm too nice. Goodness me, one day my devotion to others will be my undoing," he declared. He swivelled on his heel with a satisfied smirk playing over his lips.

As he reached the doorway, he turned back:

"Dinner will be served on the ground floor in one hour's time. Evening dress obligatory, with a well-ironed shirt." He was trying not to laugh.

"Arsehole!" murmured Cédric, softly enough not to be heard.

Despite his anger, he was keeping a cool enough head not to provoke a situation that gave him very little room for manoeuvre. Perhaps none at all…

His immediate priority was to take off his wet socks, an imperative as urgent as it was trivial given the temperature of the room. Next would be to go back downstairs to get a better idea of the layout of the premises. And, perhaps, to catch a glimpse of that wonderful creature Angèle. Thanks to Karl, he now had an excuse – finding an iron!

Shutting the bedroom door, he went down the stairs deliberately slowly, trying to memorise his surroundings as best he could.

In spite of the impressive size of the mansion, there were only four rooms on the ground floor, all leading off the entrance hall. This formed a corridor, on the right of which was the large drawing room where he'd been received, and on the left a sparsely furnished dining room. Opposite the staircase he'd just come down he saw a door to what was in effect a continuation of the drawing room. He tried to enter but it was bolted shut. At the end of the passage, on the left of the staircase, was the glass door of a large kitchen.

He heard voices having a conversation, or rather an argument, which ceased immediately he entered. Angèle and Karl turned towards him.

"Sorry to interrupt, I'm just having a look round my little holiday home and was hoping to find an iron."

"Thinking of going to a night club this evening?" said the henchman sarcastically.

"If you can find me an escort, why not?"

"Let's all calm down," said Angèle. "There's an ironing board and an iron in there," she continued, indicating a cupboard to the right of the door, "but on no account is it to leave this room! Accidents can happen so quickly."

"I'm as good as gold, gentle as a lamb. Even Karl hasn't managed to rile me, and it's not as if he hasn't been trying."

Cédric spoke without thinking, staring at this young woman who exerted such a magnetic attraction. He was impressed, intimidated and excited by her all at the same time, experiencing a mixture of fear, desire and timidity that he couldn't explain to himself. How could she be having this effect on him when he'd only just met her? Was she a possible ally, or an adversary? Helpful, or dangerous?

Unable to decide what to do, he simply turned to go, saying he'd be back with his crumpled shirt.

Angèle and Karl had been arguing. At least, that was how it seemed to him. What about? Maybe just some domestic issue, as neither of them appeared to have any say in things when Babar was present – although Karl did seem to enjoy his boss's confidence.

He was seized by a sudden doubt: he shouldn't get carried away, make something out of nothing. His first impressions might be a long way from the real situation. He should wait a bit longer, take time to assess his position, start off by trying to get to know these three better. But would he have time to do so?

As he passed the locked office, Cédric thought he could hear a conversation going on. He stopped and listened. It was Babar's voice he could make out, muffled, perhaps because it was a double door. There was only one person speaking, interspersed with pauses, which meant that the boss was on the phone and this office was evidently his control centre. He continued quietly on his way.

Back in his room, he'd barely had time to take a shirt out of his bag when there was a sharp knock.

"That Karl is beginning to get through to me!" he growled, before opening the door

It was Angèle.

She seemed even more seductive than when he'd arrived, notwithstanding the iron she was holding in her hand. He kept his eyes fixed on her as he closed the door. This young woman gave off a provoking sexuality that awoke ancient instincts in him from the mists of time, something primordial, wild, that he found impossible to control. Making a great effort, he managed to stammer:

"I thought you said those things were dangerous. Aren't you afraid to climb the stairs on your own without putting a muzzle on that beast?"

"This beast seems a lot less dangerous to me than some others round here! Don't think I've taken pity on you, I simply felt I could keep an eye on you just as easily from up here."

She came towards him, still holding the iron, and pushed him towards the bed. This visit was perhaps not entirely innocent, but Cédric was still hesitant to interpret it in a favourable light. Bewitched by the way she was looking at him, he suppressed his fears and resolved to thank her in the only way still left to him. He took her gently by the shoulders and moved his lips near hers, his eyes never leaving her.

She pushed him back firmly, but her hand remained in contact for too long for Cédric to misunderstand her intentions.

"That's what I was looking for," she said, pointing to the electric socket in the corner, "and only that."

He went along with it, placed his shirt flat on the bed and turned towards her. Should he make an attempt, or not? He still hesitated; he was simultaneously surprised, disturbed and subjugated by this woman. His survival instincts were giving him two contradictory messages and he didn't know which to believe – complete and utter distrust on the one hand, or the pleasure of such a seductive conquest on the other. A conquest that had come about rather too rapidly to be genuine. Was she a danger to him, or a lone woman looking for someone to support her?

The pendulum was swinging rapidly towards the second option. Lantois approached her and seized her by the shoulders once again. She did not pull away and remained passive up to the moment when he placed his lips against hers. He felt her yield and press herself against him, not holding back in returning his kiss. He went over to the bed, ready to lie on it without bothering about his shirt, when a knock at the door followed by the sound of the latch made the young woman spring away from him. Her manner had already become very distant.

"Stop feeling sorry for yourself," she said at once, as if continuing a conversation. "In any case, your iron is hot now, so get on with your laundry."

"What are you two up to?" snarled Karl, looking at each of them in turn.

"Monsieur keeps moaning and complaining about our lack of consideration for him. I'm going, I've got other things to do than watch over him and listen to all his tales of woe. You can bring the iron down."

"Am I your lackey?"

"And do I look like a housemaid?" she said as she departed.

Cédric for his part watched the way the two of them needled each other. If he went by their conversation in the kitchen that he'd interrupted, they bitterly detested each other and could only get on to a limited degree. Perhaps Angèle really did need an ally after all, to face up to Karl.

Yes, but he was likely to end up in a very awkward position, caught between two stools in an operation the ins and outs of which he didn't yet know.

Karl turned towards him once more, interrupting his thoughts.

"If you're thinking of trying it on there, you're going to be in a load of trouble."

"From you?"

"Not just me. You're nothing here, you'll do what you're told to do, you won't attempt anything, you're invisible, you'll keep out of the way. That's all. Otherwise…

"Otherwise what? You shoot me?"

"That would give me great pleasure, believe me. A stooge snivelling because he's eliminated a witness – I don't know what to make of it, but I don't like it. However, for the moment I've no orders to get rid of you… but I can very quickly rearrange your face the way I prefer it."

"Try it!" said Cédric defiantly, clenching his fists. His instincts had taken over. However, he realised in confusion that he wouldn't hold out for very long against this vicious opponent who was certainly in better shape for a fight than he was.

"What's going on?"

Babar's loud voice was heard on the stairway.

"Karl, come down here. I told you to see what our guest was up to, not take him apart without my say-so." Karl immediately complied, not exhibiting any sign of resentment and completely ignoring the person who'd been on the point of becoming his sparring partner. Cédric noted that he seemed used to obeying orders immediately, at least those given by Babar. That provided him with some reassurance: all the while the boss needed his services, he'd have nothing to fear from his bodyguard.

"Don't provoke him," said the gang leader as he entered the room. "He's taken down some much bigger bruisers than you. If he comes at you, you don't do anything, you run away, you play the coward, but you don't react. That's an order."

"Understood. But I'd still like to know what I'm doing here and what you want from me."

There was a pause. BA's scrutinising gaze fell so heavily on him that it seemed he'd been turned to lead.

"Yes, I've taken on board that I'm on stand-by," Cédric said, to fill the silence. "At least until my little job is forgotten. But I hope I can still be useful to you because nobody knows me here and no-one saw me either."

"For the moment, everyone is staying out of sight. I shall only know from the gendarmes' investigation whether or not you were spotted or left any evidence behind. It should all be sorted in a couple of days' time, according to our informants. Until then, at least, you're not moving from this hidey-hole."

"Charming!"

"Would you prefer a bullet through your head or a hole in the ground at the far end of the park? That's another way of guaranteeing our safety."

CHAPTER 9

MONDAY

"You don't look too good," remarked one of Pascal Aupetit's colleagues. "Did you fall asleep in your archive room?"

"If only... I didn't sleep at all well this weekend. Bad news from one of my nephews who's been stupid. He's likely to find himself in a lot of trouble."

"He'll get over it. You don't need to feel responsible for what your nephew does. Especially if you're not the one bringing him up."

* * *

The town was bathed once more in the rays of a blazing sun set in a limpid sky with not a cloud in sight. All the dust had been washed away, and only the puddles and a few heaps of leaves in the gutters recorded the deluge of the previous day.

Two wide windows let the sunlight into the briefing room, giving it a spring-like appearance that contrasted with the electrically charged atmosphere that hung over the place. The tension and fatigue of the weekend had left their mark on the team and could be read on all their faces.

The recent arrival of Lieutenant Georges, brought in to

head up the investigatory brigade, was a continuing subject of discussion among his subordinates even though no-one questioned his competence. He was more experienced and of a higher rank than his predecessor, he was supported by the Section de Recherches, the specialist investigation team in Orleans, and to his credit he'd solved a complicated case the previous year, but certain of his men still wondered what the reasons were for his appointment. Some of them asked why it needed a lieutenant to manage a small team of detectives in a provincial town. Apart from his status as deputy to Commandant Dufournet, it didn't look like a promotion at all. Far from it.

Standing next to the Lieutenant, holding a mug of coffee, was Adjudant Maltier. He'd been resentful at first of the new arrival but had been rapidly consoled when he learned that he was to be promoted and transferred to his home area. He was going there in a few days' time, and was trying not to appear too uninterested in the activities of his former colleagues. He felt almost at home in this brigade after four years' service, a sure sign that it was time to move on.

While waiting for the latecomers, Georges looked over the personnel present. Some of them had already served under him, in particular Gendron and his young protégée, Patricia Blancard.

Adjudant Gendron was one of the forces of nature, a fifty-year-old giant of a man nearly two metres tall. He had twice been European judo champion, according to his colleagues – twice came second, he would reply modestly.

Having grown up in the force, he was a man ready to serve, and upright to a fault. He'd taken under his wing the most junior of his colleagues, a young woman who was full of potential but still very inexperienced.

"Is Patricia Blancard not here?" asked Georges, when the last arrival had taken his seat.

"On leave until tomorrow."

"Ok, I'll make a start," he said to the group. "I don't propose to go over the places and the circumstances, or the details of the victim and the doctor's concerns. Let's go straight away to the analysis of the photos taken by the guests. Very few were taken in the direction of the scene of the crime because most people's attention was drawn to the spectacle on the stage, which was happening at the same time and at the opposite end of the room. The result is that we have, at best, forty or so photos showing the back of the dining hall. And that with some difficulty: a camera flash only illuminates what's directly in front of it, and the background is still dark and indistinct. Nevertheless, now they've been enhanced, we can make out from some of them the silhouettes of the victim and the other Entonneur, Charles, standing next to each other. As he himself has stated, by the way. A few of the shots show him with the doctor, bending over and surrounded by several people.

"Is the criminal with them?"

"Highly unlikely. The police surgeon thinks that the torture was inflicted around 15:00 to 16:00, and the drug injected after 18:00. The person, or persons, responsible had plenty of time to go to ground, which may explain how the Doyen was able to free himself and get away. They were confident the poor old boy would want to end his days while the soirée was happening."

"A last glimmer of consciousness?"

"Something like that. On the other hand, we still don't know where he was at the time he was put into that state. Not at his home, anyway, although his attackers went there. And for what reason? We don't know that either. Everything was in a total mess, but the Doyen's daughter says that nothing valuable is missing."

"They turned everything over but didn't try to take anything? That's very odd. Either they didn't find what they were looking for, or the Doyen's daughter doesn't want anyone to know what it was."

Georges didn't bother to reply. The disappearance of small objects or documents could go unnoticed for quite some time. Including the owner of a house or flat.

He was about to continue when Gendron's phone started to vibrate, obliging him to leave the room to answer it.

The Lieutenant went on:

"To conclude with the photos, all I can say is that they confirm the witness statements. Four of the diners noticed the two Entonneurs at the back of the hall, without paying them much attention. And that's about it. As regards everything else, I'm waiting for reports from the forensic investigators and the police surgeon."

"What drug was injected?"

"Not yet identified, but it seems to have been a complex mixture according to the quack. We might possibly be able to identify a repeat offender..."

He didn't finish his sentence as he was interrupted by the door suddenly opening. Gendron came in, brandishing his phone, and thundered:

"Now the shit's hit the fan!"

"What's the matter with you?"

"Nothing's the matter with me, but another old man's just been topped!"

CHAPTER 10

Georges looked at Gendron incredulously. There was a stunned silence, then the others began to inundate him with questions.

The murder of a second octogenarian less than two days after the first would cause a furore. All the politicians and government officials would be down on them, whether or not they were directly involved, as would the media. The investigation team had a disaster on its hands!

"I've taken it upon myself to notify forensics and the police surgeon," Gendron went on, noting the lack of reaction on the part of his two superiors.

"You did the right thing," Georges said at last, "but are you sure it's murder?"

"We were notified by the municipal police. From what they've described, and assuming this isn't the first of April and they haven't been on the booze any more than usual, I think you'll be horrified!"

"I'll call the Procureur's office."

"I'm going to the scene," said Maltier, getting up and grabbing the big man by the arm. "Will you be joining us later?" he said, turning to Georges who was already on the telephone.

* * *

The surrounding area was full of inquisitive bystanders and neighbours who'd turned up when they'd heard the news. Two municipal policemen were being bombarded with questions as they tried to keep the area clear.

"You can go in," said one of them, on seeing the two gendarmes. "Given the situation and the number of people who've been wandering all over the place in there, it won't make much difference. But before you do, if you're interested, that short woman over there is the cleaning lady who discovered the crime."

He pointed out a middle-aged female sitting on a chair away from the crowd. She was being protected by a third policeman, who greeted them as they came up. The woman was profoundly shocked, sobbing her heart out and muttering some incomprehensible words.

"Fetch a doctor, I think she needs one. Was she the person who called you out?"

"No, it was a neighbour who'd heard her screaming. She was hysterical. I have to say it's not a pretty sight. One of our colleagues went in there and couldn't bring himself to look."

"Did the victim live here on his own?"

"Yes, he was a widower. An old boy in retirement. We used to see him from time to time."

"Another one," thought Maltier. "Are they doing it to reduce pension pay-outs, or what?"

"Unless it becomes absolutely necessary to move her, keep the woman here until we have a chance to question her."

"Shall we take a quick look inside before the forensic team arrive?" Gendron suggested.

"Yes, come on," agreed Maltier.

"The bedroom's on the right, off the hallway," said the policeman. "But the smell is coming mainly from the cellar. The door on the left, under the staircase."

A strong stench of burnt flesh caught their throats as soon as they entered the house. The victim was lying naked on his unmade bed, smeared with traces of blood. He had no nails on his hands or his feet – swollen feet, which exhibited marks seemingly made by a red-hot iron. The man's face bore the signs of extreme agony.

Constrained by the investigatory procedure, they held back from going into the bedroom and covering up the unfortunate man. Nevertheless, even for hardened professionals, the sight was almost too much to bear. Allowing a corpse as mutilated as that to be seen naked went beyond any notion of decency. It was somehow adding to the torment of this poor broken creature who'd been killed after undergoing indescribable torture.

Seeing the traces of fresh mud that were spattered along the corridor and at the top of the stairs to the cellar, they held back from going down so as not to increase the difficulties for the forensic team.

"What a bloody mess!" murmured Maltier.

"I have the feeling that our friend Jacques and his colleagues are going to be about as happy as they were on Saturday evening…"

Gendron said this with so little conviction that he managed to get a smile out of his colleague. The big man was nearing retirement, making out that he'd been looking forward to it for a long time without sounding very convincing, and he sometimes put on this false air of disillusionment.

Some ten minutes later, in a room put at their disposal by a neighbour, they tried to get a few details from Louise, the cleaning lady. She was sitting in front of them and sobbing like a damned soul. In between groans, she managed to explain that she'd found her employer's body in bed. She thought at first that he'd died in his sleep – "You know, a gentleman as old as that" – before seeing that there was blood all round him and his fingernails had been pulled out. She'd only noticed his feet after that, when she'd pulled back the sheet.

Why had she pulled back the sheet? She didn't really know: perhaps because of the blood, perhaps to see if he'd been assaulted. Perhaps just an automatic reaction.

And after that? After that, her recollections were confused. She'd screamed and run outside to get help, but she couldn't remember anything else. Not even the names or faces of the people who'd arrived just afterwards. Neighbours and passers-by had rushed into the house, but she'd stayed outside. Go back in there? Never!

Leaving Gendron to conduct the questioning, Maltier scrutinised the woman anxiously. He had the impression of watching a chicken running down the middle of the road, frightened by a car but unable to decide whether to go right or left to avoid its wheels. He could see all the symptoms of emotional trauma caused by a violent shock that the poor lady had certainly not been prepared for. Her make-up, a surprising piece of coquettishness for someone dressed in a work overall, had run because of her tears. A few wrinkles were taking advantage of this to reappear round her reddened eyes.

Louise had been doing the cleaning twice a week for this retired gentleman, who was very old but still active. She wasn't aware that he had any enemies, and there were not many visitors except for a few equally aged friends.

"Poor Monsieur Laurent," she groaned again. "Who could have done this to him?"

"Did he have any money in the house, jewels, gold items, valuable objects?" Maltier interrupted.

"No, I don't think so. He was quite well off, he had some money, but nothing to attract attention. Anyway,

I've never seen anything out of the ordinary in the house, apart from a few wartime souvenirs. Are they worth something nowadays?"

"How did he behave towards you?"

"Oh, Monsieur Laurent was always very correct, he would never have done the slightest thing that was out of place."

She was getting on her high horse. Gendron frowned. His question had only been intended to find out whether this 'Monsieur Laurent' was an aggressive or intransigent person, or acted in a way where he might have made enemies. She'd misunderstood the point of his enquiry. Or had she done so deliberately?

Given the state she was in, he opted for the first interpretation. She could hardly have carried out the torture indicated by the condition of the body. And a jealous husband would have resorted to some other method than pulling out the guilty party's fingernails.

"You should go home as soon as the doctor has seen you. I'll have a gendarme accompany you," said Maltier, trying to calm the woman down. "I'll need to see you later to question you about what was in the house and find out whether anything's been stolen. All right?"

"I can't go back in there," she moaned, starting to cry even harder.

"I'll leave you with my colleague," said the Adjudant, not responding to this. "He'll read your statement back to you. You can correct it if you need to."

He got up with a sigh and went to join Lieutenant Georges, who had just arrived along with the forensic investigators. Their team leader, Jacques, was in an agitated state:

"Correct me if I've got this wrong. As is generally the case in Chinon, scenes of crime are open to public view. They provide local entertainment. I hope you're selling entrance tickets, otherwise I'd have some difficulty wondering what the hell you think you're playing at! Is this for your end of year party? Is there going to be a raffle?"

"Ok, that's enough!" said Georges in annoyance, irritated by the biting sarcasm and the cold anger shown by his colleague. "We can't take any action before we receive the information. The scene was cordoned off by the municipal police when they were first called out, and they're the ones who contacted us. Unless we put a gendarme or a policeman on every street corner, I don't see what else we can do, other than commit the crimes ourselves and wait for you to arrive. If you want to spend the rest of your life just dealing with textbook cases, then you'd better go back to training school!"

Maltier was amused by all this. He would never have believed that the Lieutenant could take such a firm line. There had been one or two little contretemps in the past, but nothing like what had just occurred. Georges seemed to him to be a hesitant man, disinclined to involve himself in any kind of dispute, but the events they'd lived through since Saturday appeared to have raised his adrenalin level.

"I'm sorry," the officer went on, "but you touched a raw nerve. We're dealing with two complicated cases at the same time and we're all living on edge. I simply hope that every one of us will do the best he can, and as quickly as possible. That's how the members of my team are operating, at any rate."

"And mine," said Jacques, hard faced. "A lot of call outs, a lot of work and very few people to do it. And when the scene of crime has been totally interfered with…"

CHAPTER 11

Lantois took the opportunity of lying in bed, as the morning promised to be very quiet. At least he hoped it would be, after the restless night he'd just spent. It had been a bad night, entirely due to unpleasant dreams interspersed with bouts of insomnia. He'd been hoping to conjure up the enticing vision of Angèle, but it was Karl who'd wormed his way into his subconscious. Enough to give you nightmares even when you were still awake.

It hadn't been brought on by any thought of what he'd done to his victim. He wasn't sufficiently bothered about that to let it disturb his sleep. There was no actual malevolence in his attitude, just a kind of selective screening that allowed his mind to concentrate on his own problems to the exclusion of other people's. And he already had enough to contend with from Babar and his bodyguard.

He was, of course, unaware that at that very moment the Gendarmerie's forensic experts had begun their investigation. Even had he known, it would hardly have troubled him as he was completely convinced he'd left no trace evidence for them to find. There was nothing to link him with his victim, he was totally unknown in Chinon, so what was there to worry about?

The evening meal had not been as he'd anticipated. Babar was missing, for one thing. "As usual," added Angèle, when he raised this with her. It didn't really matter anyway, but even the presence of a beautiful woman hadn't helped him digest the food, straight out of the fridge and barely cooked. Catering packs, probably from the local supermarket, with each member of the team taking it in turn to reheat them in the microwave oven. A miserable piece of cheese was the only thing not to come out of the microwave, and that was probably a mistake.

In the absence of the boss, the atmosphere in which the meal had been consumed was akin to that of a deep freeze. Barely a dozen words had been exchanged during the course of the entire evening: just inconsequentialities, between himself and Angèle or between Angèle and Karl, who'd responded only with grunts, as cold as ice. He could have combated global warming single-handed.

Sitting in the chilly, half-furnished dining room, Cédric could easily have imagined he was involved in the making of some vampire film. Even the splendid seductress was maintaining her distance. That at any rate was how he summed up the situation, which was not at all what he'd been expecting.

Babar. Babar was absent most evenings. Cédric suddenly realised that no car or scooter had ever left the grounds. An electric or hybrid vehicle, then? But he hadn't noticed one, and the deluge on Sunday together with the isolation of the house made it unlikely that Babar would have set off on foot. So how did he get out of the house?

Only Angèle could tell him, but would she?

He stretched out, got up and, naked as Nature intended, made an obscene gesture towards the cameras which might or might not have been watching him. He gave an anxious look towards the bedroom door, which he'd jammed shut with a chair. It was a rudimentary precaution, but one that always worked. The bathroom was only a couple of paces away, and he left the door ajar.

After he'd washed and shaved, a sudden craving for a coffee and a cigarette came over him. This was very strange, as he'd hardly smoked at all for several years. Probably brought on by stress. He cursed himself for not having thought to ensure he had a packet before entering this hornets' nest. Angèle seemed too careful about her skin and her make-up to be a smoker, and as for asking Karl… he'd rather die first.

He made his way downstairs to the big kitchen, which was empty, and found an ancient filter coffee maker, which was also empty.

"Not even an espresso machine!" he said in disgust.

"As it's only a holiday home, what else did you expect?" Cédric gave a start. She'd come into the kitchen as noiselessly as a cat. He forgot his coffee, waiting to see whether she would spring at him. He was ready to take her on, with or without coffee, or a cigarette!

There was an ironic smile on her lips as she added:

"It's usually the macho seducer who comes out with that line, not the ill-fated beauty."

"But only after someone's nicked the coffee. "

"You poor little thing, how can we make it better for you?"

"I have my own idea how to answer that."

"Me too... The coffee is in the cupboard to your right, with the filters. The water supply is miraculous: the tap is full of it, and it flows out all by itself. You'll see, even a man can do it."

"And I thought I was being invited to join the Club. What a disappointment!"

He accompanied his words with a laugh and a wink. He was an inveterate seducer and knew that humour would help him achieve his ends much better than recriminations. She was moulded into a clinging T-shirt and a pair of black jeans, and looked even more attractive than when he'd first arrived. Attractive, but always surrounded by a mysterious air of *je-ne-sais-quoi* that made her presence disconcerting. Despite his aborted attempt the previous day that she seemed ready to overlook, Cédric still couldn't work out whether he was confronting an ally or someone dangerous, a cruel dilemma in his situation as a virtual prisoner.

"Karl's not here, then?" he asked, surprised that he wasn't already rushing out to separate the two of them.

"Are you missing him already? Well, I'm not. Those two get on with their own business and only give me one or two small and unimportant tasks – but they're well-paid, and that's enough for me. I don't want to know any more than that."

"Unimportant? When they've got someone like you available?"

"Whoa, just hang on. Don't try to muddy the waters, I'm not having any of that. I don't take any risks, either. The less I know, the better it is. No-one's looking for me, and it's mutual."

He took hold of the packet of coffee and began to pour it haphazardly into the filter.

"I do everything, but it never quite seems to work out. Such as now, when I've done the job but I'm still being held prisoner."

"It's for your own safety, isn't it?"

He stopped short, about to point out that it was much more likely to be for the safety of the other three. If he was arrested and started to talk...

The words were quivering on the tip of his tongue. But if he drew attention to that possibility, she'd probably stop talking, and sooner than he wanted. It would be better to take advantage of this intimate session with Angèle to find out the answers to his questions. He might well not get another chance for some time.

"So, Babar isn't here? Is he coming back late?" he asked disingenuously.

"Babar comes and goes as he pleases. In fact, the boss is NOT here, any more than we're in this town.

"Meaning what?" asked Cédric in surprise.

"Meaning that we can't let you, me or Karl be seen, and that BA isn't here."

"So we're none of us in Chinon."

Well, that was clear enough – none of them could be seen in the area until the job was over.

"That's not what I said," she responded, breaking into his thoughts.

"Oh? I must be going deaf."

Lantois had to ponder over this for a few minutes until he finally got it. Only one of them could go into Chinon without attracting attention, and that was Babar, the boss. On the other hand, he mustn't be seen in this house. So how, then, could he pull the job without going out at night, and in disguise?

"You make things very complicated in this old ruin," he said at last, trying to give the impression that he still didn't understand.

"It doesn't matter. With your lack of grey cells, I can see I couldn't rely on you in an emergency."

"Don't worry, I can still provide you with stiff support," he said, giving what he hoped was a lecherous smile.

"I prefer not to have heard that."

"So how does the boss get in here if no-one's supposed to see him?" he continued.

"I suggest you put that question to him direct, my lad, but you probably won't be given a chance to ask it twice!" Cédric passed her the coffee pot.

"Would you like a cup? It's hot, fresh and prepared with love."

"I only drink one cup in the morning, and I've already had it, thanks."

"Hard luck, then. What annoys me most here," he went on, "is this feeling of being permanently watched. There must be cameras all over the place, even in the bedrooms…"

He'd decided to go for broke. He needed to make her talk.

"In the bedrooms?" she retorted in surprise. "Of course there aren't. We don't need them for what we're doing here, we aren't making a porn film."

"But I saw cameras downstairs…"

"On the ground floor, yes – they're back-up for the ones that cover the park. There are two in the middle of the hallway, watching the entrance, and the others are near the windows of the drawing room and the kitchen, where the shutters are open during the day. That's all."

"That's reassuring to know. But I imagine BA's office must be under surveillance too…"

She gave him a mocking smile, probably to show she wasn't taken in by his questioning and could see where it was leading.

"His office is permanently monitored by a video recorder. Does that reassure you?"

"Yes, I'd hate to think that something might happen to him. What about the park?"

"Infrared sensors as well as the cameras."

"And why the closed shutters? To give the impression that the place is empty?"

"How perspicacious of you! I'm lost in admiration," she said sarcastically.

Angèle had told him everything he wanted to know. But was it to manipulate him, or to get him on her side?

They heard footsteps in the corridor.

"Karl," she whispered, moving away from him.

The young woman looked worried.

"Is that you, Karl?"

It was Babar. Angèle's face relaxed a little.

"Would you care for a coffee?" asked Lantois

"No, thank you. I just came to tell the three of you that the gendarmes are swarming all over the scene of your exploits yesterday. We shall know in two or three days' time whether you're a professional or a dangerous amateur."

His tone of voice was neither threatening nor affable. His face remained impassive, not betraying any emotion whatsoever.

The torturer was frightened: if Babar thought he needed to bump him off, he'd do it without any qualms, simply to protect his business. Just as you might kill a rabbit because you needed to eat.

"I understand completely. I'm not moving from here."

He had the impression that Angèle was looking at him as one might at a condemned man.

CHAPTER 12

In the town, near the house belonging to 'Monsieur Laurent', the murder victim, the investigation team was beginning to piece together the information gathered from witnesses.

Georges watched as the two forensic experts, Jacques and his colleague, came out with the police surgeon and made their way towards him. He gave them a questioning look.

"The poor old boy was put into bed after being tortured," said the surgeon. "He died there shortly afterwards."

"As a result of the torture?"

"No, from the effects of a mixture of alcohol and a powerful psychotropic drug, possibly buprenorphine. I also suspect there may have been some traces of cyanide in what he swallowed. The analysis will tell us more. I place the time of death as yesterday between 15:00 and 16:00, perhaps 16:30. Before 17:00, at any rate."

"So now we have two old men dying within a space of forty-eight hours, after being tortured and ingesting noxious substances. That's hard to take in," said Maltier.

"It will certainly cause comment. We ought to feed this to the local press, they lap up all the juicy stuff happening in the area," joked the surgeon.

"You have a strange sense of humour," said Georges, gritting his teeth.

"A word of caution, though" said the surgeon. "I'm not sure that the drugs used were the same each time. Also, on Saturday night it was an injection, whereas here it's a case of pills or powder dissolved in alcohol. The injuries are different too. It's possibly the same gang but not, I think, the same perpetrators."

"And what's your opinion?" asked the Lieutenant, turning to the forensic team.

"More or less the same," said Jacques. "The victim was tortured in the cellar and then put into his bed. He died there some time later. On the other hand, from the point of view of a technical investigation it hasn't been brilliant. All the rooms in the house have been contaminated by rubberneckers, and most of them had left before we could find out who they were. It's a waste of time looking for fingerprints anywhere other than on the body. These people have gone all over the place and meddled with everything."

"Is there no way of finding anything at all?"

"There is, fortunately. No-one went down into the cellar. If we do find any evidence it will be there, and only there. Our only hope is that the murderer wasn't wearing gloves or a hood, or he's left behind some object he used without taking any precautions before he came here."

Georges and Maltier looked at one another.

"We may possibly find some witnesses," the Adjudant suggested, turning towards the surgeon. "It all depends what time it happened."

"As I told you, between 15:00 and 17:00 at the latest."

"Between 15:00 and 17:00 on Sunday afternoon. Given the foul weather at the time, there can't have been many people out and about. I'm afraid our enquiries aren't going to take us very far. I'm also surprised at your conclusion: I can't recall any other instance of someone being tortured and then killed with drugs and alcohol," Lieutenant Georges remarked.

"Just so, I've never seen a case like it in this area," said the forensic officer, "but the national database might suggest some suspects, someone who's used a similar method. Especially if it was the same substance. The worst thing was putting the poor old man into his bed after mutilating him like that. These people are either insane or lacking in any sense of decency."

"Or they were following a ritual of some kind," Maltier suggested. "But what did they hope to find? Jewels? Money? Gold bars? If you believe his friends and neighbours, as well as what his daughter and the cleaning lady have said, there wasn't anything like that here. So was this some sort of macabre rite?"

At that point Gendron arrived and they all turned towards the imposing figure looking down at them from his impressive two metres as he approached. He was holding a notepad which appeared tiny in his enormous paddle of a right hand.

"As usual, no-one saw anything untoward yesterday afternoon or this morning until the cleaning lady started screaming in the street. But tongues are certainly wagging in the area."

"Have any of the neighbours gone out?"

"Yes, they've gone to work. Let's hope that some of them may have seen something. Otherwise, all the accounts are the same: the victim had nothing to justify a break-in with such appalling consequences. Laurent seems to have been a private, reclusive sort of man. He spent all his time ferreting about in the library, according to the witness statements."

"Is that the lot?"

"More or less. Except for one thing," Gendron went on, glancing at his notebook. "One old lady says that his activities during the war weren't totally above board. Old local grievances of little interest, particularly as she couldn't have been more than four years old in 1945, while he would have been about fifteen."

"If we have to go that far back to find a motive, we're in trouble," Georges murmured, shaking his head. "And we'd have to find an old man who also had a grudge and who wanted to have his revenge some seventy years later. If he was twenty years old at the time, that would now make him…"

"If that's the case, I hope the murderer didn't forget his walking frame," joked the police surgeon. "At least it proves he wasn't suffering from Alzheimer's!"

Gendron shrugged his shoulders.

"I'm simply reporting what the witnesses said without omitting anything."

"Gentlemen, I must leave you," said the surgeon, waving a hand at all those present. "I have a patient coming to see me at the end of the morning. You'll have my report by this evening, and the results from the lab … when they get their funding allocation."

It was his usual way of complaining about the lack of finance that medico-legal services had been subjected to for the last ten years. Only those who hadn't known him for a long time still found his remarks amusing.

Georges saluted and turned to the forensic officer:

"Jacques, I'll leave you to get on with investigating the cellar, unless you need me or Maltier for anything?"

"That'll be OK. No point in too many of us piling in. There may be something that will open up a few leads, so we'll proceed slowly and carefully. It will make a change…"

CHAPTER 13

Georges ended the call and stood up with a sigh. Always the same! Phoning his wife at the end of the day was no easier than in the morning.

Of course he wasn't going to help her pack the removal boxes, of course he'd been out all night drinking with his mates! No, he still hadn't made arrangements for their flat to be let. Yes, he would sort it out. But not today.

He blamed himself for not having got on with it when he'd first arrived, having opted instead to make various vital contacts in his new appointment and to forge links with his team. It was now too late, and time was slipping through his fingers.

His wife was on her own looking after the children, as well as making all the arrangements for the move. Georges could understand that she was tired and annoyed, but he wasn't prepared to be attacked like this every time he phoned her. He had his own problems and work to do. He too would have preferred to have moved house before his transfer. And he would certainly have appreciated a less stressful start to the job...

He looked through the window at a sky devoid of any vestige of cloud. A magnificent sun was trying to eradicate all traces of the puddles and was warming the straw-coloured walls of the houses. It was a very peaceful sight, but too beautiful; he suddenly found it excessively so, even obscene. How could the sun appear so bright and clear when it was shining on a town that had just witnessed such foul crimes?

It was all an illusion, mere surface appearance. The real truth was a world of dark cellars and underground labyrinths covered in a veil of fine stonework and attractive frontages.

There was always the wine, of course. The proverb said that the truth was to be found in it. If only that were the case!

It wouldn't take much for him to go back to Orleans to resume his rather mundane duties with the Section de Recherches. And this appointment wasn't a promotion anyway, just a sideways move.

All the same, he had to get a move on. In less than ten minutes, it would be time for the next briefing session with his team. After that, everybody would go back to their own homes and families. No point in doing overtime when there was so little to go on.

He was still lost in his thoughts when Gendron and Maltier came along, joined shortly afterwards by Patricia Blancard. The young blonde was in plain clothes, wearing a blue and white outfit in almost the same colours as her regulation uniform.

"I thought you were still off today," he said.

"I'm supposed to be, but I've come to lend my helpless teammates a hand. I read on the Internet that the killers were trying to keep pension costs down, and the Gendarmerie had no idea what to do about it. So I rushed back here!"

Her humour was normally of a higher standard, but her playful manner made her colleagues smile, even the Lieutenant.

"Yes, I can just see it," he responded, in similar vein. "Without you…"

"I know, I know, but I'm very modest!" she interrupted him.

In one year, she'd acquired confidence and a certain status in the group, he noted. She had good potential in the Gendarmerie.

He motioned to them to sit down before launching into a quick round-up of events since Saturday evening, intended essentially for the young woman's benefit.

"We've nothing tangible to link the two cases we've got on our hands, even though they occurred over the same weekend, but we must be on the alert for any evidence at all of that," he concluded.

"If I may quickly summarise the witness statements from Sunday", Gendron said, after Georges had finished. "As usual, nobody noticed anything, except possibly for the woman in the neighbourhood bakery. She remembers a man with a hood and gloves – he bought a *pain aux raisins* at just about the time the police surgeon indicated."

"Did she know who he was?"

"No, she didn't pay him any particular attention. Given the weather, she wasn't surprised at what he was wearing."

"I'd like to go back to the events on Saturday night," said Patricia. "If I've understood correctly, we've no idea as to when the Doyen arrived or the route he took that evening. And the only person to notice him was this individual Charles?"

"That's right," said the Lieutenant. "In any other circumstances, he'd be the prime suspect."

"So why isn't he anyway?" she asked. "Just because he's an Entonneur?"

"No, simply because witnesses saw him in the hall before the incident. There are photos to prove he was standing on the steps with the others when they were providing the guard of honour on the staircase. And also because he couldn't have tortured and killed his colleague while they were in the dining room."

"And not in any of the adjoining caves, either, because the forensic investigators didn't find anything there," Adjudant Maltier continued. "In any case, all the witness statements are in agreement that the two men were very close. Charles saw a lot of the Doyen, and not just at confrérie meetings."

"What about the other case?"

"Apart from the statement made by the woman in the baker's shop, there's very little for us to get our teeth into.

The forensic team have drawn a blank for the moment, but they still have to finish off their work back at the lab."

"No possible DNA traces?"

"They're not very optimistic," said the Lieutenant. "In any case, with the usual delays... I expect the investigation will be over before the results arrive. The man had no known enemies, although we still have to put together all the information from the witnesses."

"We do possibly have one statement there," said Gendron, "even if it does go back to tittle-tattle about the last war."

"The Algerian war? That was a long time ago," said the young woman

"The '39-45 war," Gendron corrected.

"No!" she said, almost bursting out laughing. "They certainly bear their grudges for a long time round here! Is that what Chinon wine does to you?"

"I know it doesn't seem worth bothering about, but both the deceased were around at that time, although they were young then. And, for the moment, it's the only link I can see between the two cases."

The Lieutenant paused for a moment before continuing:

"I think we might as well hold on to that idea for a while and take it a bit further. But let's not spend too much time on it, though."

"What can we do tomorrow?" asked Maltier.

"I hope we'll have some results from the police surgeon and the lab, but while we're waiting, you and Gendron are going to search the homes of the victims. Take one each, and get some assistance. You, Patricia, will go to the Caves Painctes so that you've got a picture of the place in your mind. Get the secretary talking, as well as any of the Entonneurs you might meet. I'm going to ask the Finance team to look into the bank accounts and financial background of our two customers. And if no-one has any other major questions or comments, then I suggest I take you all out for a beer. And Patricia's usual orange juice!"

* * *

Sitting in his office with the telephone to his ear, Babar was becoming agitated.

"No! We've taken every precaution. They're nowhere near making any connection with us, at least from what they've found so far – unless that cretin you recommended to me made any mistakes yesterday."

"And still no clues?"

"As to the location? No, and that's the problem. The old man's memory was full of holes and the other one was little more than a kid at the time, and dim-witted with it. He couldn't even manage to record the spot correctly."

"But you were able to get the dossier from him?"

"Yes, but it's of no interest. Just some drawings and notes made by a moron confusing what was happening in the war with stories about pirate treasure. I've reached a dead end."

"We do have one lead left. I was reluctant to put it forward before because I'm very uncertain about it, and it carries considerably more risks."

"Do we have any other choice?" asked BA in irritation.

"No. Unless you can find the Germans, which would give rise to a lot of other problems."

"All right, let's stop going round in circles and do what we need to do. I've got a character here I can't rely on and who's possibly already been identified, so we might as well use him as a fall guy while he's still available. If I have the slightest doubt about him after that, I'll get rid of him without leaving any traces."

"Very well, I'll explain things to you."

At that same instant, ignorant of the fact that other people were deciding his fate, Cédric Lantois was freshening up. He wondered whether there was any point in going down for dinner. The midday meal had been as unappetising as the one the previous evening and he did not enjoy the atmosphere, which was as sinister as ever.

He could have made do with a sandwich but then, on the other hand, there were the smile, the breasts and the figure of Angèle. Enough to unbalance anyone, even a Buddha in full meditation.

Angèle... Her banter had a certain elegance to it. And her way of giving him information while at the same time showing she wasn't taken in by his questioning. What was her actual role in this affair? Was she acting on her own account, or was she trying to manipulate him on behalf of the other two?

He kept wavering between doubt and reassurance, unable for the moment to place his total trust in this gorgeous creature. Although he certainly wanted to.

Taking advantage of the time left to him before dinner, he stretched out on the bed to reflect on what he'd discovered during the day. The short walk he'd taken behind the building, on the pretext of stretching his legs, had shown that the frontage was flat. Babar's office was in between the kitchen and the drawing room and had to be about the same size as the latter. Unfortunately, because the basement was only partly below ground level, the height of the office windows had prevented him from getting a glimpse inside. From the same spot in the park, he'd noticed another house over the boundary wall on the side facing the town. The shutters were closed, so it was probably unoccupied. Perhaps it was an old annexe, or servants' quarters.

Inside the residence, he'd been interested to discover a barely noticeable doorway under the staircase in the hall. Conceivably, it led directly into the basement. He just needed some excuse to be able to find out tomorrow.

It suddenly came to him that he'd completely forgotten to ask Angèle what Babar's real name was. Did she actually know?

These thoughts swept the last remaining hesitations from

his mind. He got up. With or without Karl to ruin the evening, he was going down for dinner, even if only to glean some more precious pieces of information. He walked slowly, almost regretfully, down the dusty stairs and entered the dining room, which was empty. A few snatches of conversation emanating from behind the door to Babar's office caused him to turn his head just as the two men came out, along with Angèle. This unexpected turn of events made him frown, but he restrained himself from showing any emotion at all. The beautiful girl might be more deeply implicated in this affair than he'd thought. Against her will?

"Well, speak of the Devil…" Karl sneered.

"We have some problems to sort out before we eat." Babar spoke in a brusque tone, accompanying his remark with an impatient wave of the hand indicating that Cédric should go into the drawing room. He was now very fearful and was already beginning to wonder what mistake he could possibly have made. Was it his account of what had happened at Laurent's house, or when he had cased the place during the afternoon?

He glanced swiftly at Karl, who stared coldly back at him with a supercilious smile before entering the room first, followed by Babar. Cédric was the last to go in, and he would gladly have slammed the door on the two of them and run away. But where to?

He took hold of the door handle at the same time as Angèle. She let her hand slide over his, giving him a hint of a caress which sent an electric shock through him.

"I'll shut it," she felt it necessary to add, pushing the door closed before heading off to the kitchen.

Stupefied, Cédric stared at his hand as if the girl was still stroking it. That contact had been so delicious that his worries almost disappeared.

"Perhaps it was the last meal for the condemned man," he thought.

CHAPTER 14

Georges was alone in his office. He hung up the phone without making the call and slumped back in his chair. He'd been incapable for some while of making any move where the outcome might be in doubt.

What should he do now? Go out for a meal, or make himself a pizza and slouch in front of the television watching some moronic programme?

He found himself more or less by chance at the Café National. It was a local institution. Once a house of ill repute, it had become a restaurant, then a bicycle repair shop and finally a night club at that already distant period when there were still American GIs around. It had since been transformed by its new owner into a sort of café-theatre. Georges had been there before, the first time he'd had to deal with a case in the town. A few young people were hanging around outside smoking, and they stared at him for a moment before resuming their conversation and laughter. He thought the establishment looked like one of those cafés from the good old days with its wood-panelled bar and display of glasses and bottles in front of a mirror. The walls were adorned with a few framed cartoons and a series of signed posters recalling the time when some local or even national celebrity had performed on the little stage at the rear. It was June, and the high season had brought its usual horde of tourists taking up all the tables, leaving just a couple of places squashed in front of the bar. Georges held back. He was about to go out again when the waitress, the owner's wife, appeared in front of him with a broad smile on her face.

"I'd heard you were back in Chinon!"

"Yes, that's right."

Surprised at being immediately recognised by the young woman, he didn't have time to think up some evasive reply.

"The town's lucky you've come. Especially given what's happening here at the moment."

"I'm officially debarred from talking about it," he said defensively, afraid of being bombarded with questions and surrounded by people wanting a scoop.

"Don't worry. Do you want a table?"

"Yes, but I think…"

"I've got just one left, next to the stage, you can't see it from here. You won't be bothered there."

Taken in hand firmly but with a smile, Georges could not do other than comply as the café proprietor looked on in amusement, giving him a little wave of the hand by way of greeting. He ordered a croque-monsieur and a beer.

From where he was sitting, he could only see part of the room. Customers were engaged in their various, sometimes animated, conversations and didn't pay him any attention. He made out a few lively exchanges, occasionally followed by rude jokes and laughter, and savoured for their true worth these moments of relaxation.

"I've just come over as it's my turn to say hello to you," said the proprietor. He shook his hand after setting down two croque-monsieurs and a small salad.

Georges hesitated a moment before replying.

"Have you got a few minutes?" he said at last, indicating the chair opposite him.

"Not many, but you can have two or three of them, *pourquoi pas?*"

"I presume the news is all over the town, so you know about what's happened this weekend?"

"Everybody's talking about it, but…"

"I was just wondering whether you knew the two victims and could tell me anything about them? Any information, even gossip, might be helpful."

"There's not much to tell. Neither of them patronised this establishment, except maybe around six o'clock just for a small glass of Chinon or a coffee."

"Anything else? You'd have the odd chat occasionally with your customers, wouldn't you?"

"What can I say? Everyone liked the Doyen of the Entonneurs. He had a good memory for past events. He'd stopped driving, but there was always someone ready to do his shopping or take him for his doctor's appointments. And one of the younger members of the confrérie had struck up a friendship with him and had had a lot to do with him over the last few months."

"Charles?"

"Yes, that's the one. He's got a rather cold and distant manner about him, but he was very obliging. Well, I say that but I don't really know him. He comes in here some evenings when there's a show on, but that doesn't give much opportunity to talk."

"And what about 'Monsieur Laurent', as the cleaning lady calls him?"

"He was a totally different sort, rather taciturn. He was pleasant enough but not terribly forthcoming. He didn't have a very good reputation here after the war ended, apparently. Probably just malicious talk… In my profession, you have to listen without hearing. Or do I mean the opposite?"

"And have you any idea why people might have formed that impression of him after the war?"

"None at all. I didn't come here until forty or fifty years later. Possibly he'd been a black marketeer? Or people suspected him of being a collaborator? I really don't know."

"He'd have been too young for anything like that. And how did the two men get on?"

"They hadn't been on speaking terms for quite some time, I believe. But I never saw any hostility between them, it was more a question of them simply ignoring each other. Look, I have to go," he said, glancing towards the bar. "Anyway, I've told you pretty much all I know."

"Thank you very much."

Georges doubted that anything useful would come from this conversation. Except, thinking about it, the fact that the two men used to snub one another, or had fallen out a long time previously. And then, so what? They couldn't each have murdered the other, and their mutual detestation had nothing to do with this case, or the investigation.

He had another mouthful of beer and attacked the second croque.

* * *

In the drawing room of the old building, Cédric Lantois was feeling desperate.

"Have I done something wrong?" he asked worriedly.

"That is possible," replied Babar. "But we're not yet sure. I'm giving you one more chance to redeem yourself with another mission, this coming night."

"You mean this evening?"

"This coming night is tomorrow, between Tuesday and Wednesday. Is that easier for you to understand?

"Yes."

Upset and hustled by his boss's aggression and Karl's mocking smile, he decided to be laconic in his answers. Yes, no. That would do to defuse the crisis that seemed about to explode.

"You're going to carry out another job like the one with the old granddad you so elegantly removed from the pension fund."

"Another old man?" Cédric said in alarm, immediately forgetting his resolve to adopt a neutral tone.

"I could have told you that this wimp…"

"That's enough!" said Babar, pointing a finger at Karl but keeping his eyes on Lantois, as if he was trying to hypnotise him. "And as for you, it's a simple choice. Either you do what we want, or you'll make us run unnecessary risks. In which case… It's up to you to decide."

The statement was full of menace that he didn't even bother to disguise. His gaze was as cold and cutting as a flint edge. Cédric felt cornered. The slightest mistake, the least hesitation would certainly sign his death warrant. For the greater amusement of this fair-haired, scabby lout who was still watching him like a cobra about to strike and inject its venom.

"I've always done my work properly," Cédric said defiantly. "And up to now there's been absolutely nothing to make you have any doubts about me."

"Correct. And so, tomorrow, I'm entrusting you with a job of the utmost importance – it's down to you to prove to us that you're capable of carrying it out. This guy is about sixty years old but he's fit and quite able to look after himself.

"He wouldn't be the first one I've taken care of. And if it's at night and I can catch him by surprise…."

"Don't try to act like James Bond. It's not that simple: first of all, we want him alive, and secondly, he doesn't live on his own."

This made Lantois feel it was a case of out of the frying pan and into the fire. He was beginning to realise that the job was considered too hazardous by his jailer-associates, and they'd only chosen him for it so as to limit the dangers to themselves. What would happen if he fouled it up? They'd certainly make sure he couldn't talk.

Unfortunately, there was no alternative and he'd no choice in the matter. He was caught up in the machinery of a mill that was about to start grinding.

"How many are there with him?"

"Just him and his wife."

"Then everything's OK. If I can choose the method, it'll be a piece of cake", he boasted.

"I will decide the method. You will do what I tell you, exactly how I tell you," said BA slowly, weighing each word as he spoke.

A quarter of an hour later, armed with a glass of whisky, they went back into the gloomy dining room. The table was laid and Angèle had taken it upon herself to prepare dinner. It was major improvement on the previous meals. "Probably because Babar's here," Cédric said to himself, jealous that he was now getting all the attention.

Out of bravado, he was the first to sit down. She immediately sat at the opposite corner of the table, diagonally opposite him, as if she was trying to avoid him. He gave her a black look. She stared back, indifferent, giving him the brush off.

He had the impression he'd turned into some kind of

plague-bearing untouchable. And yet, that caress on his hand when he was closing the door… Nothing seemed to happen normally in this house.

CHAPTER 15

Cédric returned to his room at a snail's pace, almost enjoying every creak made by the treads of the old staircase. They were playing a tune that was in total harmony with the way he was currently feeling. He walked slowly – slowly enough to see Babar go back into his office, where he remained, while Karl took up duty at the foot of the stairs, evidently waiting to make sure he'd entered his room.

"Get a move on, I want to set the alarm," he said.

Alarm? Angèle hadn't told him there were any alarms inside the building, only the one at the entrance and those on the windows. And besides, he hadn't noticed any sensors, only the CCTV cameras.

"The outside alarm isn't likely to go off while I'm climbing the stairs!" he ventured.

"Just move yourself," was the only response he got from Karl.

He was bluffing, Cédric was sure of it. The bodyguard was simply trying to unnerve him again, to sow seeds of doubt, to make his every step and movement seem hazardous. He was a devious, suspicious and, most of all, dangerous character. Cédric felt increasingly resentful, but he had to control himself and not show his feelings, otherwise his existence here would turn into a nightmare. He knew he was still useful to them for the moment, even if only as the main protagonist in the kidnapping that was going to take place the following day. He tried to think of the word used in chess to describe a situation like this. Gambit, that was it – the gambit, a deliberate loss of a piece or a pawn to weaken an opponent's position without him realising. And he was the pawn that was about to be sacrificed.

And yet, Babar was taking a big risk in setting up this operation. Sending him and Karl out tomorrow to reconnoitre the place from the outside flew in the face of the principle they'd established of not showing themselves in public until all the elements were in place. So, this assignment must be important, vital even. In which case, the boss and his henchman would do everything in their power to make it work, even if they intended to get rid of him afterwards – a thought that was hardly any more reassuring.

Cédric was becoming very uneasy and started to think of ways of getting out. Perhaps he could use this kidnapping job as an opportunity to abscond: instead of carrying out what they wanted him to do, he'd escape from the premises by some other route while they were watching the entrance. Or else he'd alert his intended victims and get them to call the police. But that was too dangerous, especially given what he'd done the previous day. Life imprisonment was a very long time, even with remission.

He entered the bedroom almost backwards, convinced he was about to spend his last night on earth. He'd have preferred a suite in some grand hotel so he could at least have ended his days in luxury. A suite with a couple of beautiful girls. Angèle and her twin sister! Pity she hadn't got one. But maybe she had, after all. Angèle, the bitch who'd toyed with him and let him dream of a wonderful adventure with her, before dumping him at the first sign of difficulty.

Once again, he jammed the door with a chair before opening the cupboard to check whether anything had been hidden in it, then doing the same with the wardrobe and the drawers, and looking under the bed. Nothing. He was about to go into the bathroom when the creaking of the stairs told him someone was coming up. He automatically stepped away from the door. He didn't want to be shot like an idiot by someone firing through it.

The noise of a key turning in the lock made him leap over to the chair to stop it giving way from the shoulder charges he was expecting to be made. Then the unmistakeable sound of a door catch, followed by a second click, made him heave a sigh of relief. Karl had just double-locked the door to shut him in!

He listened as Karl went back down the stairs, no doubt satisfied. He'd become sure of one thing: Babar and his accomplice wouldn't trust him until this job was over, and they wouldn't let him anywhere out of their sight.

Having a shower was out of the question: if he was naked, he wouldn't be able to stand up to them if they came after him. He rinsed his head under the tap and then lay down fully dressed, determined to keep his eyes open all night: it was better to be ready for anything.

He was resentful and racked with anxiety, but after spending some time chewing over the bitterness he was feeling he eventually dozed off.

Screek…

He was roused from sleep by a kind of furtive sliding or scraping sound. He kept quite still, all his senses on alert.

Do nothing, don't look as if you're awake, don't let them know you're listening and ready to react. Had there really been a noise? Perhaps it was a mouse, or he'd imagined it as part of a bad dream?

Anxious, almost panicking, he forced himself to breathe more regularly and peacefully as if he were still sleeping. Pretending to be asleep, but with his nerves jangling and ready to defend himself.

Survive.

He had no weapon, nothing to fight back with other than his fists. If he'd only kept one of the drawers near to hand, he would have had something to smash in the hardest head. He hadn't even thought about that, having put too much trust in that chair and the double-locked door.

But it was impossible for anyone to have got in without making one hell of a racket. Even the key turning in the lock would have woken him up. And with the chair as well…

He breathed out with a sigh of relief. There couldn't be anyone in the room about to attack him. He was having nightmares for no reason. This simple bit of common sense made him relax.

Another creaking sound, closer to him near the cupboard, made his pulse rate shoot up. There WAS somebody there! And close by.

Although he was engulfed by fear, instinct kicked in and he turned over suddenly onto the opposite side of the bed from the noise, let himself drop and slid underneath.

CHAPTER 16

Patricia Blancard was restive and tired. Thoughts had been running through her head all evening, alternating between her ruined weekend and the details of the investigation that she'd just caught up with. Her presence at the briefing had been neither accidental nor premeditated, but dictated by her need to be with other people and to put a brave face on things.

The intimate dinner she'd been so enjoying had ended in a row. Whose fault had it been, hers or Paul's? She no longer remembered.

It was his fault. Obviously. Why had he kept going on like that when previously he'd always appreciated that she had work responsibilities? And hadn't she done the same to support him? Hadn't she helped him whenever things became difficult?

No, it wasn't his fault. She'd started it. She'd spoiled everything. She ought to call him and apologise. He'd understand.

Phone in hand, she paused as she suddenly remembered the way he'd ended the argument. The rat! It was inexcusable. She couldn't lower herself that far to forgive him. Not just like that, she wouldn't make it so easy for him. He must make the first move. It was up to him to apologise.

Patricia stared at the muted television set without seeing it. In any case, she needed something else to think about. It wouldn't have taken much to make her start crying. It was all so stupid. Everything had come to an end because of tiredness, a few trivial comments, a few misunderstood remarks. Just a few words that had erased the hundreds of thousands exchanged between them over the course of several months, and in just a few seconds.

She was single and still too young to take the competitive examination to become an officer, which was her eventual aim. She'd gained a good degree and she had an outgoing personality and a quick enough wit to have gelled very quickly with her team mates. She'd brought them her freshness, enthusiasm and humour. Although the team still told blonde jokes in their off-duty moments, they were no longer aimed at her. Instead of taking offence, she'd added to the jokes, and gradually a kind of self-censorship had established itself within the team. It was as if her own repartee stood bail for all other women with fair hair.

Unable to think straight, she turned her mind to her parents, humble working people who'd raised their only child as best they could, encouraging her to pursue studies they could never have imagined possible for themselves. Like millions of other parents, they'd been worried that their daughter would suffer the ravages of unemployment and were relieved when she'd obtained her position in the Gendarmerie. Succeeding in your career was all very well, but what if your love life suffered as a result?

That had clearly been the reason for the rift – her job, which took up a great deal of her time, too much of it, in fact. Irregular working hours, an unattractive salary and the risk of disciplinary action even when you tried to follow all the rules in spite of being terrified. Some of her colleagues had paid the price, treated like criminals for having misunderstood the significance of a comma in the regulations, or because they'd acted too quickly in order to save their own lives. And now it was her turn – her private life was bearing the brunt of professional demands that were becoming less and less manageable.

She stood up, trying to think about something else. Such as this investigation.

First of all, why had there been two crimes over the same weekend in such a peaceful town, both committed on old people? Why had they been tortured? Although the Doyen had not been subjected to the violent atrocities that were inflicted on 'Monsieur Laurent', he'd nevertheless been assaulted and injured, and then had his jaw broken.

Was it a deliberate fracture, to prevent him from talking?

That was a ridiculous idea, given that he'd been turned into a dying zombie unable to do anything at all to attract attention. Unless it was just an extra precaution, in case he was discovered before his death?

And there was still that nagging question: how had the man got there without anyone having seen him come in?

She awoke with a start at about two o'clock in the

morning, still troubled by bad dreams. Restless and with a stiff neck, she got out of bed, turned off the television, put on her clothes and placed a capsule of coffee in the espresso machine. A quarter of an hour later, she was crossing the courtyard of the Gendarmerie building, intent on reading the whole case file even if she fell asleep in the process.

* * *

Lying under the bed, his shoulder hurting from his deliberate fall, Cédric was scared out of his wits.

"Shush," Angèle murmured, "don't make so much noise. You'll attract attention."

Angèle? What was Angèle doing in his bedroom? What was she up to? How did she get in?

But it was indeed the young woman's voice. Was she alone, or was there somebody with her?

"Put the light on," she whispered.

"What the hell are you doing here?"

"Charming welcome, I must say. Aren't you pleased to see me?"

"I'm not sure. Are you on your own, or with that Pitbull terrier?

"I'm on my own, in my night clothes. Now stop fooling around and put the light on."

In her night clothes? Baby doll, nightshirt or burglar's outfit with stocking mask and balaclava?

In the end it didn't matter, all three versions were equally pleasant to contemplate. Since the two of them were being intimate. He wavered a moment longer, but then his resolve melted away like snow in sunshine. He was not in an ideal position, still half asleep, unshaven and lying under the bed. He was unable even to defend himself. He cautiously extricated himself and got up slowly from beneath the side opposite his visitor, listening out for the slightest sound while he fumbled for the bedside lamp.

"Are you going to put it on, or are you waiting for me to bang into the bed?

"All right, I'm just looking for the switch."

His fingers found it at that same instant, and light filled the bedroom. It was indeed Angèle, alone, fully dressed, standing in the middle of the room. Gasping in amazement, he checked the bedroom door. The chair was still in place!

"But how…" he stuttered.

"How what?"

"How did you get in here? The door's locked!

"Don't speak so loud! I'll explain. But first say you're pleased to see me."

"Yes, I am, but you've given me the willies. If anybody at all can get in here…"

"So I'm just anybody?" she asked sarcastically.

"No, but you might have warned me. You scared the crap out of me."

"Yes, perhaps I should have asked permission first from Karl and Babar…"

She came quietly over to him. She was almost touching him. Like some toxic plant that paralysed its victim before finishing it off, he thought. Now she was touching him, arousing his desire, a mad, uncontrollable desire. Banishing from his mind the image of a spider spinning its web, he took her in his arms and sought her lips, panting.

"Shush," she said, freeing herself. "Don't you want to talk first?"

First? And then what? The next rebuff?

"We can talk before and after, in that order," he corrected her, very sure of himself.

"Monsieur has no doubts in his mind!"

She came up to him again, touching him, her head tilted backwards, looking him in the eyes.

"I have the impression that a few neurones have… gone astray," she murmured. "Perhaps we should help them get back into this creature's brain."

"That's all this creature is asking for."

"Shush!"

He could restrain himself no longer, pressing against her and seeking her lips. She did not refuse and slid over slowly towards the bed.

Subjugated, dominated, he held back as long as possible, caressing this beautiful woman in the way she seemed to be expecting before abandoning himself completely. A few minutes later, the floor was strewn with scattered garments and moaning noises accompanied the creaking of the bedstead.

* * *

Patricia was going through the hundreds of digital photographs from that evening. Almost all of them came from memory cards handed over voluntarily by the guests but several others, of better quality, had been supplied by the confrérie's official photographer. She was hoping to find at least one picture where the Doyen appeared somewhere other than where everyone had seen him.

Even if she did find it, she would then have to work out when it had been taken, a task complicated by the fact that most cameras had very approximate settings and some were totally wrong. Luckily, the ones from the official photographer could serve as a datum point, but for the rest she would have to find at least one shot that could be used as a time reference for the others. And then compare all the remaining ones with each other. It was a monumental task even for the lab, which had specialist software. And after that, all you had to do was change the parameters on each of the photocards so that they were sorted correctly.

For the moment it was of no consequence anyway, as a picture showing the Doyen 'somewhere else' could only have been taken before his collapse. There would be plenty of time later to determine when that was.

Footsteps in the corridor followed by the creaking of the office door presaged the arrival of Gendron. He stopped short, looked at her for a moment and then came over.

"Don't tell me you've got insomnia, I won't believe you. That's an affliction that only old people like me suffer from, not pretty young women," he growled.

"Oh, but they do. And here I am to prove it!"

"Did your weekend go as badly as that?" he put to her, not beating about the bush. "I noticed this evening that you were not exactly on the most scintillating form."

"Was it that obvious?" she answered anxiously.

"I don't know about the others, but it was to me, yes. I don't like to see you like this."

He'd taken her under his wing since she'd first joined the brigade, helping her to fit in and giving her the wise counsel of an extremely experienced gendarme. His assistance and his knowledge of the local area had been invaluable on a number of occasions. And yet he'd never imposed on her, simply making himself available rather than breathing down her neck. Like a father figure. Possibly because his own children had not wanted to join the Gendarmerie? She'd often wondered about that.

His words had got through to her, opening up the wound again. She was almost crying.

"It was nothing much, just a big argument. We'll get over it."

"Is that it? You're afraid of splitting up? Don't worry, you've been together too long for things to end for a stupid reason like that. You need to think about something else, and you can start by calming down and getting some sleep."

"Not now, I don't feel tired any more and if I go back to bed…"

"What are you looking for? The solution to this puzzle?"

He changed the subject, adopting a light-hearted tone. She followed his lead.

"I'm trying to find a photo that shows the Doyen somewhere other than the place where he fell down. Even a simple outline would do, provided we can make a positive identification."

"Have you seen how many pictures were taken?"

"I know. And if you can't sleep either, you could help me!"

* * *

Cédric, calmer now, very definitely seduced, and with Angèle's warm body clinging to his, was trying to clear his mind. Once again, he missed his morning cigarette. Was there no way of getting out of this once and for all?

"Aren't you going to ask me anything?" said Angèle, trying to break the silence several minutes later.

"Yes. How was I?"

"Hopeless. As I'd expected."

She pretended to punch him in the chest before continuing:

"And there I was hoping that a few neurones might eventually have surfaced…"

"They have. I've got two questions. The first is, I'd like to know how you got in here so easily. And the second is: why? Unless you were simply offering me a condemned man's last wish."

"You bastard! Do you know what a risk I'm taking if anyone was to find me in here, or if they discovered I wasn't in my bedroom?"
The young woman was furious, abruptly raising the tone of her voice.

"OK, OK, I was only joking."

"You can keep that sort of joke to yourself!"

"Sorry. I'm still worried by what's happening to me because of Babar and his Pitbull. You can rely on me, I won't betray you."

"In a moment, I'll show you how to get in and out of here without using the door," she said, not responding to his comment.

"And the 'why'? Is it simply because you fancy me? I'm drawn to you by some kind of magnetic attraction, but I'm surprised you're taking so many chances to be with an individual like me."

"You're wrong. I need you just as much as you need me, and not simply for sex. You're a prisoner here and you'll be running a lot of enormous risks tomorrow, but I'm in no better position with those two unscrupulous gangsters. They're relying on me for the moment, but once they've pulled this job they could finish us both off. They've known each other for a very long time and they won't give a damn about anyone else if they need to protect themselves."

"So how did you get mixed up in all this?"

"Through a friend of mine, the one who organised this whole business. They needed a female in the gang to give them the opportunity of making up a couple, if necessary – a man and a woman together always look less suspicious. But the fact I'm of mixed race rather unnerved them: in this town, I can hardly go around without being noticed."

"Nor anywhere else, I can assure you!"

"Anyway, for the moment they haven't needed, or wanted, to make use of that option. As a result, I've been permanently stuck here for over a week."

"And what's the reason for this dangerous job tomorrow?"

"They didn't find what they were looking for, either directly or through you. They're now being forced to take things further but they don't want to get in too deeply themselves, particularly as Babar goes into town and would risk being recognised."

"But I wouldn't. And if…"

"If you screw up, you're dead."

"I thought I might use the occasion to leave them without saying goodbye."

"You're off your head. They know everything about you, and they're pure evil. The only hope you've got is to pull this off – then they'll let you live, at least until the whole thing's over. You're still useful to them. And I can back you up if necessary, they need me too."

"What's it all about, anyway?"

"A very big operation, worth millions of Euros. The problem is, they don't know where to find the stuff – yet."

"Are you having me on?"

"Do you think I feel like joking?"

"Sorry, but it's difficult for me to get my head round. Organising a heist without knowing where to carry it out is not a very usual way of going about things."

"No, but it means they still need you to help them – and that's our only chance of survival. You mustn't fail tomorrow."

Lantois frowned. She was urging him to make a maximum effort on behalf of Babar and his acolyte. Was it on their orders, or to get him on board as her ally?

"Who are you working for?" he asked suddenly.

"For myself, and now for the two of us. If you aren't prepared to trust me, neither of us will come out of this alive."

"So tell me how Babar gets in and out of this ruin without being seen."

"I don't know yet, but I shall soon. Through the garage, possibly."

"Find out for me. And as soon as possible. Do you know what," he said, looking down at the parquet, "I love your lacy panties. Particularly when they're lying on the floor."

"Idiot!"

He turned towards her, stroking her shoulder and moving his hand slowly downwards, following the curve of her breasts as tenderly as he could, and kissed her on the lips. A few moments later, the moaning started up again, only partially muted.

CHAPTER 17

TUESDAY

A tired and hollow-eyed Patricia suppressed a yawn as she sat in the meeting. She glanced across at Gendron. The big man didn't look very bright eyed and bushy tailed either.

"If I've followed all this correctly," she said, when there was a lull in the discussion, "the forensic lab hasn't managed to find a single incriminating fibre, hair or trace of DNA on the Doyen's body?"

"That's so, once you exclude those from the people who were round him after he collapsed."

"I don't have much experience in cases like this, but that's rather unusual, isn't it?"

"Not really. It just means that the person or persons who put him into that state had taken precautions – balaclava, gloves, overalls, mask. Anything that would reduce the chances of detection. Everybody knows what to do now, because of all the films on TV."

"It's one thing to know what to do, but actually doing it is quite a different matter... There's another possibility," she said. "Let's suppose that the guilty person, or persons, was present in the group round the Doyen. I know, we've already discussed this, but..."

Everyone looked at her. She felt embarrassed, not liking to

be stared at when she was not feeling at her best with her drawn features and tired appearance.

"Yes, that's an important observation, but unfortunately not a very plausible one," said the Lieutenant, after a moment's hesitation. "The same question was raised by the lab, but the outcome of their investigation was that all the guests involved were in photos taken during the aperitif, and then at their respective tables. Including the Entonneur, Charles, as I've already pointed out."

"Unless one of them went out just long enough to fetch the Doyen and bring him into the cavern?" Maltier interjected.

"If that was the case, then we ought to be able to find at least one or two photos showing them together at some given moment – but there are none. It would also need the Doyen to have been held in a place near the cavern where the ceremony took place, but the forensic team haven't been able to identify anywhere like that."

"This whole case is totally crazy," said Patricia. "I went through all the photos last night with Gendron. There isn't a single picture showing the Doyen anywhere other than where he collapsed, or just next to it."

"It's like *Star Trek*. Teleportation," joked Fauroux, one of the older but less prominent members of the Brigade.

"I know, it does your head in," Georges agreed, going along with his humour. "On the other hand, we might strike lucky with what's been found in Monsieur Laurent's cellar. Hopefully enough to identify someone from the DNA trace evidence – unless it comes from the householder himself, members of his family or the cleaning lady! We'll know in two or three days, anyway."

"And has Charles got an alibi for the Sunday afternoon?" continued the young gendarme.

"Have you just taken against him, or have you got some idea at the back of your mind?" asked Gendron in amusement.

"Neither, but as he's the sole person to be seen with the Doyen in every one of the photos, I was just wondering."

"Charles does in fact have an alibi for Sunday," Georges went on. "He had lunch with two friends at a restaurant in town and then took part in a bridge match until around six o'clock."

"He doesn't seem very bothered by his friend's death."

"Have any of the substances used in the two cases been identified?"

Gendron had been watching his young colleague before asking the question. It seemed to him that she was concentrating too single-mindedly on the idea that the Entonneur was implicated. Due to tiredness, probably. He wanted to move the discussion into other possible avenues of enquiry.

"Partly. They detected a large dose of buprenorphine along with some other substance from the benzodiazepine group, administered either as a powder or through an injection. It's a very powerful narcotic drug. The thing is that combining the two substances can prove fatal. Even mixing the first of them with alcohol could be enough."

"Given the ages of the two men and their weakened condition after what they'd been put through, they'd have had no chance of survival," Maltier agreed.

"And the narcotic might explain the Doyen's passive state, as well as his lack of reaction when he was in the cavern."

Silence fell. None of the gendarmes present had ever come across such sophistication in the art of destroying human life.

"Right, let's get going," said the Lieutenant at last, to shake the group out of the lethargy that seemed to have infected them. "Every team has its allotted task. We'll take stock this evening of everything we find out."

* * *

Still stunned by Angèle's nocturnal visit, Cédric continued to savour its pleasures, regretting that nights were so short. Never before had he experienced such passionate and expert kissing. He didn't usually remember his conquests for very long, but this beautiful, distant woman with her air of mystery and that hint of venom he always felt in her presence was something quite different. She was unlike any other woman he'd ever known. Perhaps she was a snare, but she was also his only hope of getting out of this insane mess.

He got up, took away the chair that was still jamming the

door and then stopped himself just before making his usual gesture to the cameras. The light! She'd got him to put on the light. So there were no cameras in the bedroom, just as she'd said.

He stepped into the shower. Shaved, fresh and rested, he was about to go down to the kitchen for his morning coffee when he came to a halt in front of the cupboard. Now that he knew the bedroom wasn't being monitored, he could take a quick look at the mechanism his new associate had told him about, which had enabled her to come into the room without his being aware.

The rear of the cupboard consisted of brick and plaster covered in ancient green wallpaper. On one side, there was a wooden panel butting up against a vertical beam set against the back wall. The other end was fixed to the wall of his bedroom and fastened between two upright brackets.

That side of the cupboard served to separate two adjoining bedrooms, as he'd suspected when he'd first arrived. He pushed it with both hands towards his own room. One part of the panel slid back a few centimetres, revealing several studs on a decorative upright support. The other part, fixed to the vertical beam of the back wall, could now pivot on an invisible hinge, leaving just enough room to get through.

It was an ingenious contrivance. Perhaps it had been dreamed up by a former owner to be able to get at the maid, or his mistress, without the rest of the household knowing. Was it the only one of its kind in this strange building?

Satisfied with his experiment, he took the opportunity of taking a quick glimpse inside the neighbouring bedroom. He was hoping he might discover his new confidante's own cubby-hole, but it was empty – not a stick of furniture in it. It was dark and narrow, with a view from the side of the house. He examined his surroundings very carefully. The two rooms had clearly formed one single one before the long cupboard had been put in place. The space needed for the mechanism had required the erection of a fairly thick party wall, intended to disguise the gap of about seven or eight centimetres required for the panel to move.

He put the pivoting part back as it had been and refastened the other. The two halves were now solidly fixed again, held rigid. It would have taken a very experienced eye to detect the narrow slit along the edge of the support. He took the precaution of pushing the cupboard door shut – no point in drawing attention to it.

The kitchen was still imbued with the smell of coffee but there was nothing left except its aroma and a few drops in the bottom of the pot, barely luke-warm. He took the filters and was preparing his daily dose when he saw Angèle come into the kitchen. She motioned to him to be quiet, raising a finger to her lips. It was almost erotic.

"I can't imagine how you can trust someone to carry out a job when he can't even get up before nine or ten in the morning, after doing sod-all the previous day. You've backed the wrong horse there, if you ask me."

He looked at her, flabbergasted. Her face was cold and hard in a way he'd never seen before. He was about to make some curt reply when he saw Karl emerge behind her.

"Don't worry. I'll be keeping my eye on him, and if he doesn't go in the right direction, or not fast enough, he'll be the first to feel nervous."

"I hope so. I don't want to stay in this place for another two weeks. It's creepy."

"Just say when you've finished using me as the duty punch bag," said Lantois angrily. "And if you've got any suggestions apart from sending me on this suicide mission tonight, then let me know!"

"It's just as well for you there isn't another option," said Angèle, turning her back on him and stalking out of the kitchen.

"I told you you wouldn't get anywhere with her," said Karl sarcastically, after she'd left. "She's a real wild one. You can't make up to her like that. One day she's all charm, the next she's more ferocious than a tigress."

"I wasn't planning on setting up home here either. I just want to get out and be free to go with my pay-off. I'll find someone else just as good as her, or better."

He decided to play Karl's game, to avoid any suspicion. Besides, confronting him would only have made the situation worse – for both of them, because he had no choice but to link his own fate to that of his paramour.

* * *

Patricia walked through the Caves Painctes accompanied
by the secretary of the confrérie. She examined everything
carefully, not wanting to miss any little detail. She took on
board as best she could the information she was being
given by her companion, who told her that whenever the
grand chapters were held, she installed herself in a small
office by the access corridor so she could check invitation
cards and let the guests know where to go. It was
impossible for anyone to get into the first cavern where the
vin d'honneur and speeches happened without going past
her. On the evening the incident had occurred, there'd
been two of them on duty at the entrance, and neither of
them had seen the Doyen come in. Her colleague had
already said as much to the investigators.

They passed through two corridors, noting some mossy
ironwork decorated with old flagons that were as dusty as
they were empty. After a glimpse at the 'Fontaine de la
Dive Bouteille', the Fountain of the Holy Bottle and its
spring, so named from the writings of François Rabelais,
they emerged at last into the first cave, which was longer
than it was wide. At the other end was the great staircase
that led to the next cavern, where the induction
ceremonies and dinners took place.

"And there's no other entrance?" the young gendarme
asked insistently. "Do the kitchen and waiting staff come
in this way too?"

"Ah! That's right, I was forgetting about that. The kitchens are on the left at the top of the stairs, and the other cavern is on the right. There's a passage between the kitchens and the outside porch. That's where the caterer delivers the meals and unloads all his equipment, crockery, table decorations and so on."

"Could your Doyen have come in that way?"

"No, your colleagues have already asked me that. Once the meals are being prepared, people are flying about all over the place and any intruder would be unceremoniously ejected. And a fully-robed Entonneur could hardly have gone unnoticed in the middle of the kitchens."

They continued on their way, climbed the steps and entered the second cavern. Stripped of its tables and decorations, it seemed even bigger than normal. Right at the end, to the right, was the stage and, on the left, two alcoves carved out of the tuffeau. At the opposite end was a stone wall with a passage at either side.

"That's the access to the toilets," said the secretary, noticing that the gendarme was looking towards that area.

"And to get onto the stage, there must be a corridor of some sort, I suppose?"

"Yes, it comes out in the first cavern, the one we've just passed through."

"At any rate, he can't have come in by the stage entrance. Everyone would have noticed him. I'm going to go round it all again and have another detailed look. And then you can show me how the kitchen and delivery personnel get in."

∗ ∗ ∗

With Karl sitting beside him, Cédric was driving the car he'd been allocated. Not his own – they were still unsure whether or not it had been spotted – but one of those that had been parked underneath the house.

To get into the basement, they'd gone through the little door under the staircase. The garage was dimly lit, and all that was visible were the spaces formed by an enormous structural wall that followed the line of the rooms it was supporting, the big drawing room and Babar's office, and presumably the bedrooms and the attic above those. There was a small room set against this wall, the door into which was closed, offering no clue as to what might be inside or what the room was used for. It had been the only point of interest in the basement, other of course than the cars and the fact that they could be accessed without having to go outside the house.

Proceeding at a steady speed, they followed the corniche road that ran beside the river. Angèle had set off before them, with instructions to call them in case of any danger or a Gendarmerie checkpoint. On their left there was only the Vienne, flowing in all its majesty, and on the right a few houses clinging to the hillside. Some of these were large, ancient mansions, others more recent buildings or old abandoned ruins. Just a few caves used as wine cellars still resisted being turned into dwellings.

"Slow down, we're nearly there. It will be on your right where I tell you."

"Yes, I'd assumed it would be on the right rather than in the middle of the river!"

"Shut it! Watch out, it's behind the next wall, after that small deserted house."

"It would be easier if I wasn't driving! Shall we pull up?"

"Yeah. Why don't you ring the doorbell and ask if you can take a look round?"

As they drove past the wall surrounding the property, Lantois caught a glimpse of a large house dating from the '70s or '80s in the middle of parkland planted with trees. It was situated half way up the slope and had an outstanding view over the Vienne as well as the meadows and hills stretching beyond it. The wall was less than two metres from the road.

"Are you off your head? Do you really expect me to go in there? On my own? And where will I park the car?"

"Never mind that. You'll do what we've planned, and that's all. Go right at the next roundabout, I'll show you the way from there. We'll have a look round the back."

"What about the dogs?"

"What dogs?"

"You think a place like this won't have guard dogs?"

"No. Babar says there's a burglar alarm, but no dogs."

"And he's never wrong?"

"No!"

They turned right at the roundabout, went past a fire station and then took a narrow, climbing road. They drove through a hamlet where the majority of the buildings were hidden behind high walls.

"This is the road I took when I arrived," Cédric remarked.

"Could well be, but who gives a damn. Look over there, on the right, there's a rusty gate five or six metres past the last house in the village."

They came to a metal railing fence, set into which was an old iron gate. In the distance was an ancient abandoned chapel, outlined against the blue of the sky. A dirt track ran down from the gate towards the house, of which only the roof could be seen.

"Is that it?"

"Obviously! And you'll come along this deserted road to get here. I'll be driving. I'll drop you to the left of that gateway, where there's a gap in the fence, and after that you're on your own. Have you got the layout of the house fixed in your head?

"Yes. And when it's over?"

"You come back with your package. We'll be waiting for you. Don't worry, we'll be close to you all the time. And don't get any stupid ideas, you've nowhere to run to from here."

"And what about the woman?"

"Tie her up, give her a seeing to, do what the hell you like with her so long as you bring back the goods."

They had scarcely slowed down as they passed the fence.

"Keep driving, we'll go round again."

CHAPTER 18

The bell of the St Etienne church clock had just struck six when Georges hung up the phone, looking towards his group.

"I think you all heard that. The Procureur has now allocated an examining magistrate to the case. A female judge, as it happens. I'll be going to see her tomorrow. That's the end of the good life, from now on it will be all reports and minutes of meetings. But for the moment, may we summarise where we've got to so far?"

"That won't take long as far as I'm concerned," said Maltier. "There was nothing of interest to my team in the Doyen's house. None of the witnesses had seen anything out of the ordinary in the last few weeks, but all their statements are in agreement on one point: the two men, that is, the two victims, had known each other for a long time. They were very close after the war but apparently fell out a few years later. But we need to be careful here – apart from one old lady who knew them at the time, all of this is just hearsay."

"And the statements I've collected say pretty much the same thing," said Gendron, interrupting. "However, one of the men would have been twenty or twenty-one years old at the end of the war, and the other one about fifteen or sixteen. Given their ages at the time, they wouldn't have had the same interests."

"They were aged twenty and sixteen respectively in 1945," Georges stated. "A difference of four years."

"I would have said more than that," the big man murmured, "but it doesn't really matter. If we're going to start taking into account every altercation that's happened since the 1950s, we'll never get to the end of this case!"

"That's for sure," Maltier responded, grudgingly.

"You may well be right," said the Lieutenant, "but I heard the same thing said last night when I was in town. As it's the only link between the two cases, we shouldn't let go of it."

He was silent for a few moments before continuing:

"Patricia? Haven't you got anything to say?"

"As regards that issue, no. On the other hand, I've been going through all the witness statements and those made by the Entonneurs, the ones from Saturday night. I haven't finished yet, but I've come up with one or two points of interest."

Her eyes were tired and she could barely stifle a yawn as she went on:

"Sorry, I didn't sleep very well. I discovered that the last Entonneur to be admitted to the confrérie was none other than our friend Charles."

"You're not going to give up on him, are you?" laughed Gendron.

"He was inducted in Chinon just under six months ago. His money comes from businesses he's set up in Africa and Asia. At least, that's what I was told."

"It's on his file," Georges interjected. "I've already asked the Finance department of the S.R. to look into the money situation and bank accounts of the two victims, and I'll add Charles to the list if you think it'll help. That said, even if his income did come from dubious sources, it wouldn't make him a murderer. Particularly as he has alibis."

"If I may continue," said Patricia. "He'd hardly been in Chinon for any time at all before he approached the Entonneurs. The secretary says that he made up to members of the confrérie so he'd be accepted immediately. And who was the first person he contacted, other than the Grand Maître? Got it in one – it was the Doyen. After that, he used to run little errands for him."

"Just hold on a minute, Patricia," Gendron interrupted. "If you want to join an association in a place where you don't know anybody, you start by approaching the president and then one or two senior or representative members. That's perfectly normal behaviour. I think you're misdirecting yourself here."

"Possibly, but I can't believe what everybody claims to have seen. How is it that no-one, no-one at all, noticed this old man dying in a dining hall full of people? Except for Charles, at the point where everybody was looking towards the stage. Doesn't that surprise anyone? Don't you find that odd?"

She said all this with such conviction that everyone stared at her.

"You've put your finger on the question that we've all been asking from the very beginning, but no-one is able to answer it for the moment. Making Charles a suspect still doesn't solve that problem."

"If nobody wants to see anything, we might as well not bother investigating!"

She stood up in agitation, her words coming out with such increased vehemence that all the other group members looked at her in astonishment.

"We all agree that some kind of trick was used here that we don't understand," she said, almost angrily, "and the one person who was in a position to have seen anything, or indeed to have done it himself, was Charles. But no, nobody here wants to listen to me and take any notice of that. I'm being treated like some kind of obtuse idiot when it's the only lead we have."

She sat down again, embarrassed by her outburst and not daring to look at her colleagues. She felt tears welling up in her eyes. Why on earth had she done that?

A few moments passed, then Gendron decided to break the silence.

"Patricia has taken this case very much to heart and has stayed up all night working on it. I agree with her – if there's anyone who can help us understand how the Doyen got in, it's the person who first noticed him. And even if there's nothing in his statement from Saturday, we should press him a bit further, he might remember a few extra details."

Georges waited before responding. Going down that road meant he would lose some degree of control over his team, perhaps for nothing in return. He doubted that the Entonneur would now remember very much more than on the evening the crisis had occurred. On the other hand, questioning him again wouldn't take up much time.

"Patricia, you've convinced us," he said eventually. "I leave you to pursue all matters concerning how the Doyen got into the cavern."

"Thank you," she stammered, standing up.

Tired and at the end of her tether, upset by her own reaction, she was ready to burst into tears. She made her way towards the door without saying a word, while everyone gazed at her in astonishment.

"Have I dropped a clanger there?" asked Georges, turning to Gendron.

"No," he said, getting up. "She's tired, and she has a few personal problems. She'll get over it. I'll sort her out."

He too went towards the door.

"You take on all the hard jobs!" said one of the other gendarmes, jokingly. A scornful shrug of the shoulders was the only response.

"Can we please get on?" asked Georges, who could feel the meeting slipping away from him. "The other lead we have concerns the substances involved. They're the same as were used in several cases in the Paris area several months ago. Those investigations are still ongoing, and the perpetrators haven't yet been identified. On each occasion, it was a domestic burglary with violence. There's nothing in common with what we have here."

"Given the lack of anything else to go on, I propose we take these war stories a bit further. There may be some link there," Maltier suggested. "I'll take responsibility for identifying those Chinon residents who were around at the time."

"Why not? Considering the stage we've reached..."

CHAPTER 19

It was two o'clock in the morning. A car without its lights on, travelling at low speed, had just entered the lane that Karl and Cédric had reconnoitred a few hours earlier. It slowed down as it passed the closed iron gate. The passenger door opened and a dark form emerged, making an approximate attempt at a forward roll.

"Shit," groaned the form, moving towards the gate as the car door slowly closed again. "The bastard made sure I'd land on the road instead of the grass."

A few minutes later, Lantois the hit-man was approaching the house from round the back. The dim moonlight was just sufficient to illuminate his progress and prevent him from falling over the drum of a spraying machine that had been left on the path. He ended up on a small terrace carved out of the hillside, now plunged into darkness because of all the vegetation and trees growing round it. He turned back towards the track he'd just come down. The slope had turned out to be much steeper than he'd anticipated. He doubted he'd be able to carry his victim up it as he made his escape.

Stifling an oath, he walked round the side of the house, where he found the small cellar door he'd identified on the plan. It was the work of a few minutes to force the lock and release the three bolts. Child's play! He proceeded to examine his surroundings with a small flashlight. There was a horizontal freezer cabinet, two rows of cheap cupboards, a washing machine and a laundry basket. Nothing to prevent him from opening the door leading to the kitchen, or to impede his escape if it all went horribly wrong. Cédric was ready to begin work less than ten minutes after he'd got here. Not bad. Now that he was back in action, he felt his spirits revive and he could even summon up a degree of pride in his performance, as if he were some kind of top-ranking athlete. He forgot all the constraints and threats – Karl and Babar couldn't do this as well as he could, they'd chosen him for the job because of his abilities.

He switched off the torch and carefully opened the kitchen door. Although there wasn't a glimmer of light, it was best to be cautious. The tiniest noise or untoward movement would have him out of here and disappearing into the night. As he gradually became used to the dark, he moved from the kitchen into the hallway, then waited a few moments before briefly shining his torch round about him. It was always advisable not to collide with a piece of furniture or trip over the edge of a mat.

The bedroom was opposite him, on the left. The door was closed. He went over to it, hoping it wasn't going to creak. He slowly turned the handle, and it didn't creak – but it wouldn't open, either. Surprised, he tried lifting it up slightly and pushed a bit harder. Still no result. Was it bolted on the inside?

He was about to give up when the door squeaked and opened a fraction, scraping on the wooden floor. Then it suddenly gave way with a crash that seemed horrendously loud to him in the stillness of the night. Losing his balance, he almost fell flat on his face in the middle of the room. His eardrums were shattered by a scream, that of a woman who has suddenly woken up in terror. Her husband didn't make any utterance, but Cedric realised at once that he was on the right-hand side of the bed from the sound, muffled by the bedside mat, of two feet violently striking the floor.

He was disorientated and had dropped his torch. He got up as quickly as he could to face his opponent and regain the initiative. Light suddenly issued from a bedside lamp, half blinding him. He had no time to react as the man jumped on him and began trying to punch him to the ground. He didn't manage to avoid the blows completely and fell on his side, pulling his adversary down with him. The man he'd come to kidnap had found an energy born of fear and, spurred on by his wife's shrieks, had turned into a furious aggressor. He had one knee on Cédric's arm and was hitting him in the face, preventing him from reacting as he would normally have done. Protecting himself with his hands, the torturer came back at him, twisting onto his side and giving him a violent kick in the private parts. The man screamed in pain and collapsed against the foot of the bed, which checked his fall and allowed him to get straight back on his feet. He began raining punches again, although now with less force. Unfortunately for Cédric, the woman had got out of bed and joined in the fray as well, trying to hit him as best she could. Her blows were not very powerful, but added to those of her husband they were beginning to overcome their assailant, forcing him to use his hands and forearms to protect himself. He'd been in the bedroom for less than a minute and the operation was already heading for disaster. Overcoming the panic that was starting to take hold of him, Lantois made a supreme effort and managed to raise himself up a little, smashing a blow at the woman's jaw. She fell sideways, banged hard into the wooden bedpost and dropped senseless to the floor. Taken by surprise, her husband diverted his gaze for a few tenths of a second, just long enough not to anticipate the straight right that caught him on the point of the chin. He sat back, his eyes vacant, unable to make any movement. Taking immediate advantage of this, Cédric struck him a second blow which sent him sprawling on the floor to resume the dreams that had been so brutally interrupted a few minutes earlier.

The torturer's heart was pounding and he felt half dead as he took the handcuffs he'd brought with him and fastened the man's hands behind his back. He carefully tied his legs together right down to his ankles, leaving just enough play in the bindings to allow him to walk slowly. He finally took a length of orange adhesive tape, the sort used on building sites, and decorated the man's mouth and ears with it, removing a few hairs from the nape of his neck in the process.

Cédric bent over the woman, who was still unconscious.

She was too overweight for him to lift her up and tie her to a chair as he'd planned. Glancing round the room, he saw in a mirror that his balaclava had hardly moved, just revealing a few stray hairs. The bitch couldn't have seen his face. Reassured, he decided simply to tie her up, gagging her with the same adhesive tape. He checked the bonds on her wrists, making sure they weren't so tight that she wouldn't be able to get free after a few hours of struggling. In spite of his unscrupulous behaviour and his recent activities, Cédric could never bring himself to go beyond the level of violence necessary to achieve a 'professional' result.

He picked up his torch and dragged the still groggy man to the kitchen. Having rinsed his face in cold water to soothe his bruises, which luckily had been attenuated by his balaclava, he then splashed some over his prisoner to rouse him from the mists of oblivion.

"I don't want to hurt you," he said, failing to appreciate the incongruity of his remark. "It's just that some friends of mine would like to have a little talk with you. After that, you'll be allowed to go back home."

"Mmmmmm."

"That's right. We can leave here quietly, just the two of us. Don't worry, you can walk, not very fast, but enough. And don't try anything on, or I'll make sure that you won't do it ever again."

"Mmmmmm."

"Calm down! Oh, you're worried about your wife? It's all right, she's fine. She'll be able to get free tomorrow some time. Don't worry about that, I've taken care of her."

Three quarters of an hour later, the car driven by Karl, not showing any lights, had made a long detour and deposited them in the basement of the sinister house.

"Where's the woman?" asked Babar, as soon as they arrived.

His manner betrayed both impatience and nervousness. He too was wearing a balaclava – a precaution only necessary if he thought the prisoner might recognise him, Cédric thought.

"It was impossible to bring them both here," he said. "She's still in the house, tied up and gagged."

"That's not what I wanted. If we'd taken both of them, that would have given us a few days' leeway before their friends and neighbours became worried."

"I did what Karl told me to do."

"Shall we go back?" said Karl, not making any riposte.

"Of course not," growled B.A. "Everything went off all right, so we're not going to risk being spotted now. Take him in there."

He indicated the little room adjacent to the structural wall that Lantois had noticed a few hours before.

The room contained just some dusty shelving, three worn-out chairs and two large chests filled with various items. These included handcuffs and other implements, amongst which Lantois noticed some leather foot straps for bicycle pedals. These were no longer used very much, but they could fasten just about anything if they were slightly stretched first. Once they were tightened round the wrists and moistened, it was impossible to get out of them unaided.

Their hostage had also realised this, and started to struggle. He took advantage of a moment's inattention on Cédric's part to try to kick him in the shin. Hindered by the bindings round his legs, his attempt failed and the kick did not make contact. Karl delivered an uppercut which immediately calmed him down.

"Tie him to the chair so he can't move. Karl, make sure that our amateur does it properly."

They waited for the man to come to. He no longer seemed in any state to resist.

"What do you want from me? Money?" he groaned, a few moments later.

"Better than that," replied Babar, turning a chair round so that he could sit facing him.

His features were outlined by his black balaclava so that he resembled a bird of prey. Or perhaps, with his arms crossed over the dossier and his chin leaning on it, he looked more like a cat staring at its latest catch before delivering the final deadly blow with its claws.

"We're going to talk about your father," he said, after a few seconds.

CHAPTER 20

Georges hesitated, his lips having barely touched his second morning cup of coffee. He ought to phone his wife back and explain the situation, make her understand that in the present circumstances he couldn't possibly take two days off to help her finish packing the boxes. And perhaps they ought to put the removal date back by a week, or a couple of weeks. But that was likely to lead to a major confrontation that he didn't feel up to taking on at the moment. At least, not this morning. This afternoon then, that would be easier.

He was about to leave when his mobile started vibrating.

"We've got a new humdinger of a case," said the caller.

"Another murder?" the Lieutenant asked anxiously.

"No. Well, possibly not. It's an assault and a kidnapping. A member of the Entonneurs, Monsieur Derouchy."

"A third Entonneur?! And is he an old man?"

"Yes, fairly old. He and his wife were attacked in their home last night. An individual acting on his own. The wife was knocked out and tied up, but she managed to free herself this morning. From the preliminary evidence, her husband and the attacker left up the hillside path behind the house. He was obviously trussed up, there are signs of feet dragging along the ground. I may have overstepped the mark, but I alerted the forensic team before phoning you."

"You did the right thing. I'd much rather have them called out for nothing than miss any evidence. I'm on my way."

He hung up, swearing.

An elderly Entonneur... Maybe he'd been around in the war as well, and had contacts with the other two. But why would they have been killed and not him? Perhaps it would only be a matter of time, long enough to torture him and extract the information they wanted. What bloody awful luck! Three tortured bodies in just a few days. The pressure in the cooker was mounting...

And why had they taken this one away, rather than deal with him in his own home as they'd done with the second victim? Because of his wife?

Something was wrong there. The attackers had been quite unscrupulous up to now and were prepared to leave a trail of corpses, so why not this woman? Unless... Unless this was a pseudo-abduction, a fake kidnapping, intended to put the guilty party in the clear by making him look like a victim.

Georges grabbed his phone. He would need to check out this Derouchy's alibi immediately and identify him on the photos taken during the evening.

At that same moment, Patricia Blancard was making her way towards the house where Charles lived, on the assumption that she was free to pursue her enquiries as she saw fit following the decision taken the previous day. She was determined to extract the maximum possible information from him. If she put a little pressure on him, she should be able to make him remember a few more useful details. Or even get him to contradict himself?

The young detective was becoming more and more convinced that her prospective interviewee was one of the key figures in this case, and she was determined to find out exactly what game he was playing.

Charles's house was old, quite large and in an isolated location. The surrounding parkland was minute, more like a large garden than a real park, and it was very badly maintained. Unusually for this part of the world, there was no wall to separate it from its surroundings other than the one that could be seen to the rear of the property. One could imagine that some penurious landowner had gradually disposed of the adjoining plots before being forced to give up the house itself.

Alternatively, it might once have accommodated the staff of the mansion on the other side of the wall, which allowed just a few glimpses of its roofline to be seen between the treetops.

Seeing that the shutters were open and a car was parked outside, she presumed the occupant was at home. The wide front door was made of heavy wood. The upper part consisted of opaque glass windows reinforced by iron bars, making it look more like the gateway to some fortress. She saw the doorbell on the wall and rang.

There was no answer.

She stepped back a little to take stock of her surroundings. Perhaps the Entonneur was out in the garden. She rang a second time.

"All right, all right, I'm coming," said a dull voice from inside.

There was the sound of a key turning and two bolts being drawn back one after the other, then the door opened. She immediately recognised the man from having scrutinised so many photos of him. He looked tired. Wearing a black dressing gown, unshaven and with his hair uncombed, he gave every impression of having been dragged out of bed by his visitor.

"You'll have to excuse me, I went to bed late last night. Or rather, this morning. I was having dinner with friends. At my time of life, we don't recover as quickly as you young people."

This speech was accompanied by an engaging smile which rather disconcerted his visitor.

"To what do I owe the honour of this visit?" he went on.

"Good morning, sir, Gendarmerie Nationale."

"Yes, so I see," he interrupted, looking over towards her car. "You're required to say what brings you here and so forth. But I thought you people always went round in pairs?"

Patricia hadn't been able to say a word or to identify

herself before being wrong-footed by this man's aplomb and outgoing manner. He was forcing her to justify herself even before he knew who she was or why she'd come.

"But of course, it's your investigation into the death of our unfortunate Doyen," he continued, not allowing her time to say anything. "I must be stupid. Do come in."
What had she got herself into here? Was it to be him dictating all the questions and answers, or herself?

"Please let me state my identity and the reason for my visit before accepting your invitation. Those are the regulations, and I have to follow them."

"Of course. Go on, then."
Was this character ever going to shut up?
She went through the required formula before explaining, as best she could, that she was permitted to come here unaccompanied as it was simply a matter of confirming various items of information. He pretended to believe her and showed her into a small study off the hallway, which contained a jumble of books lying open or upside down, and piles of papers and old documents stacked in a haphazard way.

"Excuse all this mess. I'm engaged in some historical research," he thought it necessary to add by way of justification. "It makes a considerable change for me from my business affairs in Africa. I'll clear an armchair for you," he went on, picking up a heap of volumes lying on one of them.

The young woman stopped herself from remarking that his

filing system was probably not any different now from what it had been before his return to this country. She glanced round the room while he was tidying it up and noticed some of the titles of the books and folders.

"What would you like to know?" he asked, as soon as they were sitting down.

"I have your statement in front of me. You are actually the sole witness who was near the spot where the Doyen collapsed. At any rate, no-one saw or photographed him in any other place. You're the only person who could have noticed anything, some detail, however tiny, that might help us understand how he got there."

"I'm afraid I haven't the slightest idea, and I believe I've already said all I know. Perhaps you should have another look at the statements made by the kitchen staff?"

"He couldn't have come in that way, we're sure of that. On the other hand, you noticed him near the toilets, that is, on the opposite side from the kitchens. Did you see him before that point?"

"No, and I've already said so."

"Where were you before that?"

"I don't remember," he said, frowning. He seemed surprised by the question.

"From the photos we have in our possession, you went over to the area near the toilets as soon as you'd left the main stairway, when the group of Entonneurs broke up," she said confidently, without being at all certain of this. "You must surely have noticed something?"

"I assure you, I did not."

"And then all of a sudden, Hey Presto! A wave of a magic wand, and the Doyen appears next to you?"

"Er… Yes, you could put it something like that."

"And does that seem likely?" she asked sarcastically.
She could feel him hesitating, and she wanted to back him into a corner.

"You see, I was looking mainly at the stage and the guests. You have to be on the alert all the time to make sure everything goes off all right. I assume he came from the toilets, that was the nearest place."

"You didn't make that assumption on the night. Or else you forgot to mention it. Never mind, it's understandable, you were in a very emotional state. So he could have been in the toilets during the whole of the start of the ceremony, or even before the kitchen staff arrived at least two hours earlier. Does that seem feasible to you?"

"Not really. But it's your theory, not mine."
His face had changed: it was now harder, less welcoming.

"It's not mine – you're the one who came up with the idea that he might have been in there. But it's an interesting possibility. I shall need to check whether any of the WC cubicles was permanently closed before the guests arrived. One of the catering staff might have noticed."

"But even if that was the case, there's nothing to prove that he was actually in there. And it certainly wouldn't explain how he got there. All that does is move the location of the problem," he said, with the hint of a scowl.

"Perhaps so, but when you start unravelling a tangled ball of string, you always find the end of it eventually. Even if at first you don't know where it is."

Not bad, my girl, you'll have to remember that one!

She got up and turned towards the door, convinced that it was pointless to pursue this interview until new evidence became available.

"I'm really sorry I can't be more helpful to you. The Doyen was my friend, and I did what I could for him," said Charles. "But not that night, unfortunately…"

"I know, all the witness statements say you were very close. By the way, he didn't drive, and you said you were the one who was supposed to pick him up from his home before the ceremony?"

"Yes, I was, but he'd already left. I assumed one of my colleagues had taken it upon himself to do it."

"I shall certainly need to come back later to resume this morning's conversation," she said, just before going out of the door.

"You're always welcome."

Patricia got back in her car feeling satisfied with the way the interview had gone, and also relieved. Acting solo like this was against the regulations and she'd certainly receive a reprimand from Georges, but she'd been able to regain a degree of independence. By freeing herself from all these ludicrous constraints she could do things her own way, be herself again, and perhaps make it up with Paul. Constraints and regulations… there were so many of them.

But what a profession she was in! Information of the sort she'd extracted this morning was worth all the effort of getting it.

She drove off and headed towards the Entonneurs' building.

CHAPTER 21

Patricia was excited when she met up with the rest of the team, despite feeling anxious about having acted on her own. She was looking forward to sharing the new information with her colleagues but was rather taken aback by their attitude. Maltier and Gendron seemed in unusually good spirits and exchanged a few jokes on their way to Georges' office.

The latter was the only one who seemed to be in a bad mood.

"I don't know what's got into you all – maybe you're tired, maybe you've been having a laugh about these cases before the meeting, but I can't myself see anything about them to cause hilarity."

"Is Derouchy's kidnapping as serious as that?" Maltier asked in concern.

"Of course it is," said the Lieutenant angrily. "Three major cases in four days… And you ask me if one of them is less serious?!"

"That's not want I meant," Maltier explained. "I was just anxious to know whether we had any leads, or if a ransom demand has been made."

"No, no ransom. At least, not as yet. But when the two of them were struggling with their attacker, his balaclava slipped slightly, just enough to reveal a few wisps of hair, according to the wife. The forensic investigators hope that some of them may have been pulled out during the fight."

"That could be useful," Gendron remarked. "Does the wife have any idea why her husband was abducted?"

"None at all. She's completely distraught. She thinks it may have been a failed attempt at burglary. We can't link this case to the other two as the method isn't the same, and the victims are from different generations. Derouchy was born four years after the war. I had thought it might have been a put-up job to avert suspicion, but their alibis for Saturday and Sunday are rock solid. Besides, we've nothing at all to suggest they were involved, so it would have been stupid of them to attract our attention."

The Lieutenant waited for the group to fall silent, perhaps expecting a few ideas to be forthcoming, but none were. He sighed and went on:

"And what about you? Who shall I begin with – Maltier?"

"Has the financial investigation department come up with anything?" asked Maltier, as if he hadn't heard the question.

"We won't have anything until the end of the week at best, unless I put some pressure on them, but I'd like to hang on a bit first."

"OK. As for Gendron and myself, we've been concentrating on the possible links between the two cases with the help of the forensic team and the archivist, and we've interviewed all the older people we could trace in the area. The outcome is not without some interest."

"The two men were considered as rather wayward youths at the beginning of the war, young tearaways who were always up to something," Gendron went on. "They were as thick as thieves."

"Anything serious?"

"No, just petty pilfering which increased after the refugees came. They quietened down when the Germans arrived – it became too risky after that."

"That doesn't get us very far…"

"Yes, it does," Maltier interrupted. "We're sure that something very serious occurred. Almost all our witnesses are convinced of it. Before the occupying troops got here, there was complete chaos in the area and, apparently, a group of men pulled a big job. A very big job."

"And?"

"They were all subsequently arrested by the Germans and sent to a prison camp. None of them ever came back, but – and there's always a 'but' – the Doyen and Laurent were suspected of having unwittingly seen whatever it was. We definitely know that rumours were circulating at the time claiming they were looking for some kind of treasure hoard that had been moved later on without them knowing where. When the occupying forces settled in the town and started taking an interest, they had to lie low: it was very dangerous to provoke the Germans. After the war, Laurent continued looking for it on his own."

"Which could have been the reason for their quarrel," Gendron concluded.

"Right," said Georges thoughtfully. He gazed across at Patricia, who looked as though she was bursting to say something. "But do you know exactly what this 'big job' was?"

"Not for certain, but if the rumours turn out to be true, it's a bigger lead than you could possibly imagine."

"OK, you can explain all that to us in a moment. Patricia?"

"I went to see the Entonneur, Charles – I'm very curious about that man."

She paused for a few moments, noticing the smiles forming on her colleagues' lips. Georges pursed his.

"You went there... on your own?"

Seeing his protégée hesitate, Gendron swiftly intervened.

"I was with her."

"That's what I wanted to hear," growled Georges, his face relaxing. "And did you find out anything new?"

"Yes," Patricia said. "I don't think he's quite as clean as he makes out. When you press him, he retreats behind his stance as the victim's best friend."

"That doesn't mean much."

"No, of course not. I haven't got anything definite on him for the moment. But his study's crammed with books, half of them dealing with the history of the area during the last war. Strange coincidence, don't you think?"

Maltier seemed interested at this, but Georges looked unimpressed.

"That's not all," the young gendarme insisted. "Let's go back to the Caves Painctes. Everybody's noticed that the Doyen was never seen or photographed anywhere except near the entrance to the toilets. So I thought he must have come in from there. I don't know if I'm the first person, perhaps I'm the only one, to wonder whether the Doyen had been shut up in there before the guests arrived."

"In his statement, Charles said that he'd gone to the Doyen's house to fetch him more than an hour before the ceremony, but he'd already left. Your conjecture is plausible, but it would tend to show that Charles was not guilty."

"Yes and no. Let's stick with my idea. So, the Doyen goes missing in the middle of the afternoon and reappears next to the toilets in the Caves Painctes. It seems to me he must already have been locked in there before the kitchen and waiting staff arrived."

"And apparently he got out of there on his own, in that condition, after spending two or three hours in a WC cubicle?" Maltier interrupted. "Difficult to see it, given that someone would have had to take him in there and then ask him to close the door!"

"Let me continue, even if I haven't got all the pieces of the puzzle as yet. I went back to the members of the catering staff, and three of them confirmed that one of the cubicles was locked shut. There was a little notice saying it was out of order. Now, the Entonneurs' secretary states that the toilet cleaning had been completed at the end of the morning, and inspected by herself. None of the cubicles was locked or malfunctioning at that time. She also confirms that no-one had access after the arrival of the caterer and his team."

She paused, appearing to enjoy the silence that had come over them all. Georges got up with a baffled look on his face, turned his chair round and, still standing, stared at his file.

"That's interesting. So we have all the toilets working at midday, but one of the cubicles was locked by the end of the afternoon and nobody knows why. And you're certain that no-one, absolutely no-one, came in afterwards? Is that right?"

"Exactly."

"There's one problem," Gendron interposed. "You say that the Doyen was shut in there, and he never moved or knocked on the door – yet, at a given moment, he was able to get out without drawing any attention to himself. That's difficult to believe."

"Seeing what he'd been injected with, I don't think that's a valid objection. Somebody else must obviously have helped him to get out. But the real problem was clearly how to put him into the toilet block in the middle of the afternoon when everybody claims the entrance to the caves was closed off.

"That's correct."

"He must have come in through the emergency exit! That's sited behind the toilets and opens out near the door used by the kitchen staff. The forensic investigators did follow that up, but they weren't very interested because the door only allows people to leave the premises, it won't let them in. Unless, of course, it had already been opened some time earlier and fixed so that it couldn't close again, or else some mechanism had been rigged up with nylon thread to allow it to be opened from outside."

Surprised at the determination and insight of his young colleague, Georges thought he'd better try to regain control of the meeting. He whistled through his teeth as he went on:

"Let's try and picture the scene. Here we have an elderly man who's well known to everyone. He's been drugged and tortured, on top of which he's got a broken jaw, and he has to travel half way across town carrying his Entonneurs' robes over his arm, go up the cul-de-sac leading to the Caves Painctes and then through an iron gate, the key to which I do appreciate he had in his possession, to end up in front of an emergency exit which only opens from the other side – to which no-one has access. Quite a nice little challenge, that!"

"Unless he was driven there. In the back of a van, for instance. I interviewed the delivery drivers and the chefs about this. They confirmed to me that there was a vehicle parked near their space, and it drove off as they arrived. It was a beige utility van, apparently a Citroën, but they couldn't tell me anything else. It's something that happens quite frequently so it didn't particularly surprise them, and they didn't mention it in their statements. As far as they were concerned, it had nothing to do with this case."

"So it appears that at least one vehicle came out of there an hour and a half to two hours before the ceremony began," murmured Georges.

"If you'll let me, I'll tell you how I think it goes after that," Patricia went on. "We now have the Doyen drugged and asleep in the toilets. The door is locked, but it can be opened from the outside if you have a little tool you've brought with you for that very purpose."

Her ensuing description was as vivid as if she'd lived through the events of that evening.

"The induction ritual begins. All eyes are glued on the stage. Even the waiting staff are watching while they wait to start serving. Charles has surreptitiously placed himself near the toilets from the very start. Nobody is taking any notice of him, and the ceremony is taking place at the other end of the cavern. When the Official Cupbearer starts to fill the new members' glasses from his enormous bottle and everybody is staring at what is happening on stage, Charles slips into the toilet block, fetches the Doyen and helps him to walk out. It's not the first time he's attended a chapter so he's well acquainted with the ceremonial, and he's aware that at the very moment he comes back into the dining hall, the new members will raise their giant glasses and all the camera flashes will go off. Nobody, but nobody, is looking at anything except the stage at that point. Then the Doyen collapses, or at least Charles lets go of him so that he falls down. Now all he has to do is to shout out, call for help, and he's performed the trick. I presume he administered the lethal drug just before coming out of the toilet block. He'd broken the Doyen's jaw to stop him making any sound at all if he'd been discovered before he could be given the injection that was intended to kill him."

It was a masterly presentation, but the way the crime had been carried out was no less so. By staying close to his prey, the Entonneur escaped detection: no investigator would be surprised to find his hair or fingerprints on the victim's person. His presence near the body, as if by chance, removed any risk.

Gendron was looking at his protégée like a father proud of his clever daughter, but Georges remained pensive, surprised by the way the young gendarme had set it all out. Patricia had given the three of them a lesson in tenacity and logic. He'd regarded her as someone showing promise for the future but not yet ready to be fully operational quite so soon. Gendron was a very good trainer and she was a remarkable pupil, he thought, looking at each of them in turn.

He ought to do something, immediately, but how could he sum up and give directions as to who should do what after he'd just received so much unexpected information?

He stalled for time by standing up, pretending to pick up the phone and then replacing it after looking at his watch.

He turned his chair the right way round and sat down again.

"It's too late now to call Jacques and his forensic team," he asserted. "On the other hand, we now have two propositions which are both interesting. The first, thanks mainly to Patricia and her brilliant presentation, is that our Entonneur could be implicated in the Doyen's murder. And he would have had an accomplice, because he'd have needed a driver for the van."

Georges paused.

"This gives us a lead on the 'how' of the case," he went on, after a few moments' silence. "The other conjecture concerns the 'why' by offering a possible link between the two men and a very old crime that takes us back to the beginning of the war or thereabouts – a link to that 'big or very big job' that you now need to give us more information about. Gendron? Maltier?"

"I was with Patricia when Maltier was following up that lead," Gendron lied, looking over to his colleague under the surprised gaze of the Lieutenant.

"Right, then," said Maltier. "Now, Lieutenant, hang on to your hat: this is either totally crazy, or it's a very serious matter."

"Carry on. Having got to this point, I could believe anything!"

"In 1939, just after hostilities had broken out, the government took the decision to remove the most strategic services, other than Defence, out of Paris. The first of these, obviously, was the Ministry of Finance: it was the nerve centre of the war effort, and it was immediately relocated to the provinces."

"OK so far..."

"Yes, but like quite a lot of people round here, you'll be surprised to know that the destination was... Chinon!"

"No! Is this some kind of joke?"

"Not at all. It may seem surprising, but when you think about it, the town is protected by the Loire and the Vienne, it's within easy reach of Paris, and there are cellars and underground passages all over the place here, which certainly helped sway the decision. There were some excellent reasons for making that choice."

"And our two victims allegedly participated, here in Chinon, in a heist from the Bank of France or the Ministry of Finance? But they were only youths at the time!"

"Our witnesses think they'd simply been around when it happened. Perhaps by accident. But we can't find any trace of a robbery being carried out during that period. And, curiously, no-one in the area seems to have come into a sudden fortune. It seems as if all those involved in this affair disappeared after having stashed the loot away somewhere."

Georges stood up, his head spinning, and made a gesture to his team to keep silent. There were too many pieces of evidence that kept coming without any obvious link between them. Was it really feasible that this strange historical event, already largely forgotten, might have any connection with the current cases? A few indications such as the age of the victims meant that it could be a possibility, which then made it difficult to ignore. But devoting too much time and effort in going down this trail risked delay to an investigation that had already started off on the wrong foot. He looked at his colleagues for a few moments before making up his mind.

"Maltier, I believe you said you hadn't found any evidence of a robbery. Have you checked with the Archives?"

"Archives and local newspapers. Those for that period, obviously. Nothing. It was wartime, and a lot of things dropped out of sight then."

"Wartime or not, an affair big enough to raise its head some sixty years later must have left some traces somewhere!"
Stretching out his hand with fingers apart, he turned to his deputy:

"The Ministry of Finance archives! That will be the best place to start. Even if the matter was covered up at the time, there may be some vestiges to be found there. Aren't they near Melun?

"At Savigny-le-Temple," Patricia told him.

"Yes, that's right," said Georges, with the hint of a smile. It had just occurred to him that Orleans was on the way there from Chinon.

"We should be able to consult them online. If not, our colleagues at Melun can check the archives on the spot," suggested Maltier.

"I'm a bit reluctant to ask them. We still don't know exactly what we're looking for, and they aren't even aware of the scope of our investigation. They might well miss some little detail. I have to go and see the judge this evening, in Tours, and I might as well go on to Melun straight after that. I'll be able to start first thing in the morning and be back here tomorrow night. It shouldn't interfere with what you're doing."

None of his team failed to notice his smile of satisfaction.

"Maltier," he continued, "don't forget to contact the forensic team tomorrow morning. Explain to them the leads that Patricia has opened up. If they could unearth some evidence, however slight, to show that the Doyen was in the toilets... And as for myself, I'm going to phone the examining judge and then bring the Commandant up to speed."

The meeting broke up.

A few moments later, the young protégée was anxiously going through her mobile phone messages, failing to find the one she was hoping would be there. Gendron suddenly tapped her on the shoulder, making her jump.

"Come with me, I think you have some explaining to do!"

CHAPTER 22

Karl, Cédric and Babar were holding a council of war. Despite their violent interrogation of the hostage, he'd given his tormentors virtually no useful information. They weren't sure whether he was being deliberately obstructive or whether he was genuinely ignorant of the facts they were interested in. Lantois wondered privately whether it was the man's own survival instinct that was keeping him from talking. He was probably convinced that Babar would kill him after he'd obtained all the answers he wanted.

"He's hiding something from us," the boss thundered, "and I need to know what it is. As soon as possible."

"I could rough him up a bit more," said Karl.

"No. We'll have to wait for him to become weaker. No food, no water. It's been twenty-four hours since he left his house and all he's had since then are beatings. He won't to be able to hold out much longer. He'll crack tomorrow morning."

"I don't know why you didn't let me do it," said Cédric. "I have my own methods."

"The stench of grilled pork and a lot of screaming turns my stomach," Babar cut in. "And I don't want to risk finishing him off before he tells us what he knows."

"Perhaps he doesn't know anything else."

"His father told him what he'd done in the war, and afterwards," said Karl. "However much he claims it didn't interest him, I'm convinced he must be able to remember some of the important facts."

"In any case, we need to move quickly, it's becoming urgent," Babar insisted. "The pigs are beginning to stir themselves. They may be floundering about in the dark for the moment, but eventually they'll move in on us. Assuming they haven't started to already. There's a young female gendarme who seems to want to play it on her own. We'll have to take care of her if she gets too close, but that's likely to cause an avalanche of cops to descend on us."

"Is she pretty?" joked Karl, unperturbed.

"I'd say so, yes."

"Am I not enough for you?"

Angèle had just come into the drawing room and was watching them with a sardonic look on her face.

"It's dinner time," she continued.

"Angèle, you're going to do something very important for us tomorrow morning," said Babar. "When we go to give our friend in the cellar his wake-up call, you'll bring in a large hot coffee and some toast. I want it to smell strong and appetising."

"Is that to give him a treat or by way of mental torture?" she scowled, disgusted.

"Never mind, just bring them in, put them down, and we'll do all the rest. You don't have to stay."

Without anyone saying so, Lantois had now been provided with confirmation that his lover was not involved in any way with their scheming. And although the boss spoke to her using the formal 'vous', he seemed to tolerate the beautiful mixed-race girl. Did he have a soft spot for her?

When they'd finished their meal, Babar returned to his lair and Karl went down to the basement to check that everything was as it should be. Cédric decided to go into the drawing room. He was more laid back now, and certainly more alert. He'd noticed a few DVDs and a player, the only way he could spend an evening relaxing before going to skulk in his bedroom. And in any case, Angèle couldn't come to him, assuming she was going to, until everyone was presumed to be asleep.

He skimmed through the list of what was available. Nothing remotely pornographic, not even an action film!

There was a collection of American musical comedies from the fifties, obviously bought at a flea market, together with a video of *Doctor Zhivago*. He hesitated. He'd always been fascinated by Julie Christie's face and her role in this film to the point that he couldn't bear the way it ended. He, the soulless torturer, lacking in any kind of human feeling, always found himself on the verge of tears whenever he saw her sad, pretty face. Not a very good idea, then, to have that on if Karl and Angèle were to come and join him. He took a quick look at the last DVD case: it was *Mary Poppins*, a film he'd often heard mentioned but had never seen. Something for kids. *Faute de mieux*, a good way of winding down before going to bed.

"Haven't you got anything better to do than watch crap for rug rats?" snapped Karl when he arrived some ten minutes later.

"Yes. Collect my dosh and get out of here. But as I can't, I make do with looking at the garbage you've got on the shelf."

"At least if you do that you won't get any uncontrollable urges, and I won't have to prove to you I know how to look after myself," Angèle laughed, as she entered the room. "That suits me perfectly."

* * *

'Feed the birds, tuppence a bag,
Tuppence, tuppence, tuppence a bag.
Feed the birds,' that's what she cries
While, overhead, her birds fill the skies.

The slow, sad song inviting the children to give food to the birds made the beautiful Angèle lift an eyelid; she sat up in the armchair in which she'd been dozing. Looking round the room, she saw Karl stretched out drowsily on a small sofa, while her lover, in an armchair next to hers, seemed fascinated by the film. She shifted her position, and then decided she would be better off in her bedroom than on an uncomfortable seat. She tried to attract Cédric's attention. Leaning forward slightly, she noticed with surprise that he had tears in his eyes as he listened to the song. She watched him for a moment. He was like a waxwork dummy, oblivious to everything else around him.

Angèle just smiled and stood up.

"He's perfect. I couldn't have hoped for anyone better," she murmured inaudibly.

Half an hour later, the tender-hearted torturer went back to his bedroom under the questioning gaze of Karl, who had been ordered to sleep in the basement as a precaution. The boss was unwilling to take the slightest risk with his prisoner and trusted nobody except his right-hand man, so Karl wouldn't be on either the ground or upper floors that night. It was a rare opportunity. Would Angèle take advantage of it to come?

He hoped so. He had no doubts from now on. He was convinced she needed him, in the way that the children had needed Mary Poppins. Except that he had no magic, even if his mission the previous night had been accomplished without any problems, which was almost a miracle in itself...

Cédric slowly closed the door to his room and blocked it once more with his chair. It had become a ritual. Less than two minutes later, it was locked through Karl's good offices, provoking only a scornful shrug from his supposed prisoner.

Switching off the bedside lamp, he stretched out and watched the ray of light on the staircase disappear in its turn, plunging the house into darkness. A quarter of an hour later, tired out by his nocturnal foray and a trying day, he fell into the sleep of the just.

In the middle of the night, the sound of the panel pivoting

round made him rise up quickly from the depths, all his senses on alert. Angèle? Maybe, but at night all cats are black. He instantly turned over on his side and slid under the bed.

"Switch the light on!" whispered the voice of his mistress.

"Angèle?"

"Who do you think? Switch the light on, idiot, and get dressed."

The light came on.

"Get dressed? I already am, but don't worry, I can take it all off very quickly."

"Try to move your brain up from below your belt. Karl is in the basement, and Babar has left."

"I know, so we can get on with it without having to worry about anyone at all!"

"How long have you been mentally defective? All you think about is having it off when this is probably the only night I can show you something important on the ground floor."

"You've got a new coffee machine in your magnificent kitchen?" he said sarcastically, grabbing her round the waist.

"Take your paws off! It's a matter of our survival, so cool it and come with me."

CHAPTER 23

THURSDAY

Seven-thirty a.m. The previous day, Georges had gone along with the arguments put to him by the examining judge. She didn't want to risk charging anyone prematurely and was insisting on some tangible evidence to back up the gendarmes' deductions, such as locating the van and finding traces of Charles or the Doyen in that, or being able to prove that the latter had been in the toilet block. The Lieutenant had experienced greater difficulty in convincing his team, especially Patricia, of the good sense in this decision, which avoided putting the suspect on his guard too soon and ending up with a fiasco on their hands. As he left Melun and followed the long, straight road that led to the Archives Centre in Savigny-le-Temple, the Lieutenant checked his satnav. He was a quarter of an hour early. At least. He had no illusions about how strictly they would keep to time in an administrative office whose main activity consisted of filing and retrieving bumf that most people couldn't give a damn about. And did government ministers have any interest in archives that related to the past, when all they cared about was the future? 'To govern is to foresee', the saying went. Except that leaders nowadays seemed more concerned with predicting their own immediate political future than anything else, using opinion polls as their new science along with crystal balls whose scope extended only as far as the next election. And a stunted future at that, its branches too short to allow new shoots to form and give it a chance to grow.

He spotted a little café conveniently placed next to a car park, and stopped.

The night had been too short. The twins had been waiting up impatiently for their Daddy and had gone to bed later than usual. They'd been too excited to go to sleep, and Georges had needed all his patience and skill as a reader of children's stories to calm them down and eventually get them off. Telling stories. He who spent his life taking apart the ones told by the criminals and murderers he interrogated, each of whom thought they'd given the perfect, unshakeable account that no policeman or gendarme would ever be able to prove wrong. He'd heard many unlikely tales in the few years of his career to date. Tales to make you fall asleep from sheer boredom, or so incoherent that he sometimes wondered which piece of nonsense to demolish first.

Staring at his luke-warm coffee, he cast his mind over the few cases he'd wrestled with for a long time, and occasionally failed to solve. Those had been the work of true artists, Masters of Lies, experts in pulling the wool over people's eyes, but sooner or later the axe had fallen even on them. And that without his having recourse to clairvoyants specialising in reading coffee grounds. Like the ones now lying in his cup.

"You should change your machine, or your filters. There's a lot of mud at the bottom of your coffee," he said to the *patron* as he paid.

"Nobody ever complains," the latter replied. He was an unshaven, rough-looking individual clearly uninterested in any comment made by a passing customer.

Georges got back in his car, checked his destination on the satnav and continued along the Route Nationale. Ten past eight, and he was there. Perfect. It was essential for him to obtain the information he expected to find as soon as possible, so he could spend a whole evening with his wife and children instead of yet another truncated night. It was imperative. When he'd arrived yesterday, he'd barely had time to get his feet under the table before going to bed and getting up early, which had provoked a family crisis. He hadn't even had the wit to compliment Jeanne on the boxes she'd already filled, still less found any time to help her with the task. If the same thing happened again this evening there would be a few angry looks, even if he did hide in the children's room on the pretence of putting them to bed.

Lost in his thoughts, he didn't hear the directions the satnav was giving him and failed to take the little road on his right, driving straight past.

"And a free ride on the merry-go-round!" he said angrily, as the imperturbable voice of his guide told him to make a U-turn at the next roundabout.

Eight-thirty. The car park was almost empty, and the

barrier was down.

"Yes?" came a garbled voice over the intercom.

"Lieutenant Georges, Gendarmerie Nationale. I've come to consult your archives."

"The archives are open by appointment every day between 09:30 and 17:30. Have you made an appointment?"

"No, but…"

"I am sorry, sir, you can only enter by appointment, and in any case you're too early, the public is not admitted before 09:30 as I've just told you."

"I'm not 'the public', I'm involved in a homicide investigation and I don't give a damn about your opening hours! Either you raise the barrier now, or I'll be putting you in handcuffs at 09:30!"

As Georges had observed several times before now, a firm threat from a gendarme to put the metal bracelets on generally proved much more effective than a lot of official blether about obtaining a court order. The tension rose a tad in the few seconds that passed. Just as he was about to press the intercom button again, he saw the barrier quiver and then open. At last.

A security guard came out to meet him and accompanied him to the reception hall.

"Not everybody's here yet but most of the section managers are in. Who did you want to see?"

"The one responsible for the archives from 1939 to 1940. And I hope there isn't a different person in charge of each year!"

"No. I'll show you up."

The section head's manner was as austere as the modern furniture he was surrounded by, and Georges took an instant dislike to him. He noted that the office had two windows. In any government department, that was a sign of a certain level of importance in the hierarchy. Unpleasant or not, this official was in a position to help him find what he was looking for, so he decided to be accommodating and sat down after the introductions. The man was unable to look at him directly for more than a few tenths of a second, giving the Lieutenant the disagreeable impression that something else was going on behind his back all the time.

"Have you understood what I've just explained to you?" he asked eventually, in a tone that failed to conceal his irritation.

"Absolutely, Lieutenant. I'll call my principal archivist, but I believe all the documents from that period have been digitised and you can consult them on line.

A few minutes later, wrapped in the overall coat he always wore, Pascal Aupetit made George's acquaintance and was apprised of the reason for his visit.

"Come back and see me before you leave," said the manager as he saw Georges out. "I have every confidence in you, Pascal, do the best you can. And you might get our guest a coffee."

Confidence in him? That hypocrite was capable of anything.

"I suggest you come with me to my room," said the archivist, not replying to his section head. "The documents from that time have all been computerised but I think the originals provide the best source material. There are sometimes tiny details such as manuscript annotations that the scanner doesn't pick up, or doesn't transcribe very well. And because they were only recently digitised, there might still be some corrections needing to be made to them."

"Go for the paper versions," said Georges, giving his companion a surprised glance. Here was a civil servant making work for himself rather then planting his visitor in front of a computer screen. He was a rare breed, trained in the old school. His too-premature retirement on a small pension would no doubt allow him to be replaced by some overqualified and frustrated incompetent.

"Are you looking for anything in particular? If so, I can help you. I know my field pretty well."

"That's the problem, I'm not quite sure what I'm looking for. Something like an attack or a break-in that the Ministry might have suffered at the beginning of the Second World War while it was in Chinon, or during its transfer there."

The archivist frowned.

"When it left for Chinon?"

"Yes, or while it was located there."

"That doesn't ring any bells with me," he said hesitantly, "but I'm not familiar with the content of what was produced in any detail. Fortunately for you, the number of filing boxes from that period is extremely limited. No more than two or three, I think. It was when the Germans invaded, and not many people were interested in archives then.

"I don't doubt it."

A quarter of an hour later, George was installed at the archivist's desk wondering which of the six enormous cardboard boxes lying at his feet he should start with.

According to the archivist, the sixteen hundred employees of the Ministry had arrived in Chinon on the evening of 3rd September 1939, the same day that war was declared. One thousand, six hundred persons, plus their families, in a town with a population of only... how many at that period? Less than eight thousand? It must have caused an enormous upheaval.

He gave a sigh, and started on the first box.

Trying to look busy, the archivist was unsure what stance to adopt. That of the three Chinese wise monkeys seemed the most appropriate: see nothing, hear nothing, say nothing.

Three hours later, lying cocooned in paper with two cups containing coffee of unacceptable quality even if it was free, Georges was pulled away from his reading by Aupetit.

"Madame Pellegrin, the head of department, would like to meet you. I thought you must be getting a bit saturated with it all by now and you could go and see her as she's available at the moment."

"Yes, a short break wouldn't do any harm. Are you coming with me?"

"Of course."

As they walked along the corridors, the archivist complained about the lack of interest in traditional record keeping since computers had arrived on the scene, but Georges' mind was elsewhere and he was only half-listening. He was thinking in particular about the documents he'd gone through that morning without finding anything of interest. Except possibly for one small detail.

"It's in here," said Pascal, showing him into a secretary's office.

"She's expecting you," said the secretary, pressing a button on her phone system.

A door at the side opened a few seconds later to reveal the departmental director, Laure Pellegrin, in all her glory. She bestowed a large smile on them.

"Please come in, Lieutenant. Although it's lunchtime I won't offer you a whisky, I know you don't drink on duty, but perhaps you'd like a coffee? My secretary makes an excellent brew, not like the stuff out of the vending machine. Céline, would you bring it in? Monsieur Aupetit, I'll call you when we've finished."

In just a few seconds, she'd managed to impose a coffee on the gendarme, issue orders to the secretary and eject her subordinate from the room. And all with a beaming smile. He didn't bother to reply.

Her office was very large. Four windows, Georges noted automatically. The dark wooden furniture and a few quality pictures on the wall gave a clear indication of the occupant's status. A status of which, it seemed to him, she was rather too conscious. A huge desk with a computer screen on a ledge to the side took pride of place at one end, in front of a series of glass-fronted cabinets whose shelves were covered with books and bound folders. There was a small pile of documents in her work space, while others, open towards an armchair with a leather headrest, were patiently enduring their temporary abandonment.

She indicated that he should sit at her round conference table placed in front of a bay window, where six wood and leather chairs quietly awaited their chance to be of service.

"I was surprised to learn of your visit," she continued, pulling out a chair for him and choosing to sit opposite. "Normally, investigators phone before they arrive, even several days in advance, and I can then arrange for them to be received appropriately."

"I only decided to come here late yesterday evening. An unexpected turn of events in our enquiries."

"I understand. But surely files as old as that could wait a few more days?" she suggested.

"It's not so much the events at the time that interest us as what they can tell us about some major crimes that have been committed now. If we can get to the bottom of that, we've a much better chance of catching up with the perpetrators. And that can't wait."

He was irritated at the way she was attempting to lead the discussion but he could only regain the initiative by telling her about the current investigation, which he had not the least intention of doing. The secretary knocked on the door and opened it. A tray appeared, shortly followed by the girl carrying it. Coffee pot, cups, plate of biscuits. This was somewhat different from the way the Gendarmerie Nationale normally received its guests, even when they weren't dealing with miscreants.

"I'm impressed by the excellent way you welcome people," he said politely.

"You're an important visitor, Lieutenant. Have you got very far with your enquiries?"

"Yes, but not with very much success, unfortunately."

"Really? I'm very sorry. Maybe a little later. Perhaps I could help you with some particular issue?"

"Possibly you could," he said hesitantly. "In the boxes of documents, I noticed that the filing system lets you put back any document in the right place after you've taken it out."

"That's how archives work," she laughed. "What do you mean?"

"Simply that, if I've understood the system properly, there's one file missing in the June 1940 series."

Georges had been trained in NLP, neurolinguistic processing, and immediately noticed a fleeting movement in her eyes. Casting his mind back to his classes on the subject, he recalled that this meant she'd been searching her memory for a particular event linked to his remark before deciding how best to respond to it. Unfortunately, her facial expression had remained impassive: it was impossible to tell whether or not she was remembering anything.

"That's strange," she said at last. "Our archives are particularly well maintained, and by competent professionals. Especially Aupetit, even if he is allergic to information technology. But maybe the file wasn't of any interest to you anyway, or doesn't relate to the period you're interested in?"

"I'm afraid it does. That's precisely why I noticed it was missing."

"I'm sure it must have been mislaid by a work-experience student. We get a lot of them here in the summer. We're forced to take them by the powers that be. Sons or nieces of employees or... higher up. They aren't all conscientious. This sort of thing does occur from time to time, but we usually end up finding the document again."

"That could be too late for what I need."

"I'm really dreadfully sorry. I'll ask Monsieur Aupetit to carry out a search for it, but there is another way. Since nearly all that period has been digitised, your document might well be available as a computer file. We'll take a look after lunch. Allow me to invite you, you can tell me all about your job and the investigation you're working on."

"I'm afraid I haven't enough time for that. I need to get back to Orleans and Chinon as soon as possible."

"Just a buffet lunch then," she insisted. "We have an excellent caterer who'll be delivering to us in half an hour's time. We can eat in my office to avoid being disturbed. That's what we do for some of our meetings."

She pressed the button on the intercom to alert her secretary.

"If you'll excuse me, I want to put my notes into some sort of order first. Let me know when the food arrives."

"Of course, Lieutenant."

The caterer's buffet meals were perfect. Best quality plastic plates, glasses, top-of-the-range prepared dishes, nothing was lacking. Except for any warmth in their exchanges, despite the efforts of Laure Pellegrin to get him to talk about the present investigation. Georges even refused to taste the claret that had been delivered with the meals, claiming that some official regulation preventing him from doing so. Unlike the departmental head, who seemed to be enjoying it. He felt uneasy. He'd been troubled by a sense of distaste ever since meeting this woman. She was too sure of herself, too assertive.

Perhaps she didn't have enough to do in a department that was entirely devoted to the past? In that case, an out-of-the-ordinary visitor engaged in a criminal matter could only excite her interest. Georges abruptly gave way in the face of this evidence: he would entertain her!

They were interrupted by the phone ringing.

"I've come to a conclusion," she said, after hanging up. "The computer technicians have just confirmed that no document was digitised in between the two you mentioned, so it had obviously disappeared before the filing box was sent for the contents to be scanned. It's possibly been missing for years."

"That's most annoying, it's from exactly the period that's of most interest to me."

"All I can promise you is that I'll do everything in my power to try to find it as soon as possible."

She remained standing, maintaining her welcoming manner but clearly indicating that Georges should get up and go back to the archive room.

"You said you were in a hurry. I don't want to rush you, but if you want to get back early…" she said, looking at her watch.

"Thank you for this very pleasant lunch. I shall leave as soon as I've finished here. I've got your contact details, of course, just in case, but above all do please try to retrieve that missing document. I'm convinced it could help us."

"I shall do my utmost."

He went back to Pascal's room, reflecting on this

departmental director who was just a little too pushy for his taste. She could make his task easier, but at what cost? Compared to her, the archivist seemed a good sort, conscientious in spite of his aversion to computers. Perhaps he would have to rely on him, being careful not to annoy his boss. It was a risky game.

His musings were cut short by his mobile phone ringing.

"Yes, Maltier?"

"We've found the beige van. At any rate, for the moment we're assuming it's the one we were looking for. It was burnt out during the night of Saturday-Sunday on an isolated industrial estate in the middle of the forest. No-one noticed it until yesterday. It's a vehicle that was stolen in Saumur last week. With false plates, of course."

"Nothing to be got from it?"

"No, because of the fire and then the torrential rain on Sunday. It won't be enough for the judge, in my opinion…"

"That's what I was afraid of."

* * *

It was four p.m. and Georges had resigned himself to returning empty-handed. He left instructions for the archivist to try and find the mislaid document as soon as possible, and to check whether some other ministry might have a copy of it. A very faint hope, but one he couldn't afford to neglect.

Watching from her office window several floors up, Laure

Pellegrin watched his vehicle leave the car park and disappear into the distance. She sat at her desk and looked up a number on her smartphone. She was interrupted by a call from her secretary on the intercom.

"Yes, Céline?"

"Monsieur Aupetit would like to see you."

"Is he in your office?"

"No, he just phoned. It sounded important."

The director hesitated a few moments before coming to a decision.

"Tell him I'm in the middle of a telephone conference. Make him an appointment for Monday or Tuesday."

"Very well."

"Thanks. Oh, hang on a second, get me Xavier Bompart at the Ministry of the Interior. You've got his direct dial number?"

"Yes, I'll get on to it right away."

A few minutes later, Laure had him the other end of the line.

"Xavier, I have a favour to ask you."

"Anything you like, my darling."

She gave a little smile of satisfaction. Whenever he answered her like that, her ex-lover was hoping that one small good deed might deserve another... of a different nature. A good basis for negotiation.

"It's a rather delicate matter, but important. We've lost a document from 1940."

"So nobody gives a damn," he said sarcastically. "But if you think I'll be able to find it here, you're in cloud cuckoo land."

"That's not the issue. This document could potentially help in solving a police case, although I don't know the details. A Gendarmerie lieutenant from Chinon came over today to look for it. He seemed to be a rather difficult, pig-headed character. A trouble maker."

"So what?"

"So what? But don't you understand? If this document has disappeared after being entered on the record, it can only have been lost by one of my staff or a work-experience student. They're all MY responsibility and I don't want anyone accusing me of not running my department properly, when I'm coming up for an important promotion. If we let this cop have his way, he'll be like a Pitbull terrier with all this, he'll do everything in his power to screw up my career. And all because of some ancient piece of paper which probably won't tell him anything."

"So what exactly do you want me to do?"

"Can you get him taken off the investigation? Any other normal cop would be OK, but not this one."

"Hold on, you told me he was a gendarme, not a National Police detective. If that's the case, then it's complicated."

"Can't you at least try?"

"Yes, but I'm not promising anything. The Gendarmerie Nationale comes under the Army, not the

Ministry of the Interior. You're talking about rigid minds there."

"I did notice, as it happens. But I know your abilities and your skills of persuasion, my pet. Are we having dinner together this evening?"

"Well, if you're going to play on my feelings! On Friday, OK?"

CHAPTER 24

Maltier was standing in front of his office window, staring at all the hustle and bustle in the Gendarmerie courtyard without taking it in. He was plagued by doubt. The phone call from his boss saying he was returning empty handed did not augur well.

Although Georges had said he'd come straight back to Chinon without stopping off in Orleans, Maltier had used all his powers of persuasion to convince his superior that it would be a bad decision. It would do him good to have a proper evening at home with his family, whereas being alone in an empty room, mulling over failure, would only cause him to dwell on all the uncertainties and setbacks. Given the investigation he had on his hands and its various twists and turns, his chief might not get another chance to spend a quiet moment with his wife and children for quite some time.

He'd gone there on a wild goose chase, looking for a document that perhaps didn't exist. Or else no longer existed. But, just supposing the event had actually happened, was it mere chance that the file should have disappeared without trace?

The coincidence worried him. As Georges had pointed out, the witness statements all referred to the time when the Germans had arrived in the town: so, if the classification system was reliable, the missing document must relate to that crucial period, the week they came or the one before. There was no reference to this in the municipal or departmental archives, as he'd already been able to establish. The local history society, Les Amis du Vieux Chinon, had no papers from this period as it was too recent to interest them. And it was wartime, so possibly many documents were still classified as secret by the military.

Military secrets. That thought provided a sudden inspiration. They needed to consult the Army archives, or even just those of the Gendarmerie. Perhaps Patricia would be able to find something there.

* * *

In the basement of the sinister house, Derouchy was drunk with fatigue and famished. He'd resisted his tormentors for a long time and hadn't been broken until the end of the morning, letting slip, one by one, bits of information that Babar was still trying to piece together, word by word, sentence by sentence. The boss at last let out a sigh and ordered that the man should be given something to eat. Karl immediately objected, as he felt that if the beatings were continued it should be possible to extract more from him.

"If he's dead, you won't get anything from him at all," Babar replied with a shrug. He then left, and was absent for the rest of the afternoon.

Cédric felt that the boss had looked more relaxed when he'd arrived in the morning. He'd not reacted when Angèle had refused to have any part in the torture, albeit mental, of the prisoner – a prisoner she'd never met, Cédric thought. She kept resolutely to her walk-on role in this production and refused to be involved in its brutal side. That was something in her favour, and he could only appreciate her all the more for it. But if the operation came to a bad end, what would the judges say?

He couldn't bear to think of such a beautiful creature, caught up against her will in this sorry affair, spending the rest of her days in a sordid prison. He had to protect her. That was his true mission from now on – indeed, the only one.

The nearer it got to evening, the more impatient he was to see her again. Having dinner while she was present would be sheer torment, making him avoid her gaze and pretend not to be interested when he was becoming more and more passionate about her. Karl was going to stay down in the basement again that night to guard the hostage, so she'd be able to come to him without risking anything.

A frown clouded his brow: unless, of course, she was intending to show him yet another of the unlikely things in this house!

Lantois was very resentful about their abbreviated session the previous night. Of course her discovery was of major importance, but for the moment he couldn't see it was of any practical use. There was no point in making plans to escape if they didn't have money or a car. They were stuck here and couldn't even grass on their accomplices to the police. And if they did, he'd get life imprisonment, while she …

Coming up from the basement, still lost in thought, he almost bumped into Babar and stammered some words of apology. He always felt the boss looked through him as if he could read his mind.

"After tonight, you'll pack your belongings and we'll spend the whole of tomorrow evacuating the place. We'll be moving our H.Q. in the evening. Not this evening, tomorrow evening," he added, as if he wanted to remind Cédric of their little exchange two days previously.

"You have an elephantine memory," Cédric joked, which only drew a glacial look from the boss.

He fell silent immediately, wanting to pull his thoughts together and not get himself further into the mire. An elephantine memory. Perhaps that's what would help them get out of this. There were three possible outcomes, the first of which was a complete and utter fiasco. And the other two came together into one, thanks to his memory and what he'd learned that morning.

"So why are we leaving? We've got everything organised here, and we're out of sight." Cédric was worried, and thought about the two hidden passages his lover had shown him. They represented a kind of life insurance policy for the two of them.

"Out of sight, but for how long?" Babar interrupted. "We've been using this hideaway for nearly two weeks. Neighbours or passers-by are bound to notice the presence or movement of vehicles eventually. I need another two or three days to finish this job, and I'm not going to take any chances at all."

"But we'll have left trace evidence behind – fingerprints, hair," Cedric responded anxiously.

"By the time they get here, and when they've eventually pieced together the results of their investigation and received the analyses from the forensic lab, we'll be long gone, out of their reach and in the sun. I'd have preferred to torch this old ruin before we go, but that would run the risk of attracting attention too soon. On the other hand, if we do nothing, it's possible that no-one will come looking here for another two weeks, perhaps months. Or even longer."

He stopped speaking and stared at Lantois, as if waiting for him to agree.

"Karl!" he called out suddenly.

"Here," said the henchman, emerging from the basement.

"I'll take you over to Saumur before dinner this evening. We need a new vehicle. You can deal with it… in the usual way."

He left without bothering to say anything else.

Two or three days. A hiding place well away from here, in the sun. Cédric had deduced rather more from this information than the fact that they were getting a new means of transport. Were they proposing to drop him in it and get out? There'd never been a suggestion that he should receive any payment other than the large amount agreed at the beginning of the job. Karl and Babar had known each other a long time, they were a partnership. How could he believe they'd share anything at all with their other two associates?

He and Angèle were certain to be on the list of passengers who would never get on the plane to faraway sunny beaches. More likely they'd be the perfect suspects to be shopped to the police by their accomplices.

There was no point in raising any of this with Angèle, not yet. He needed to calm down and think about it first. And besides, she'd come to him as her protector. He ought to act like one and not frighten her unnecessarily.

He went back to his bedroom.

CHAPTER 25

FRIDAY

During the night, Angèle had rejected the idea Cédric put to her of running away. She refused to budge on this. All the while they had no money and no car, any attempt would be doomed to failure, even if they were to shop their accomplices. Especially if they shopped them, she insisted, because they would then immediately grass on them to the detectives. Although there was the van Karl had brought back from Saumur that evening, they didn't know where it was being kept. Not in the basement garage, at any rate. And even if they did take it, the small amount of cash they had on them wouldn't get them very far, particularly in a stolen vehicle with a possibly empty fuel tank.

Cédric had reluctantly gone along with her arguments and given in. His lover's plan was probably the best: to go on doing as they were told, keeping out of the way as far as possible, and taking advantage of the first opportunity that presented itself, once Babar and Karl had their hands on the loot. That would be the only moment when their attention would be distracted.

The preparations for leaving the house were already well in hand. Both Cédric's and Angèle's rooms on the upper floors were emptied. The doors, including the doorframes and handles, had been cleaned with disinfectant to remove all possible useable fingerprints. The vacuum cleaner had also reduced the chances of the investigators finding any vestige of DNA that could be too readily analysed. These measures had reassured the torturer, who took them as proof that he and his lover would at least be included in the forthcoming move. Otherwise, what was the point in eliminating any trace of them?

Karl had just brought the prisoner up from the basement, which he asked them to clean out immediately. So, they would be leaving through the main entrance and not the garage, as Cédric had first thought. They'd presumably take care of the ground floor last, starting right at the end with the kitchen and working their way along to the front door. The sheets and towels had been rolled up into a ball and doused in disinfectant behind the house. Babar was showing all the signs of being a careful and experienced organiser.

Except that he hadn't asked them to clean out his office. That was a rather surprising omission. Was he going to do it himself?

* * *

Georges was more rested and relaxed after his brief family visit, allowing himself the luxury of being almost late into work. Shortly after 08:30, he'd sounded the rallying call for his troops round the coffee machine before taking them into his office.

He didn't mention his *tête-à-tête* with Laure Pellegrin, but he praised the support he'd received from Pascal Aupetit, saying he'd found him to be a very effective archivist.

"I'm convinced he'll very soon find that document for us," he said confidently.

His colleagues' faces did not register the same degree of enthusiasm. They'd been told how his day out had gone, and they all felt that this excessive display of optimism was intended to cover up his deep disappointment.

"Quite apart from the question of the archives, there's another important piece of information," Georges continued. "The Police surgeon confirmed to me earlier this morning that that the Doyen was definitely given an injection in his forearm about ten minutes before his death. It was a dose of buprenorphine. On top of the narcotic already injected and his state of fatigue, it was a death sentence."

"That confirms Patricia's theory," Gendron affirmed. "But won't the judge expect more than that?"

"I'm afraid she will. The ball is now firmly in the forensic investigators' court. I'm going to chivvy them up this morning."

Round about midday, the phone rang. He was expecting the call to be from the forensic lab, but instead it was Colonel Lepic, his former superior at Orleans. Colonel Lepic was a complex character, believing in old-fashioned hierarchical rigidity and the enforcement of strict discipline, but also giving credit where it was due and rewarding work that was carried out well. For quite some time, he'd considered Georges to be an excellent prospect – until the birth of the twins, which had caused problems for the Lieutenant's wife and started to interfere with his professional work. In view of this, he'd supported his request for a move, thinking that if he was involved in operational work in a small district it would help him over the bad patch he was going through.

"Hello, Colonel. Very pleased to hear from you."

"Well, I'm not pleased, Lieutenant."

The conversation was off to a bad start. Since Georges' departure, the Colonel had called him informally by his name. Use of his rank implied a more official and more worrying discussion. The investigation might have faltered a little, but even so…

"Is there a problem? Have I missed something, forgotten about some file when I left?"

"No, nothing like that. But I want you to finish your investigation at the double, not just sit around twiddling your thumbs like they do in the rural areas! I supported your nomination to Chinon because I wanted you to show them what someone trained by the Section de Recherches is capable of."

This harangue seemed very strange to Georges. Obviously, Lepic never missed a chance to bang the drum for his unit, but the present investigation did not concern him directly and he rarely became involved with case files unless he was specifically asked to look at them. It was his way of ensuring that other people did likewise in respect of himself.

"I don't understand, Colonel. What is the problem, exactly?"

"This morning, I received a lunatic call from Paris. Those paper-shufflers haven't got their records up to date yet, they think I'm still your commanding officer. You went to the Finance and Economic Archives yesterday, didn't you?"

"Yes, but…"

"You must have done something really outstanding because I've been asked to kick you off this case. What have you unearthed over there?"

"To be honest, nothing. I came back empty-handed, but there's a file missing and they've lost it. I insisted they locate it for me, that's all."

"Then try to find it, and quickly. I don't give a stuff what the Ministry of the Interior says unless I receive an order in writing, but this is going to end up with it coming at us from all sides. I've no idea what's in your missing file but whatever it is seems to be upsetting everybody, so get on with it! And if you need any help from the S.R, give me a call on my direct line.

"What do I do as regards Commandant Dufournet?"

"Nothing, because I haven't phoned you, so you don't know anything. I'll tell him myself. He doesn't have to take any action at all as long as he doesn't receive an official notification, and since he isn't about to get one…

Always remember that a wet hen may leave marks on the

ground but it puts nothing on paper."

"Thank you, Colonel."

Not one for effusiveness, Lepic had already hung up, leaving Georges feeling dejected. Could it be that his unsuccessful visit to the Archives had provoked a tidal wave?

The only person able to get through to a minister's private office could be none other than the departmental director, Laure Pellegrin. The section managers wouldn't have sufficient clout, and the archivist even less.

It was one more upset that Georges could well have done without. He'd only just arrived to head up the investigatory brigade when he'd had this tortuous case wished on him, and now an attempt at intimidation. Not bad for someone who'd come here for a quiet life!

Patricia entered the room at exactly the right time to pull him up out of the black pit of his thoughts. She was proudly holding a small sheaf of paper that had just come out of the printer.

"Have you got something? The document?"

"No, Lieutenant, but I looked in the Military Archives and found some traces of an enquiry carried out at the beginning of 1945, a few months after the liberation of Chinon. There's a reference there to an event that occurred in June 1940, but unfortunately it doesn't say what it was."

"There must be a jinx on this case!"

The young woman brandished the sheaf with a smile.

"Perhaps not. Those three men won't tell us anything else, but you'll be delighted to learn that on his return from a German prison camp, a man named Derouchy was interviewed in connection with this affair! He was the father of the one who was kidnapped two days ago."

CHAPTER 26

Madame Derouchy's face was haggard, and she greeted the two gendarmes in an anguished voice:

"Have you found my husband?"

"Not yet, Madame, but you may be assured we are doing our utmost," Gendron said in a very confident manner.

Standing next to him, Patricia kept her face impassive. She still found it very difficult not to share the grief and pain of the victims she came across in the course of her enquiries.

"Can I help you?" asked the unhappy woman, holding back her tears.

"We need you to confirm an important point which could assist us in our investigation."

"Come in."

They followed her into the kitchen, after acknowledging two neighbouring women friends who were sitting in the drawing room. One of them froze when she saw them, her teacup hovering in front of her lips, perhaps feeling that some major catastrophe was about to descend on the house. Patricia went in last, firmly closing the door before taking a seat.

"My colleague has discovered a document that mentions the name of your father-in-law in an investigation that took place in 1945," Gendron explained.

"So that's it!"

Madeleine's exclamation was accompanied by a gesture of annoyance. She sighed, stood up suddenly and pushed her chair back. Then she went over the kitchen door, much to the surprise of the two gendarmes.

"Wait there, I'll be back," she said without turning round.

A few moments later, she placed a small folder consisting of just a few pages on the table and pushed it towards the big man.

"I'd thought that all this business was over and done with a long time ago, but this morning I began wondering whether it might have anything to do with the two murders and my husband's kidnapping."

"What are you talking about?" asked Gendron, nonplussed.

"In 1940, my father-in-law was entrusted with an important task. It turned out very badly for him and he was imprisoned by the Germans. In 1945, on the way back from the camp where he'd been interned, he felt his reputation had been impugned and he decided to make a statement, possibly the one that you've now found.

"Unfortunately not," said Patricia. "All I have is a report that refers to that statement and to the year 1940. I don't have any of the details."

"Then you should know that Captain Derouchy was exonerated. He was so traumatised by the whole affair that he settled permanently in this town to prove he had nothing to hide. He wanted to write his memoirs in the form of a novel, but he only completed one chapter. That's what's in the folder."

"Hang on, I don't understand. Why did he need to be exonerated, and what affair are you talking about?"

"Read that, it's not very long. I'll explain the rest to you afterwards."

Gendron pushed the folder over to Patricia.

"Would you read it out to us? You are young, but my arms are getting shorter…"

"It does certainly look like a novel," the young gendarme confirmed.

The Night of 13th-14th June 1940

The colonel halted in front of the door and buttoned up his cape. Despite the mildness of the June days, the nights still retained something of that terrible Siberian winter that had lain over the country until the beginning of May. He hastened over to the Ministry building. The matter was urgent.

Fifteen months earlier, the decision had been taken to transfer all services to Chinon. At that time, it was still believed that war could be avoided. And, if it came to the worst, the

Maginot line and the confident stance of the high command would keep Paris safe until the final victory, of which everyone was certain. Unfortunately, the situation had developed rapidly in the other direction, caught up in a maelstrom from hell. Reassuring speeches had been interleaved with diplomatic meetings but, from the start of the German offensive five weeks earlier, the false claims and certainties in the official statements could no longer sustain the illusion: the populace was in full flight, and so was the Army!

A few hours earlier, the meeting in Tours between Churchill, Paul Reynaud and De Gaulle had ended in failure, throwing the country into chaos. Paris was declared an undefended 'open city' and was occupied by the Germans the following day.

The instructions we had just received in the middle of the night confirmed our worst fears: although plans had been made for a final evacuation to Quimper, inside what the strategists had christened the 'Breton Redoubt', our orders now required the immediate move of all State services to Bordeaux!

We had just five hours to organise the transfer of the reserves of the Ministry of Finance and the National Lottery to their new destination, urgently and at night. It was to be a total evacuation, made worse by a catastrophic situation that, for too long now, had been inexorably deteriorating.

The operation was perhaps feasible for those services where it was just a question of moving paperwork, but the Ministry of Finance was a different matter.

There were several storage sites scattered around the area, and many lorries had been commandeered and held ready: but at one of the depots, the four reservists charged with loading the vehicles were missing, and the lorries that should have turned up were nowhere to be found. That was all we needed! How could a difficult mission be accomplished when the vehicles hadn't arrived in time and there was nobody to load them?

"So this business was linked to the evacuation of the ministry and its reserves to Bordeaux?" Gendron interrupted, in surprise. "I thought something might have happened before that, like a robbery."

"Hang on, I haven't finished."

The Colonel did not wish to leave anything behind for the Boche, but how was he going to find replacement troops in the middle of the night? Or lorries? They were already in short supply everywhere. The outcome of the brilliant idea to resite the various ministries all over southern Touraine was that, by the same token, the means of doing so had been dispersed, complicating the already difficult communications between services at a time when each of them had for some while been trying to secure all available resources for themselves.

And who had decided on Chinon as the place to relocate the Ministry of Finance? Clearly, the natural protection afforded by the Loire was of some importance, and there were countless caves in the Chinon area, ideal for storing… that which needed to be stored. But the end result was a mass of complications!

A motorcycle was heard to ride up and stop.

'Colonel', said the NCO despatch rider, 'I have bad news: there are no troops at all left at Depot No. 3. They've all gone over on foot to Depot No. 5.'

'What the hell are they doing there? Who gave that order?' the officer interrupted.

'But it had your signature on it. It came about an hour ago.'

'Complete bullshit – I signed nothing of the sort!' swore the Colonel. 'And that's another depot where there are no men to do the loading, and no vehicles.'

'Derouchy', he said, turning to me, 'send a squad over there at the double. If we don't get this sorted out in the next two hours, we shall have to blow up the cave. So that it doesn't fall into German hands', he added after a few seconds.

I ran over to the guard post as the Colonel watched the despatch rider depart.

Given the disorderly upheaval that was going to be caused by this removal in the middle of the night, there could well be opportunists ready to try anything, ready to risk their lives that, in any case, were already endangered by the bombing and the imminent arrival of the German army. If one of them had intercepted the messages about the urgent evacuation and had worked out how to take advantage of it by making this shambles just a little more shambolic…

It suddenly occurred to me there might be another explanation. What if an enemy commando was already in action here during the night?

At six in the morning, a long caravan of heavily-loaded vehicles was proceeding under orders along the road towards Bordeaux. All that was missing were the lorries from Depot No. 3.

The Colonel had told me to remain there with two men and do all in my power to find and execute the looters, then to blow up the depot before the enemy arrived.

A week later, during the night of 20th-21st June, and despite the heroic defence of the bridge at Port-Boulet, the German army entered Chinon. By the 1st July, they had occupied Bordeaux. On 3rd July, the colonel died during the battle of Mers el Kébir. He probably never learned that no depot or cave was ever blown up in Chinon, nor that I, Captain Derouchy, was reported missing as from the night the occupation began.

"If I've understood all this," Gendron went on, "the upheaval caused by this sudden departure was used to steal money under guard belonging to the Ministry of Finance. And we have Captain Derouchy claiming to be innocent but very conveniently disappearing. He was after all the person best placed to carry out any shady operation."

"My father-in-law was an honourable man!" Madeleine retorted. "He didn't have enough soldiers, so he went to the depot on his own. When he got there, he was attacked and left for dead. A winegrower found him two days later and saved his life. Then the Germans took him and interviewed him after they'd set themselves up in the town."

"And as far as you're concerned, he knew nothing about it?"

"Oh, but he did! He didn't speak about it to anyone other than his son and... to myself, to some extent. He gave the names of the looters to the German officers because he hoped they'd arrest them. He still believed in the honesty of men of a certain class – but he was wrong. By way of thanks, the occupying forces sent him to a camp in Germany. My father-in-law was convinced that those officers subsequently got their hands on the goods and summarily executed the looters."

"But rumour has it that they died in a concentration camp."

"Nobody's ever found any evidence of that whatsoever."

"If those officers were in it for themselves, they'd have had to get rid of the witnesses," Patricia added.

"That's what my father-in-law thought. He also presumed that the loot must have remained in Chinon because of the disorderly German retreat in 1944."

"So, if we're on the right track, the gang that murdered the Doyen and Monsieur Laurent must also believe that the stuff is still in this area," Gendron stated. "But with all the caves in this part of the world, not to mention all the basements, they've got a lot of work on their hands!"

"I can't say I feel very sorry for them," Patricia went on with a smile. "If they've taken as many risks as this in just a few days, it's because they must be on the point of finding it. As far as I can see, they're relying on the delays in our getting the lab results so they can finish the job before we're able to lay our hands on them. They're playing a game with us, just like they did in the Caves Painctes."

CHAPTER 27

Georges glanced down at his plate of food, which had already gone cold. All in a good cause. The phone call from Jacques, head of the forensic team, had allowed an interesting gleam of light to penetrate the fog shrouding this enquiry.

He barely hesitated before deciding to disturb Gendron in the middle of his own meal, a vital part of the day for that force of nature.

"Gendron? Sorry to interrupt your lunch. Something new has come up. Can we meet in my office? I'll be there in five or six minutes, OK?"

He was sitting on the terrace of a café in the Place Jeanne d'Arc, in the shade of the hundred-year-old lime trees. He called the waitress over. There was just time for him to settle up before going back to the Gendarmerie barracks to retrieve the document sent by the forensic team. The two men met up a few moments later.

"The hairs that were found in Derouchy's house have given a positive DNA match. They come from a character called Cédric Lantois. He's a small-time crook, not very intelligent, but capable of torturing his own father and mother."

"A torturer… So could he be the one who dealt with the Doyen, or Laurent?"

"Exactly. If the baker's shop woman or the neighbours recognise their Sunday afternoon individual from these photos of Lantois, it will remove any doubt that the three cases are linked."

"I'll get onto it. And I'll do the same with the photos from the soirée, you never know."

"No need, the forensic team have already started on those."

At that same moment, Patricia was, for the third time, checking her SMS text messages and emails. Nothing. Not a hint of anything from Paul. That made it five days in a row without hearing from him.

Spam! Always check the junk mail folder – but there was nothing there either.

She was wavering between anger, resentment and the feeling she was about to cry that came over her from time to time, particularly when she was on her own. Unable to hold back any longer, she started composing an email, then stopped. That was not a good idea. A short text message would be better. No heading, no subject, no polite formulas – just simple words, abbreviations if necessary, to ask him if everything was all right. No excuses, no weeping and wailing, simply a message from someone who is perfectly calm and wants to hear from a friend they've lost touch with.

How are you doing?

She paused, then deleted it. She'd no reason at all to enquire about Paul's welfare. He was the rat who'd dropped her. He was the one responsible for the break-up.

Yes, but she'd acted rather abruptly. She'd felt he was just about to calm down and come back to her. And it was at exactly that moment that she'd not been very accommodating and had taken advantage of the little weakness he'd just revealed. Perhaps she should have…

She began again on her text message:

Everything OK?

It was woeful. She stopped, just as her finger was about press the send button, and cancelled the message. She put the phone down on her desk in frustration, with tears in her eyes.

She sat down and jiggled the mouse to rouse the computer from its lethargic state. The screen lit up obediently. She mechanically typed in the password, which brought up a page of text from the document she'd discovered that very morning in the archives. She skimmed through it again but none of the words made any impact on her mind, which was elsewhere. Letting go of the mouse, she stretched her hand nervously over to the phone, picked it up and quickly composed a new text message:

I miss you.

Pressure from a finger that nobody was controlling caused the send key to operate. It was done, the message had gone, it would reach its addressee. She was both relieved and scared at having been the one to show weakness and take the first step. She realised that she felt rather guilty about it all, including their break-up. If Paul responded positively, they could turn the page and make a new start. But if he rejected her, she would have nothing left but bitter regret.

Patricia had been expecting an instant reply, but none came. Unable to concentrate, the young gendarme decided to leave her office and look for Gendron, her mainstay, her second father, the one who understood her best and supported her in her most difficult moments.

She couldn't find him.

Dejected, she switched her PC on again, swore mentally at all the dust that had collected between the keys, blew on it to no effect, moved the screen slightly and tried to wipe it with a cloth she found on a nearby table, then banged her fist on the desk to complete this little session of emotional release. In a rage, she filled in a request for two days' leave and left it on her desk.

She needed some air, to get out, to forget this investigation as well as her problems.

A quarter of an hour later she was wandering the streets of the ancient town, not at ease with herself, when she was overtaken by an irresistible urge to get away from it all. She hated the entire world. Her throat was tight and she stared fixedly ahead, not seeing or hearing anything. Paul was occupying the whole of her thoughts, which were swinging back and forth between feeling sorry for herself and being resentful. She had to get him out of her head, to forget him as quickly as possible. The image of Charles, the

Entonneur implicated in this affair, suddenly came into her mind. His house was in an isolated location but only about a kilometre from where she now was, or a bit over. In the state of anger and frustration that was gripping her, she felt able to make anybody confess so she might as well take it out on a genuine suspect.

Shaking with rage, unable to think straight, she walked half way there without questioning the wisdom of what she was doing. She was forced to slow down as the road started to lead uphill, and consciousness began to seep back to reclaim its rightful place.

As she neared Charles's house, she realised she was about to commit a serious error. She stopped for a few moments, then came to a decision. She wouldn't go to see this Entonneur, who was under suspicion and possibly dangerous. Instead, she'd take a walk in the fresh air to help clear her mind. She only needed to go down to the river and walk along it to get back into the town, rejoin her colleagues and start work again.

Her phone vibrated, announcing the almost simultaneous arrival of two messages and making her come to a halt, just as she was passing the house that had been her intended destination only a few minutes previously.

The first was from Paul:

Miss you too!

Patricia closed her eyes. At last! Life began to return. She was about to read the second message before replying when she stopped short, incapable of movement.

Charles had just come out of the house and was standing in front of her, with another man next to him – one of those she'd seen in the photos, among the first who'd rushed over to help the Doyen. And that man had given a telephone number and home address in Germany.

The Entonneur was the first to react.

"The girl cop's taking photos of us!"

His companion immediately sprang to life and jumped on Patricia, who was unable to do anything.

She'd not had time to read the second message, which was from Gendron:

Where U gone? Waiting for U. Urgent.

* * *

Not long after his young protégée had left, Gendron had returned to the Gendarmerie barracks with the satisfaction of a job well done. The woman in the baker's shop had confirmed that the man in the photo was indeed her customer from Sunday afternoon, the one she'd seen muffled up in his rainwear. "Almost 100% sure", she'd said. "A nice-looking chap."

The link was now definitely established between the three cases, bearing out what they had surmised – this affair stemmed from something that went back to 1940. It was beyond belief!

Gendron walked diagonally across the Place Jeanne d'Arc and entered the gateway of the Gendarmerie. People were already filling the corridor on the left where complaints were received from the public, log books were kept and other routine business transacted – pathetic brawls between drunks or problems with bad neighbours, which frequently kept two or three of his colleagues busy writing it all down. A young disabled man in a wheelchair was waiting for his turn to be seen. He was a regular, and Gendron immediately recognised him.

"Back again? What's the matter this time?"

"A bloke threatened me for going too fast along the pavement. That's the second time now. I know who he is – he's violent, he might hit me."

"Give me his name, I'll go and have a word with him. Trust me, that'll calm him down so you won't have any more to worry about. Or any more need to come and see us. But you must promise me you'll be careful too, whenever you meet pedestrians. All right?"

A few minutes later, Gendron went into the neighbouring office to greet his colleagues.

"I've sorted out the young disabled man for you."

"He'll find another excuse, today, tomorrow, in a couple of days," smiled a female gendarme of mature years. "That's the way he is. And he's not the only one. You have to understand them, it gives them a chance to talk to someone."

"And to complain," said one of her colleagues, less amenably.

"Anyway, since you're here, when was it that Derouchy was kidnapped?"

"Tuesday evening, well, night, between two and three o'clock. Why?"

"I've just had someone make a rather strange statement late this morning, and I was wondering whether…"

"Somebody saw something?"

"No – if they had, I'd have alerted your brigade, obviously."

Gendron put back on the desk the pen he'd just picked up, which had disappeared in his enormous hand.

"I only thought of it because you came in," she went on. "It's possibly nothing to do with your investigation anyway, more likely a matter for the Surveillance and Intervention squad."

"Go on."

"We were contacted by an amateur astronomer who'd been setting up his equipment in the middle of the night, about three o'clock. He saw something he thought was unusual, but it was only this morning that he decided to come to us about it."

"Get to the point," said the big man impatiently.

"Along that lane that runs the length of the hillside, there's a big house that's been shut up and abandoned for years. The shutters are always closed and you never see anybody in there, apparently. Except that, on this particular night, he saw a vehicle drive into the grounds with its lights off. He also thought the basement garage was lit up for a moment, but he couldn't be sure because of the trees in the way. Probably squatters."

"Squatters who drive without lights along a road where a kidnapping has just taken place? To hide in an abandoned house? Give me a copy of that statement, quickly!"

He was a former judoka and now regained the strength in his legs and the speed that he'd had as a twenty year old. He rushed up the stairs to the third floor, gathered all the members of the team and went to the Lieutenant's office. A few minutes later, he sent the message to Patricia that she didn't have the chance to read.

* * *

Georges looked at his watch. He'd been seething with impatience since an out-of-breath Gendron had told him the probable location where Derouchy was being held. This was no time for hesitancy and, for once, luck was on their side. Thanks to the proximity to Chinon of the nuclear power station and its security force, the renowned *Peloton de Surveillance et Protection,* or PSPG, they didn't have to wait for the deployment of the Gendarmerie's special operations unit, the GIGN. The PSPG was made up of former members of that organisation, or persons trained by it, it was on the spot, and it was immediately operational. Derouchy was going to get another chance.

"Their commanding officer, Commandant Hugo, shouldn't be much longer, but there's still no sign of Patricia. Didn't she say anything? Even to you, Gendron?"

"No. She didn't even reply to my text message. I went over to her flat, but she wasn't there either. My wife has the key, she waters the plants when Patricia's away," he added in self-justification.

"You know her very well – don't you find that she's been acting rather strangely recently, a bit depressed?" asked Georges, raising his voice.

"Let's not over-react," said Maltier. "She's got problems with her love life. She's young, she'll get over it. She's a very strong girl, both mentally and physically." He turned towards Gendron, seeking his agreement.

"All right, if you two are convinced... Everyone's here so we'll make a start without her, but I want to see her as soon as she gets back. She needs a good talking-to at the very least."

"Let's get on with it, then" said a loud, strong voice.

They all turned towards the door, which had been pushed open by the PSPG commander followed by his two deputies.

They shook hands quickly, exchanging names for those who didn't know each other already, a swift introduction made by men used to operating in the field, making rapid decisions and taking quick initiatives.

The newcomer immediately took charge.

"Lieutenant, I have two bits of news for you. I won't ask you the usual question, which is just as usually a waste of time. I'll give you the bad news first: we can't use the helicopter."

"That's a set-back, isn't it?"

"The good news," the commander continued without replying, "is that our reconnaissance of the place shows that although the location chosen by the criminals is in a remote spot, that's of no help to them. There are trees all over the park and the premises are surrounded by high walls, so we can get near to them while remaining concealed. It's almost impossible for them to get out. There are only two roads, more or less parallel, running alongside the grounds. I won't say it's a piece of cake, but it's not far off. For us, that is, not for them."

"OK, I'll let you be the judge of that. How do we go about it?"

"Blocks at each end of the two roads – that's your job. Have some men waiting at the foot of the boundary wall, on the town side. Given the steep drop, I don't think they'll try to escape that way but we're not taking any chances. We'll be in charge of all the rest. They've got CCTV cameras covering the entrance and possibly the park, but we'll take those out when we start the operation." Silence fell. Everything had been said concisely, giving those present the feeling they were already in action.

"Everybody's working flat out and the road blocks will be in position in half an hour or less," said Georges.

"There's no way you can put them in place before we begin the show. If the criminals spotted anything, the whole shebang could turn sour. You'll remain out of sight, ready to deploy, but I'll be the one to give the order when to block the roads, and I won't do it unless the operation starts going wrong and there's any possibility that they could get away."

"Then we shan't need longer than a quarter of an hour to twenty minutes."

"I'll give you half an hour anyway. Act like professionals, I know what you're capable of, even if it's the first time for some of you."

"Any comments or questions?" asked the Lieutenant, looking at the members of his team.

Silence. All the men there were well aware of what was at stake and the risks of the operation, even if most of the action would be carried out, and the hazards faced, by these special operatives trained by the GIGN.

"Gentlemen, to work," said the Commandant finally, looking at his watch. "Georges, you'll be my sole point of contact for all the teams Commandant Dufournet has assigned to you. You will carry out my orders without delay, and not do anything else. In case of doubt or if there's a problem, let me know, but don't take any initiative yourself. The hostage is possibly still alive and any mistake could prove fatal for him. Not to mention the risks for my men."

"Understood."

The Lieutenant showed none of the annoyance that he was starting to feel. These men were an elite special force, in the front line of a very dangerous operation, but his own temperament did not align well with decisions taken so swiftly and in such a curt manner.

They all rose. It was 16:00 hours. The adrenalin was already pumping and it was time to take up position.

CHAPTER 28

Patricia hadn't had time to take in what was happening. She'd been concentrating on her mobile phone when she suddenly saw Charles appear and then his henchman had jumped on her. The two men had overpowered her in seconds, before she could make any move to defend herself.

She hadn't been able to put up any sort of a fight and was now lying on a rug, bound and gagged with her legs bent backwards and fastened to her wrists. She'd been in that position for an hour already, and felt she was being smothered. And all this because of the distress she'd been suffering. She cast her mind back over her feelings of anger and disappointment. How could she have been so stupid as to throw herself into the lion's den like this?

She was, of course, dealing with a murderer. Perhaps even two: the way they'd acted left her in no doubt whatsoever. Worst of all, she was now being held hostage by the suspect, Charles, whose guilt she'd been the first to realise. It was like a bad movie.

Why had she continued walking along that road, when she knew it was likely she'd provoke him as she went past his house?

She wanted to cry. Nobody would ever believe that she'd gone there by accident. Her career was down the drain, and possibly her life as well. Just at the time when…

Paul! He would never know how delighted she'd been or how happy his last message had made her. She was emotionally exhausted and began to sob.

"You should have thought about that before, darling," said her jailer. "But don't be too worried, you're very useful as exchange currency. We'll keep you alive right up to the point where you aren't any more use to us. If your colleagues leave us alone, you've got a chance of getting out of here still living. On the other hand…"

He stopped suddenly, and looked cautiously out of the window.

"Shit! Were you expecting company?"

She shook her head as a sign of negation, or perhaps hope. Her team mates! They'd discovered where she was thanks to her mobile phone and had come to the rescue.

The doorbell rang, cutting through the silence.

"Karl!" shouted Charles, "Move yourself, we've got visitors. There are two of them. Get ready, I'm going to the door."

He unbolted the door and assumed his usual pleasant manner.

"Good afternoon, gentlemen, what can I do for you?"

"Our colleagues are going to force an entry into the house behind yours. We think it's being occupied by squatters. Nothing very serious, but the Intervention Squad is going to climb over the boundary wall to stop them getting away on this side. Don't show yourself, and stay away from the windows.

"Ah. I understand, although those premises have looked empty for a long time, certainly from before I came to live here. But that's for you to deal with. By the way, I'm going out in about a quarter of an hour to twenty minutes, with my visitor. You don't see any problem with that?"

"No, but make it a quarter of an hour maximum. After that, you'll have to wait for instructions from us and not move from here."

Charles closed the door and gave a sigh of relief.

"I knew it was time for a change of scenery," he murmured to his accomplice.

"Shall I alert the others?"

"No. They can go to hell. We've only got a quarter of an hour anyway, and they don't know what we're going to do next. Watch for the crazy cops as they come past. As soon as they've gone over the wall, load everything we need into the van, together with our lady friend here. We'll go to the new hide-out and I hope this time it's the right one. In three or four days' time, we'll be rich!

"Shall I shoot the hostage?"

"No! Are you deaf? No unnecessary risks. You'll stay here."

* * *

Angèle and Cédric were getting on with the final cleaning

of the ground floor, in accordance with Babar's orders.

"We haven't seen either Babar or Karl for at least two hours," the young woman remarked. "I hope they aren't pulling one of their stupid stunts on us."

"Perhaps they're in the office?"

They knocked several times. There was no response, and they decided to open the door. It was locked from the inside.

"We need to open it. In any case, we're about to leave this ruin and not come back, so – the door," Angèle insisted.

After Cédric had smashed violently into it three times with his shoulder, the lock give way.

The room was deserted and had been completely stripped. Only the monitoring system remained in place. They looked at each other in concern, not understanding what was going on.

"They're out in the park," Cédric suggested, without conviction.

"Look!"

The young woman pointed to the security camera screens.

"Shit!" Cédric swore. "It's the cops! The road outside's full of 'em. Both roads," he corrected.

"That's why those two stinking sons of bitches left!"

The alarm began to blink on and off.

"Look, there's two of them climbing over the back wall. We can't get away on that side," Cédric shouted.

At almost the same moment, the screens stopped showing anything at all except for grey stripes and a lot of interference.

"Get your stuff, we're off," said the young woman immediately.

"Where to? They're all over the place."

"The secret passage! Have you forgotten the passage I showed you? Hurry up!"

A few minutes later, ignoring their hostage still tied up on a chair in the kitchen, they rushed into the drawing room.

"It's this one," said Angèle, opening one of the wall cupboards. "There must be another one like it in Babar's office. That's how they got away, the cowardly bastards!"

She threw herself at the inside wall of the cupboard and pushed it, making it swing round. The mechanism was much the same as the one on the top floor. Once it had been opened, there was an entrance into a narrow space in the supporting wall, behind the cupboard. When he'd first seen it two nights previously, Cédric had said to himself that it was an old chimney hidden by the woodwork erected in front of it. There was no floor inside, but the two uprights of a ladder could be seen. Angèle was the first to get there and anxiously threw her bag into the opening.

"The torch, give me the torch."

They went down the equivalent of one storey and ended up on a platform that covered half of the available space. The other half opened onto a second rectangular shaft.

"They've taken the ladder away!"

"I hope the other one is long enough!"

Cédric took a vigorous grip on the ladder they'd just used and lowered it into the gaping opening on the other side. He gave a sigh of relief when he saw that there were still a few rungs showing after it had reached the bottom.

"Did you put the cupboard back the way it was?" his companion in misfortune asked anxiously.

"Of course I did!"

The corridor they were following smelt damp and mouldy. It was a kind of tunnel, built with dressed stone and evidently an underground refuge installed at the time of the Revolution. The low height of the vaulted ceiling made them walk slightly bent over, but it was wide enough to let them move along without being encumbered by their bags.

"Do you think they're in the building yet?"

"The cops? No," she reassured him. "The two came round the back won't try anything on their own, and the others were still deploying in the road outside. In my opinion, we've a good quarter of an hour before they come in. They'll spread out over the park and then force all the entrances at the same time. They won't take any risks, because of the hostage."

"Are you sure of that?"

"Positive. We're going to end up in the house belonging to Babar. Or Charles, if you prefer, that's his real name. People around here know him, and if he's under suspicion we could get nabbed as soon as we're inside his place."

"So that's how he was able to come and go without anyone seeing him! And you never told me…"

"I didn't trust you enough when you first asked me the question."

"Anyway, it's too late now. I presume we'll come out in his cellar, inside another of these bloody trick cupboards."

"Don't moan about the cupboards, it's thanks to them you've got a chance of getting out of this."

A few minutes later, the two fugitives emerged into the basement of a house: all was very quiet. They climbed the stairs leading to the ground floor with the wariness of cats.

"Get the girl and we'll go." The impatient voice of Babar came from above them. "They've given us a quarter of an hour, no point in getting spotted."

"Another two minutes and we can be off."

The two lovers looked at each other. Their accomplices had not yet fled the scene. Should they go and remind them they were still there, or wait until they'd left?

"I'll go," said Angele.

"Wait"

Cedric went back down and grabbed hold of a pickaxe handle he'd noticed a few moments before. The young woman opened the door and placed herself on the landing under the astonished gaze of Babar.

"Aren't you forgetting someone?"

"But how…"

"Never mind the how, we're here whether you like it or not. I hope you weren't thinking of abandoning us to the cops, to tell them all about you? We'll leave here together, or we'll finish this business together. Karl," she said, without pausing, "you can put down your shooter, it's crawling with cops all around us and you haven't got a silencer."

Galvanised by the young woman's fearlessness, her lover placed himself opposite the hit-man ready to make use of his improvised weapon.

"And I agree we should discuss things, with this," he said, looking Karl right in the eyes.

"OK," Babar conceded at last. "I see you've brought the other idiot with you," he said, motioning with his chin towards Cédric.

"You'd have preferred me to have left him up there to discuss matters with the pigs?"

"Karl wanted to go and fetch you but we were surprised by the arrival of the gendarmes. It was too late to warn you, we hardly had time to pull out ourselves before it all went pear shaped."

The boss looked at his watch. There was no more time for idle chatter.

"Karl, pack the van with our stuff and the girl cop. You know what you have to do. Your friend here can drive. Angèle, you're coming with me and you'll be driving the car. There's no time for delay, we're getting out of here while the cops are busy playing their little war game. I'll go in front. Let's move!"

CHAPTER 29

All of the teams had now taken up their assigned positions. At a given signal, six men dressed in combat fatigues, balaclavas and body armour climbed over the walls on either side of the property and advanced towards the house, taking advantage of the vegetation to conceal themselves. Everything was very still, and no suspicious movement could be seen inside the building. Guided by the intelligence received from the men who'd come over the wall by Charles's house, three gendarmes made their way round the back, on the side where the shutters were open. From their low-down position, they couldn't see into the rooms opposite them. Noticing a nearby oak tree with a suitable number of branches, one of the assault team took the risk of slowly climbing it, his body pressed against the trunk. He confirmed in a low voice that the rooms he could see appeared to be unoccupied.

"There's a drawing room on the left, and a virtually empty room in the middle. I can see a computer screen, no two. They're switched on. There's a kitchen on the right. Hang on, there's somebody in the kitchen. A bloke on a chair, wearing a balaclava. Must be the hostage?"

"Nobody with him?" came a tinny voice in his earpiece.

"Doesn't look like it."

"Can you fire from where you are?"

"Yes, but it would be an awkward shot. I can wedge myself properly after you give the attack order, but it's at long range and I'm at an angle."

"We haven't any choice in the matter. Be ready in one minute's time."

One minute later, the front door of the residence was smashed to pieces while, simultaneously, six men swarmed in through the ground floor windows, and the main gate was wrenched off its hinges.

Trembling with fear, still tied to his chair in the kitchen, Derouchy was rapidly surrounded by two of the assault group. He was taken to a place of safety just as four PSPG vehicles came charging into the grounds. Less than three minutes later, their arteries pumped full of adrenalin, the gendarmes had taken complete control of the ground floor. Surprised by the silence and the lack of any reaction from the hostage-takers, they held themselves flat against the walls and doorways, carefully watching the staircase that led to the upper floors. Tension was at its height when a dull thump from the basement told them that the garage door had given way in its turn. No shots were heard, proving that only the upper floors could still offer any refuge for their targets. A brief order was given, as if on a training exercise, and four men got into position to go up the stairs while others, already in place, prepared to give immediate covering fire. After a few more minutes, all the rooms in the house had been taken and the men who had gone into the basement came to the front door.

Disappointed, the PSPG gendarmes had to face up to the evidence: the building was deserted, abandoned by its occupants before they'd stormed it. But not very long before, judging by the equipment that had been left behind.

To the great relief of the intervention teams, the hostage was exhausted but still alive, and was already being cared for by the doctor. For Georges and his team, however, this wasn't the outcome they'd been hoping for. Their intention had certainly been to free Derouchy, but also to arrest the perpetrators. They'd put a lot of energy and resources into this, without result.

The Lieutenant could already envisage tomorrow's official press release: 'A magnificent operation carried out with great success to save the life of a hostage.' A lot of baloney, horse manure intended less to inform than to satisfy the sensationalist demands of the journalists – who would nevertheless not fail to be up in arms the day after, complaining about the way the guilty parties had been allowed to escape and forcing the investigators to go over a lot of nit-picking details with them instead of concentrating on solving the case. So much for the Fourth Estate…

He turned to the doctor who was looking after Derouchy, lying on a stretcher.

"Is he able to talk?"

"Yes, he's suffering from shock and he's very weak, but lucid. Don't take too long, though."

These people were all the same. Who did they think we were? The torturers have already left, we don't do that.

"Monsieur Derouchy? I'm Lieutenant Georges. Could you answer a few questions? We need you to help us find your attackers as quickly as possible. They might be about to do the same thing to other people."

"They're insane. There were three men, but I could only see the faces of two of them, the other one was wearing a balaclava."

"A balaclava. Did he never take it off?"

"Not in front of me. He must have been afraid I'd recognise him. But I had a good view of the others, several times."

Maltier came over with the photo of Cédric Lantois.

"Yes, he was one of them!" said the hostage, becoming agitated. "But the other one was worse, the fair-haired man."

"You need to show him the photos from the evening in the Caves Painctes", the Lieutenant told Maltier. "He may recognise the other individual."

"What about my wife?" Derouchy asked anxiously.

"She's fine, don't worry about her. We've already told her that you're safe and sound. She'll join you at the hospital very shortly."

"And there's a woman mixed up in this. I don't know if she was here or whether they communicated by phone, but they mentioned her several times. I didn't catch her name."

"Laure Pellegrin?" Georges suggested, as a sudden inspiration struck him.

"Laure? Possibly. I'm not sure."

"Did you see her or notice what she was doing?"

"No, never. But I was in the basement the whole time. With a balaclava and ear plugs… I only heard them talking between themselves when I was being interrogated."

Despite asking him a few more questions, they weren't able to obtain any more information. So, it seemed they were looking for three accomplices, possibly with a woman. And all of these wonderful characters had scarpered less than half an hour before they would have been caught inside the house!

"I did promise you," said Georges ironically as he greeted Jacques and his forensic team. "This time there are only gendarmes all over the scene of the crime. And a hostage, who didn't touch anything!"

"I knew that you people don't do anything the easy way," responded the forensic officer, with the hint of a smile. "First of all a corpse who suddenly appears in the middle of a crowded hall, and now we have the guilty parties escaping from a sealed-off room. Will you be putting your magic show on soon, or are you still preparing new tricks?"

"I like your way with words. After this case is over, we'll celebrate with a decent bottle of Chinon. OK with you?"

"Only one bottle?"

Georges smiled and extended a closed fist, which was joined immediately by that of Jacques. This superficial, almost unnecessary exchange of words cemented a man-to-man bond between them and buried the hatchet.

Now that the hostage had been freed without any blood being spilled and without even a shot being fired, all the men were beginning to relax. Save for one.

Gendron had disappeared before the assault on the house was over. He'd been minutely exploring every nook and cranny, possibly to avoid thinking about Patricia, who was still showing no signs of life. He'd called Paul, who had confirmed that he'd had heard nothing from her beyond a brief exchange of text messages an hour or two earlier. He eventually persuaded himself that his protégée's obsession had led her to go to Charles's house again. But how could he broach this with his superior officer?

Unable to hold back any longer, he decided to speak to him.

"Lieutenant? If the Entonneur, Charles, is involved in this case, he's very soon going to find out that we're on to him. I suggest we go to his house immediately with one of the men from the PSPG."

"Excellent initiative. Go on, it's time we put some pressure on him. But be careful. I'm going to call the judge and the Commandant to bring them up to speed with the situation."

Gendron was surprised to find that the suspected man lived so close to the house they'd just taken out.

"One of my colleagues rang the doorbell there about an hour ago," his surprised companion said.

"Are you sure?"

"Absolutely. He asked the occupant to stay out of sight, but he'd already left the house before we started the operation."

Gendron went straight up to the front door and rang the bell several times, becoming increasingly agitated. He was about to force the door with his shoulder when he noticed that it wasn't shut properly. Throwing caution to the wind, he rushed inside, ignoring his colleague's protests, and charged through all the rooms without stopping, shouting at the top of his voice. There was no response, just silence.

Moved by instinct and experience, he went unhesitatingly down to the basement. Still nobody, still nothing. Or rather, yes – an open wall cupboard, behind which there was no wall. A tunnel?

He thrust himself inside. The reduced height of the passage made his progress difficult and his back was scraping along the ceiling. There was nothing and no-one in here. He got out his pocket torch and saw that he had reached the end of the tunnel, where there was a ladder.

Patricia was in here somewhere, he was sure of it. He

wouldn't believe that anything had happened to her. She would be a prisoner, but her life would have been spared. He wouldn't admit of any other possibility, but he needed to act quickly.

After making use of the ladder twice, he found himself behind some solid wood panelling, squashed into a space not intended for someone of his size. He didn't have enough room to move and, in spite of his efforts, it wouldn't give. He started banging on it and shouting in anger. He was answered by violent blows from the other side.

And a miracle happened. One of the panels gave way. He used his shoulder to force the bits out of the way in front of him and, gun in hand, turned round as best he could to see through to the other side. He came face to face with two armed colleagues looking as menacing as he was!

It hadn't yet dawned on him that he was back inside the big house.

The investigation had just taken a sudden new turn, and depression set in.

CHAPTER 30

Laure Pellegrin was sitting thoughtfully in her office. She hesitated. Xavier Bompart had just told her there was little hope of his being able to have the gendarme removed from the investigation and, even if he did, it would probably be too late. Going down that road could well present more dangers than it avoided. A lot more.

She gave one last glance at the message, grabbed hold of the Lieutenant's business card and dialled his number herself.

"Lieutenant Georges? It's Laure Pellegrin, Director of the Archives Department."

"Yes. Good morning, I certainly remember meeting you. What can I do for you?"

His tone was icy.

"Well, I just wanted to tell you…"

"That you're pulling strings in the background to get me taken off this case?"

"Listen, I'm very sorry…"

"Not as much as me."

"It was a mistake, and I want to put it right. I've cancelled my request, but I've got something to tell you. Something important."

"Go ahead. I'm ready to hear anything."

"First of all, you should know that the disappearance of documents from my department could have serious consequences for my career, even when I'm not the one responsible. At my level in the top echelons of the civil service, there are too many sharks with long teeth who'll use the slightest excuse to see that you're side-lined instead of being promoted to the post you were expecting. That's why I reacted like that when you were so insistent about the document."

"The promotion of civil servants does not constitute any part of my investigation," he said brusquely.

"I'm well aware of that, I just wanted to explain things to you. More to the point, I remembered, just after you'd left, that I must have had that document in my possession a few months ago. It was given to me by Monsieur Aupetit, the archivist who looked after you when you came here. He thought it contained important information and passed it on to me. I gave it back to him a few days later after quickly leafing through it. We were right in the middle of preparing the annual reports and I had plenty to occupy myself with other than pursuing some fantasy dreamed up by a subordinate. I now recall that I asked him to prepare a summary for me, but I've never received it."

"Your archivist could have been responsible for the disappearance of the document? But what reason would he have had?

"I haven't the faintest idea. Presumably the same reason that brought you here as part of your investigation."

Georges didn't answer. He was thinking hard. Of course, if Pascal Aupetit had read that document and noted its interesting contents, and also the lack of interest by his senior managers…

"Lieutenant?"

"Yes, I was just reflecting on the implications of what you've just told me. You really have no idea what this document contains?"

"I told you, I barely skimmed through it. I'd even forgotten that I'd seen it. Mind you, I can't state categorically that it was the same one that you're looking for."

"Is there any way of checking?"

"I carried out a rapid search of all the files from that period that have been scanned but I couldn't find any document like the one you're after. Therefore, I presume we may suppose it's the one that's missing."

"Thank you for your call. And please ensure that your hounds from the Ministry of the Interior are called off in double quick time."

"I already have," she lied.

He ended the call.

This woman had a gift for making him lose his temper. She didn't give a damn about anyone else, she was obsessed with her career, and she was capable of anything to achieve her own ends. She'd be very dangerous for anyone who crossed her. Nevertheless, she'd just given him an important piece of information for the investigation.

Pascal Aupetit.

Pascal Aupetit discovers a vital document, and he's tempted to do something reckless. But how could a minor civil servant working near Melun set up an operation as complex as this, and so far away from his home town? It didn't feel right.

He needed immediate assistance from his colleagues at Savigny-le-Temple to help him find out about this archivist's background and the people he mixed with.

* * *

Angèle brought the car to a halt at the entrance to a large building. It was a chateau, with a short driveway flanked by walls that led up to a porch with a Gothic arch; this was framed by two small round towers and had an enormous wooden gate painted in red. The porch was set against a long façade pierced with mullioned windows from which, in the far distance, the royal fortress and the old town could be seen. Viewed from this angle, the ancient residence gave the impression of having been built into the steep hillside immediately behind it.

"You know what you have to do?"

"Yes, we're interested in renting a gite for tonight and for one full week in September. But what if there are no vacancies this evening?"

"I've got rid of everybody who booked up for this week and given them their money back. They think they're making way for a wedding party."

They got out of the car and walked up to the imposing gate. Charles-Babar rang the doorbell. A dog began barking on the other side, but there was nobody about.

"That's the only thing I hadn't bargained for – they might be out!"

He noticed a handle on the end of a long wire which ran across the wall at a right angle. He pulled on it, and a large bell rang out.

"All right, I'm coming," said a voice from inside.

The grey-haired proprietor was wearing a T-shirt, jeans and gardening boots. He gave them a questioning look. Angèle for her part was staring anxiously at the huge black-and-tan Beauceron hound standing by the side of his owner. It was not so much the size of the dog that impressed her as the size of its teeth, which it was continually baring at them.

"Good morning, Monsieur," Charles began. "My wife and I are looking for a gite for September. We understand that you have two here – perhaps we could see them?"

"In September? I think I've only got one week available…"

"That's perfect. We're not restricted as to the exact date. Could we have a quick look inside?"

"Of course. One of them was booked until tomorrow, but the reservation was cancelled this morning."

"In that case, would it be possible for us to have it for this evening?"

The porch extended through the width of the building and formed a kind of corridor two storeys high that led onto a large terrace dug out of the hillside. On the far side, there was a retaining wall about fifteen metres high constructed of dressed stone, intended to stop the earth behind from reclaiming its rightful place. Along the rear flank of the building, a wide gravelled area provided access and parking for cars. Between the gravel and the wall was a carefully manicured lawn, greener than English peas. The whole formed a very extensive open space that Charles estimated to be about two thousand square metres, possibly more. The place had an air of serenity about it, despite the fact that the central portion of the retaining wall had collapsed under pressure from the land it had been holding back to leave a huge rock fall, a tongue of earth and stone about twelve metres wide that protruded onto the lawn.

At either end of the wall, there were openings that revealed the entrances to caves or underground cellars extending under the hill.

"It's wonderful," said Babar, looking very pleased. "What period?"

"Thirteenth century, but the exterior façade dates from the fifteenth. Some of the beams have been traced back to the end of the twelfth century."

The pseudo-visitor wasn't listening. All his attention was concentrated on his surroundings. On the left, the courtyard was shut in by the frontages of some troglodytic buildings and a wall over five metres high abutting the gable end of the chateau. The only access on that side was through a wooden gate of impressive thickness and height. On the other side, on the right, there was a pigeon loft several storeys high surmounted by an odd-looking octagonal turret with a roof of slate tiles. Beyond that, the courtyard was enclosed by another wall topped by iron railings. It was a veritable stronghold.

"And what's on the other side of the retaining wall?" Charles asked, with feigned artlessness.

"Just above it, there's a large clearing in the woods, with deer, and I've got about fifteen hectares of woodland that extends all round it. It's all fenced in. When the porch gate is closed, we're cut off from the world. That's what my guests like."

"It's just perfect. Even better than I'd hoped… Good dog," said the visitor, caressing the hound's head, as it had been expecting. "Do you live here alone? Can you show us the gite?"

"Yes to both," said the proprietor, surprised at the two questions in quick succession.

Angèle remained silent, looking over her new surroundings with a mixture of satisfaction and apprehension. The place was secluded and perfectly protected. Too much, perhaps: it was as difficult to get out of as to get into. And she was still worried about that dog, even if it was used to visitors.

∗ ∗ ∗

Acting on Karl's orders, Cédric turned the van into a lane that ran past a lake surrounded by trees. There were quite a few anglers fishing from the banks, most of them accompanied by their families, and there were children playing all round the area. They drove slowly along the lane, where some other vehicles were parked, passed an expanse of water, slowed down at a second one without stopping, and finally came to a halt behind a clump of trees protruding from a small stretch of woodland.

"What are we doing here?" he asked, lowering the side window. "It's hot!"

"We're waiting. That's all."

Karl inserted the battery into the smartphone which he'd slipped into the door compartment as they set off, and switched it on.

"We're waiting for the boss to clear the way. As soon as I get his message, we're off."

"And the girl in the back, under the tarpaulin, who's she?"

"A gendarme who annoyed Babar. She'll be a hostage if things turn awkward."

"Are you mental? You'll have all the cops in the area down on our heads!"

"They'll arrive too late."

"You're both defective! Worse than I thought. And under a tarpaulin in this heat! Do you want to do her in?"

Not restraining himself any longer, he lowered the rear windows of the van and pulled back the tarpaulin slightly, giving Patricia a little air.

"Do that again," Karl shouted in fury, "and I guarantee you'll be feeding the fish here!"

His attention was diverted by the vibration of an incoming text message.

"It's OK, we can go," he said after reading it.

He took the battery out again as his chauffeur started the vehicle.

* * *

Under pressure from Gendron, Georges had eventually informed all the brigades in the company that it was impossible to make contact with Patricia. He'd nevertheless refused to put out a general alert until her leave period had expired. The big man had been in a bad mood ever since, and would often answer his questions with just an irritated grunt.

The 19:00 briefing saw an unusual number of participants gathered together in an electrically charged atmosphere.

Georges summarised what they knew about this grim case and the part played in it by the two victims as well as Captain Derouchy, the father of the hostage who'd been freed that morning. It only took a few minutes more to cover the start of the enquiry and the few available leads.

"Since this afternoon, we've known for certain that it's Charles, the oh-so-charming Entonneur, who's heading up this operation. He wore a balaclava helmet in front of his prisoner, but the tunnel between his house and the one where the hostage was detained leaves absolutely no room for doubt."

"And nothing gave rise to any suspicion about him before this?" one of the group asked in astonishment.

"Yes, it did. Patricia Blancard, who's currently on leave, showed how he could have gone about it. Unfortunately, the examining judge wanted some positive proof from the lab before we could take him in and charge him. To continue," he went on. "We know that there were three men and possibly a woman inside the house. I've already mentioned Charles, as well as Cédric Lantois, identified from his DNA. Less than an hour ago, the hostage also recognised the third member of the gang from a photo taken at the soirée. He's one of the four men who carried the Doyen out of the Caves Painctes! He's not on our database and he was there under a false name. We'll need a little time to identify him properly."

Georges was silent for a few moments before continuing:

"The road blocks were set up too late, but we know our fugitives can't have gone very far. I would emphasise that their departure was pre-planned and well prepared, which means either that they suspected something was up or, perhaps, that they're on the point of coming to the end of their treasure hunt."

The Lieutenant was interrupted by the phone ringing. He picked it up immediately, leaving them to talk among themselves. He hung up a few minutes later.

"The brains behind this affair has now been identified," he announced without pausing. "Charles is a former captain in the Foreign Legion. Since his retirement, he's been implicated in several major robberies in the Paris area, but never convicted for lack of evidence. We assume that his fair-haired companion served with him, or under him." He let a general buzz of conversation start up before speaking privately to Maltier and Gendron:

"Our Entonneur is also a member of the same fitness club as the archivist I spoke to you about, the one who's supposed to have lost the document I was looking for – Pascal Aupetit."

"And still no news of Patricia?" Gendron insisted. "No trace from her mobile phone, nothing?"

"Unfortunately not. Her mobile is still switched off."

"By the way," Maltier interposed, "I would remind you that I'll be away from tomorrow morning until the end of next week. Sorry to let you down in present circumstances."

"I'm very grateful to have had your support up to this point," said Georges, shaking his hand as he thanked him. "I hope this whole business will be over by the time you get back."

* * *

In the chateau he'd just taken over, Charles was patting the Beauceron, now definitely won over. The dog showed his affection by standing on his hind legs and placing his gravelly paws on his new friend's shoulders. From time to time he would start running round the courtyard for no apparent reason, then come back for a few extra tokens of affection.

"This dog is better than I'd hoped for," he laughed as greeted Karl and Cédric. "The Lord of the Manor is locked up and I've just cancelled all the bookings for next week. We're OK for the moment. You can put our careless gendarmette with him in the salon. Third door on the left as you go into the courtyard."

"What about the van?"

"Leave it under the porch for the moment. I've put the car in one of the caves. No-one will be able to spot the vehicles, even from a helicopter."

Cédric remained silent; he was hardly listening, being totally immersed in the thought of the languorous smile his mistress had just bestowed on him. He'd been so fearful of never seeing her again and not being there to protect her that nothing else was of any importance. Angèle turned her face away, afraid their liaison might be noticed by their accomplices.

CHAPTER 31

SATURDAY

Once they'd set up base in the chateau, the three men subjected the proprietor to a harsh interrogation and then organised themselves for the night. Karl was detailed off to sleep in the same room as the prisoners, while Cédric and Angèle shared an improvised bedroom with Charles. A long period ensued where sleeplessness was interspersed with bad dreams. The two lovers had to bid farewell to their long, delightful and energetic nights: in their place came memories, anxieties and, above all, trying uncertainly to think up the best way of coming out of this mess unscathed. Despite Charles' embarrassed denials, there was no doubt that he and his hit-man had resolved to abandon them to their fate. As far as Cédric was concerned, this confirmed the fears repeatedly expressed by his darling Angèle.

The beautiful woman had been unable to get to sleep, turning over and over again in her mind the responses their hostage had given them, but she still couldn't elicit from those any clear idea of what they were looking for. With so little to go on, it seemed that the search would be a long one. Too long, and therefore too dangerous.

The first gleams of a new day dawning at last brightened

their two temporary bedrooms, delivering all of them from a night that had been as interminable as it was uncomfortable.

Patricia had been partially freed and was standing next to the mattress she'd been sleeping on. She was now beginning to get over her bumpy ride in the back of the van, half suffocated by the tarpaulin, and managing to forget her fear and her bruises by concentrating on her present predicament, as well as her chances of remaining alive.

She could see that, in addition to Charles and the fair-haired man who looked like a killer, the gang included a woman and a third man who'd arrived later. If she'd read the situation correctly, her attackers had tried to get rid of the other two. The young gendarme realised that this rift was something she might be able to exploit if she could get round the woman. Unfortunately, the latter hadn't come anywhere near her, not even to accompany her to the toilet. Patricia was shocked by this. She couldn't bear having this rat-faced character who clearly fancied himself standing in front of her. He was the third man, Cédric, the one that the others had tried to ditch. However, trying to get round him or seduce him presented greater risks than she was prepared to take. At least, for the moment.

Because of Angèle's obstinate refusal to have any involvement with the hostages, Cédric took charge of them. It wasn't that he'd developed any greater sense of compassion than usual: it didn't matter to him whether he looked after his victims or tortured them, if that was what was needed. He was not indifferent to the youth and sensuality of the young gendarme but, contrary to his normal habits as a voluntary bachelor, he harboured no feelings of desire for his lady prisoner. Angèle was the only one who mattered to him. He had her under his skin and couldn't imagine life without her. They would both succeed, together. How? He didn't yet know, but from now on he was going to spend all day and night thinking about it.

Lantois set down a couple of slices of stale bread from the previous day covered with a smearing of jam, and two hot coffees. He went over to the hostages to help them up to the table, one after the other. He fastened each of them by the legs to a chair and the table, one at each end.

"It's just so you don't fall backwards," he snorted.

He then untied one of Patricia's hands, and one of the chateau owner's.

"I'm going now. I'll be back in a couple of minutes. Don't bother throwing your food in my face, or on the floor, I haven't got anything else to give you. And don't try any tricks with the bowls – they're made of plastic."

"Go fuck yourself," screamed the chateau owner, who was beside himself with rage.

"That's not very nice. I'm the only one bothering to do anything for you. The others would've let you starve."

"Yeah, you're a real public benefactor. Wait till I get free, then you'll see how I deal with people who bugger around with me!"

"My dear sir," said Lantois sarcastically, "is that kind of language worthy of a gentleman of your station? But given the way you mistreat your dog, I don't think I've very much to worry about!"

He left the room, taking the tray with him.

"You haven't had much to say since yesterday," Patricia said to her companion in misfortune. "You're the owner of this place, I gather?"

"Yes, and you're the gendarme who let herself be taken captive like some kid?" he replied rather harshly. "Is it true the only training you people get is how to set up speed traps for motorists and come down hard on them if they're not wearing a seat belt?"

"If that's what they told you, then it must be true. And if we want to work together to try and escape from this predicament, we need to get off to a rather better start, don't you think?"

"Maybe, but I can't stand the way I'm being treated."

"I can, though, don't you see?" she said sarcastically. "Look, I'm sharing a room with the master of a chateau, we've just been brought breakfast in bed, or almost, and I've got a man all to myself every time I go to the toilet. It's the life I've always dreamed of."

He pulled a face.

"You're right, you're worse off than me. That said, we're both in big trouble. Those madmen are looking for something that doesn't exist, and I'm wondering what will happen when they eventually realise it."

"Explain."

"This chateau was partly occupied between 1939 and 1940 by senior civil servants from the Ministry of Finance but, more to the point, it was requisitioned after that for officers of the German army. These mobsters are convinced that the officers used the chateau to hide the loot from a robbery carried out in 1940, and that it's still here. Obviously, there are caves and underground storage areas, but my parents never spoke to me about anything like that – other than the fact that the French civil servants caused more damage to the place than the Germans who came along afterwards!"

Cédric came in at that point and they broke off. He was wary, staying partly concealed behind the door before entering the room and freeing them from the table.

"Get over there," he said to the proprietor, pointing to the opposite corner. "And don't move! You, come here, I'm going to tie you a bit more firmly while I deal with your friend."

Patricia lay down obligingly on the mattress and he refastened her bonds.

"That's enough, not so tight," she complained.

"I'm making sure you can't get loose. If you didn't wave your hands around so much, I could go easier on you next time."

"And you, come with me," he said to the other prisoner as he stood up again.

"Now what do you want me for?"

His voice was distorted with fear.

"It's OK, we just need you while we check out some more of the caves and underground passages. And try to remember stuff – we don't want to be here forever!"

* * *

"I'm waiting to hear back from our colleagues," said Georges. "They should have brought Pascal Aupetit in for questioning by now. I think they must still be grilling him."

"And what about Patricia? Nothing yet?"

"I'm afraid not."

An hour later, while they were sorting through paperwork, variously checking for anything they might have overlooked, finishing writing up file reports or checking points of detail, Georges' phone started to vibrate.

"Lieutenant Georges here. Go ahead."

"It's the Gendarmerie at Melun."

After a few polite banalities, the conversation quickly moved on to their interview with the archivist.

"Your suspect admits that he did find the lost document and read through it. He claims he didn't make the connection when you went over there, and he also states that he handed it to his Director but she never gave it back to him. I imagine she'll say the opposite."

"She already has done, yesterday. It's because of her phone call that I asked for your assistance. Does he know our prime suspect?"

"Yes, they go to the same sports centre. He hasn't seen him there for several months and doesn't know any more. However, he categorically denies ever having met the other character, the man with the fair hair. The members and staff of the centre don't know him either."

"Very strange."

"Do you really think your man here could have organised an operation this big?" the gendarme insisted.

"I've no idea. I've been asking myself the same question since yesterday, but I don't know of anyone else who could have met Charles and spoken to him about the file. Does anybody else working at the Archives attend this sports centre?

"I asked him that. Nobody, as far as he knows. We'll go through the club membership lists to check. His phone calls don't tell us anything either, but he could always have had a phone registered in a false name hidden away somewhere."

"Would you please arrange to have his place searched. I'm going to obtain the judge's authorisation right now."

Ending the conversation, Georges remained plagued by doubt. Aupetit did seem rather small fry to be running this operation. And yet, if anybody held all the cards in his hand, he was that person: he'd found the file, and he was a member of a sports club where there was a criminal capable of carrying out the job. On top of that, he was no longer happy at work, there was a deleterious atmosphere with two of his senior managers who were more interested in their own careers than bothering about their subordinates, and he was facing retirement on what was likely to be a very meagre pension.

In that rather miserable context, pulling a big job followed by early retirement in the sun justified the taking of risks by other people he'd set up.

Struck by a sudden inspiration, he made a call to Laure Pellegrin.

"I need to ask you an important question," he said, after exchanging the usual pleasantries. "When is Aupetit due for retirement? Is he coming up to it?"

"He's got about five years left to go officially, but with all his acquired time off in lieu and banked leave, I think it can only be about four years."

"Four years until he gets a full pension?"

"That's correct, but I don't think he'll stay that long. He's already spoken to me twice, quite recently, about early retirement. Some confused story about wanting to take sabbatical leave abroad and then possibly resigning. He seemed so keen to go I wondered if he'd still be here by the end of the summer."

"That's very strange."

"Yes, because he's an excellent archivist. I have a lot of time for him. And he loves his job," she added, as Georges remained silent.

"I see," said George evasively. "It all depends on your point of view. Thank you."

"Glad to be of service. Don't hesitate to call me, I think I owe you something by way of making amends."

The Lieutenant hung up, waited for a few seconds, and then called the examining judge.

Laure Pellegrin, still thoughtfully holding her phone, wondered what to make of his approach to her.

CHAPTER 32

Angèle was still refusing to show herself to the prisoners. She was looking round the chateau on her own and, after going through all the main rooms and the attics, had moved on to the pigeon loft and the outbuildings, leaving the men to explore the caves and underground passages dug out under the hillside. The ceilings of some of these were hewn out of unstable tuffeau that had come down in places, leaving large chunks of stone on the ground big enough to have killed an ox. Just thinking about it made her shiver.

Better to leave that sort of thing to those lunatics....

Her interest was aroused by an area next to the pigeon loft marked out by a large oval of half-buried stones. When Cédric had questioned him about it, the proprietor had said it traced the outline of an old pond that his parents had filled in after the war. Interesting... checking it out wouldn't do any harm, *faute de mieux*: many novels and films were filled with secrets hidden at the bottom of ponds.

To one side of the terrace, at the opposite end from the pigeon loft, there was a pedestrian gate hidden from view by a sort of screen wall. She passed through this and started following the long track that led up to the woods.

There were tyre marks on the ground, showing that vehicles came this way occasionally. She'd already explored part of the woodland, but this park was enormous. She'd noticed many remnants of wells and shallow caves, some of them collapsed, but they didn't reveal anything for the moment. All the same, she felt she had to examine every possibility.

She retraced her steps to where there was a kind of tunnel leading underground next to an old dovecote. The entrance was through a vaulted arch built of stone, but after that there was only a handrail that disappeared below ground beside a flight of steps carved out of the solid tuffeau rock. Angèle took out her torch and started down into the depths of the excavation, after checking that everything was properly shored up. She re-emerged a quarter of an hour later, disappointed: her shoes were coated with mud, her jeans were covered in brown stains and, to complete her sartorial ensemble, they'd been torn by a small cart that she'd had to squeeze past.

The tunnel had been cleared quite recently, which proved that the owner of the place had been looking for something that he hadn't found. The narrow, curving gallery came to dead end, indicating where he'd met with failure, but the very fact that he'd been searching showed that perhaps he too…

She noticed a crowbar lying on the ground: she picked it up and used it to try to prise out the keystone from the vaulted part of the roof. If she could do that, the whole of the arch would collapse, blocking access to the passage.

After a lot of effort she succeeded, but the rest was solidly cemented in and remained in place. She then attacked the surrounding stones and eventually caused the whole thing to cave in with a thumping crash.

She checked that that the entrance to the tunnel was still quite visible. There were some white stones on top without any moss on them, which made it obvious that it was a recent fall.

"That should do it," she murmured, throwing down her improvised tool.

Having succeeded in her task, she walked on through the calmness and coolness of the undergrowth. Her route took her past a lot of oaks, a few chestnut trees and others she didn't know the names of. Angèle was brought to a halt by the alarm call of a jay as a cock pheasant suddenly took off. She stopped for a few moments to look around this oasis of greenness and tranquillity: it made a rather incongruous backdrop to the affair she'd embarked upon, which had started off badly and was stained with blood.

Climbing the hill, she came out into the huge clearing that overlooked the area behind the chateau. She saw twenty or so fallow deer lying down, some on the grass and others further on in the shadows. Two big males got up as the young woman approached, lifting their antlers and smelling her scent. There was a railing fence between her and them, but the herd was spooked by her presence. A female rose to her feet, flanked by her fawn; she was followed by the others and they all trotted off to the far end of the enclosure. One of the big males was the last to leave. He stopped to stare at the intruder, frustrated that he did not have to prove his strength to her.

Angèle continued her exploration. There had to be another gateway to the park, higher than the chateau porch, to allow felled trees to be taken out or to facilitate delivery of cement and stone for repair work. It was up to her to find it: she was the only one with sufficient room for manoeuvre and the time to do it. And above all, her survival would depend on it.

A hundred metres further on, she came upon a wooden hut. Judging by its size and the tyre marks next to it, it was obviously used as a garage. The side door had a simple catch without a lock and it didn't creak as it let its visitor inside. The garage was quite large and there were tools of all kinds, including a compressor with a pneumatic drill leaning against it. Trowels, hammers, screwdrivers and pincers were all carefully arranged on shelves as if in battle formation, while the heavier items of equipment were piled against the rear wall. In front of them was a large pick-up truck, which she hastened to inspect. The tyres and bodywork seemed to be in good condition, but what was it like mechanically?

Installing herself behind the wheel, Angèle looked for the ignition key and eventually found it under the passenger seat. The engine sprang into life immediately, bringing a smile to the face of its new driver.

She shut the garage door and continued on her way,

following a curving track for the next hundred metres, and finally spotted the gateway she'd been expecting to find. Large metal bars held the gate firmly in place, but the padlocks securing them wouldn't hold out very long against the bolt cutters she'd noticed lying in the back of the pick-up. Things were looking up. Angèle returned to the garage, opened the main doors and started up the vehicle. She drove it part-way along the track and then parked it in the undergrowth to hide it.

She needed to move quickly to have time to put on a clean pair of jeans before the others came back. Men… None of them would notice she'd changed her clothes!

* * *

"No, Paul, Patricia can't receive any messages or reply to them. She's away on an operation for a few days," Gendron lied. "We can't allow her to be tracked, so no mobile. I'll let you know when she's back, and I'll pass on your messages to her. And might I suggest that if you'd been the first one to phone, you wouldn't now be getting so worried."

He hung up in irritation, ignorant of the fact that at that very moment his protégée was making desperate attempts to free herself.

The young gendarme had got to her feet as soon as her jailer left with her unfortunate companion. She worked her way towards the door of the neighbouring room. Provided the latch of the lock didn't go in too far, she might be able to cut through her fastenings by rubbing them against it. At the moment, it was just very painful. She felt she was being flayed alive as blood started to run, and she hadn't the slightest idea whether this technique was actually going to work.

The return of her captors sounded the death knell of her hopes. She went back over to the mattress and let herself fall onto it, unable to hold back her tears. She was racked as much by despair as by the cuts and grazes she'd given herself in her abortive escape attempt. She'd been initially encouraged because they'd used string instead of handcuffs. Unfortunately, it was made from a semi-synthetic material that was proving to be much stronger than she'd expected.

"Crying, my dear?" said Charles sarcastically as he came in. "You're a right little waterworks. They let anybody into the Gendarmerie these days. If I was in your position, I'd have been trying to free myself and escape instead of curling up in a ball and snivelling."

"You've tied the string too tight, it's digging into my skin and I can't feel my hands and feet," she lied, cut to the quick.

"Lantois, see to it and do what you need to, but no more than that. We can't have her running off."

Karl for his part had still not let go of the proprietor as he waited for orders from his boss.

"Lantois, when you've finished with the little lady, join us outside in the shade with the bottle of whisky that this fine gentleman is insisting on offering us."

"What do you take me for?" Cédric protested.

"Just belt up and do what the boss tells you, otherwise you soon won't be any use to anyone" Karl bellowed, throwing his prisoner down onto a mattress ready to refasten his bindings.

"Where's Angèle?" Charles asked.

"I'm here, waiting," she said from outside the room. "Still nothing, if I've understood correctly?"

"I see Mademoiselle has changed her outfit. So we're now going in for the 'Chateau Life' look?

"What the hell's it got to do with you?" Lantois yelled, not disguising his anger.

"Shut it, you two," Charles thundered, in a furious voice. "We've got other things to bother about than worrying about Angèle's dress sense. She can change her clothes as much as she likes while she's got nothing better to do. But after that…"

"But after that, what?" asked Angèle.

Tempers were getting frayed, threatening a lot worse to come.

"Let's all calm down," said the boss, playing for time. "It's not surprising that we're all living on our nerves, we're about to reach our goal, it can only be a matter of hours. After that, we'll all be kept busy enough transferring the goods and finding a place of safety. Every one of us. Is that clear enough? We'll take a break for a moment, have a glass of something decent, then we'll start again. And we'll find it."

These few words, spoken firmly, were enough to lower the temperature, but the underlying tensions and unuttered thoughts had not gone away.

The gang sat themselves at a little round table facing the retaining wall, sheltered from the midday sun by an old arbour covered in wisteria. Lantois had become the duty maid and served them their glasses.

"Just water for me," said Angèle, simperingly.

"I've brought you the bottle, you can help yourself."

He was in a murderous mood, brought on by their hasty retreat from the house to escape the gendarmes, his lack of sleep the previous night, the way he was being treated, and this whole succession of hazards and unforeseen set-backs.

She was disturbed by his attitude and touched his hand gently, giving him a radiant smile. His infatuation for her, like some overgrown teenager, made him unable to resist her. He picked up the bottle and poured her the water.

"I'm convinced it's here," Charles affirmed. "This courtyard matches the description and all my cross-checking leads to this chateau. There have to be some leads, something, somewhere!"

"Perhaps the loot was stolen or moved later on," Cédric suggested, immediately earning himself black looks from the others.

"And what about that great heap of rubble in the middle of the lawn?"

They all turned towards Angèle as if she'd just said the most stupid thing imaginable.

"It's part of the wall that's fallen down," said Charles irritably. "Even a ten year old could work that out."

"Yes, all right – but what's behind it?"

"The hill. As you can see, I presume?"

After a few seconds, the boss said: "Go and get the chateau owner."

Lantois gave a sigh and complied. He needed to get out of here, the sooner the better, but he wasn't allowed a second's respite, not a single moment when he might get organised or work out some plan.

"What's behind the part of the wall that's collapsed?" Charles asked, as soon as he'd come back with the proprietor.

"There? The hillside, and above that's the summer enclosure for the deer. What did you think there was?"

"Another cave."

"I don't think so. No-one's ever mentioned it. As far as I know, it's been like that since about 1940 or '41."

CHAPTER 33

Georges glanced at his watch. It was gone midday already. Another Saturday stuck in his office, waiting for news, inspiration, anything that would take this investigation forward. Move about, shuffle paper, make phone calls, do whatever's needed to look as if you're working, as if the leads will finally appear. Put on a pretence – possibly to ward off bad luck, or possibly so as not to miss that little nudge that fate can give you to set you on the right track.

"Gendron, aren't you going to lunch?"

"No, and anyway I'm on my own this weekend. My wife's gone shopping in Paris with one of her sisters-in-law."

"Let's both go and grab something to eat. If we don't get some fresh air, we'll turn into zombies. And a bit of sun will do us both good."

"OK, but not for long."

"Are you still on a diet? We could just have a little light something or other on the far side of the square, so we can get back quickly if we need to."

Taking advantage of the fine weather that had settled in, they sat themselves on the terrace of a café and ordered beers while waiting for the menu to be brought to them.

"I've been working on this case nearly all night," said Gendron. "I couldn't sleep anyway."

"And? Have you got anywhere?"

"Possibly. In fact, I was wondering where the German soldiers or officers would have chosen to hide the loot without having to take any chances."

"And?"

"As occupying troops, they could only have done it at one of the sites where they were being accommodated: they weren't very familiar with the area at that time. So we need to know where they were all billeted at the beginning of the war, because they certainly couldn't have moved the stuff afterwards. Too dangerous."

"How many places have you identified?"

"Far too many. They were scattered all over the place, often in little groups. Luckily, we can eliminate quite a lot, particularly those in the centre of town – for example, the Hotel de la Boule d'Or, which housed the *Feldgendarmerie*. Any unloading carried out there would hardly have gone unnoticed. Same thing with the *Ortskommandantur* in the Place de l'Hotel de Ville, where the convenience store is now."

"What about the others?"

"There was an SS company in the old Hotel Saint Hilaire, but that lot were too brainwashed to be the sort to pull a job like this. I also eliminated a few more places like that old wooden building near the Vienne and the railway bridge that used to be a night club …"

"Now vanished, I presume?"

"Yes, but it was primarily the military brothel. Not exactly a secluded location!"

"Quite!"

"I'm left with two possible sites: the Chateau de la Vauguyon and the Fort Saint Georges, where a German anti-aircraft battery was sited. The hillside all round it is riddled with holes like a Gruyère cheese, but the streets are very narrow. They couldn't have unloaded the stuff there without being seen, unless they'd made out it was a batch of shells. I'd go for the chateau, which is quieter and, more to the point, in an isolated location.

"The problem is that we need to strike quickly and hard, but also get it right. There are too many risks."

"Are you thinking what I'm thinking? Patricia?"

"I'm worried by her sudden departure and the fact we can't contact her. She was hard on Charles's heels, and then, just at the moment when we're about to lay our hands on him, she disappears. Curious coincidence..."

"That's what I've felt since yesterday, except that..."

"Except that she's officially on leave, we haven't got a clue where she is, and I can't activate a general alert for the moment. But I'm as concerned as you are."

Their conversation was interrupted by the waitress, who meticulously set down the paper table mats, then the cutlery, then changed them all round again, then moved their two Bock's beer glasses, while the two gendarmes looked on in irritation.

"She's either been put up to it by a customer or she's had a parking ticket she's going to challenge," Georges remarked sarcastically.

"Getting back to this case, I think we're stuck with two options: proceeding slowly and carefully but risking getting there too late, or going straight in at the risk of provoking a major confrontation. I'm not quite sure what to do next."

"I'm the one who has to take that decision and be responsible for the consequences."

They fell silent as the waitress brought them the mushroom omelettes they'd ordered. Half an hour later, having finished off the apple tart and drunk their coffee, they went back to their respective offices in the Gendarmerie barracks.

* * *

Back at the chateau, discussion had been cut short after the interrogation of the proprietor, and the sandwiches had been eaten in silence. The landslip was big enough to have covered up any opening in the hillside. More to the point, it was roughly in the centre of the ones that were visible on either side, which they'd already explored at some length.

"1940!" Charles repeated. "And the wall's been in that state ever since? Nobody ever thought about repairing it?"

"My parents claimed war damage reparation but they didn't receive any, even after making several applications," the proprietor said defensively. "They decided to leave it like that as a sign of protest, and I've respected their wishes."

Given the size of the task and the lack of certainty as to whether an inaccessible cave or tunnel even existed, they discussed what to do for some long time without arriving at a solution. Cédric and the prisoner could already see themselves wielding spades and pickaxes for a week to shift several dozen tons of earth and stone, possibly causing new rock falls now the retaining wall was no longer in place. For their part, Charles and Karl were wondering how to do it as quickly as possible without a mechanical digger, while Angèle seemed totally uninterested in the whole business.

"I think I've found the best solution," said Charles, putting down his cup of foul coffee. "We need to go in at ninety degrees."

"A shaft from up on top?"

"Sideways! From one of the two neighbouring tunnels, using a pickaxe to make an opening in the tuffeau. The other galleries are spaced less than fifteen to twenty metres apart, and are four to five metres wide. If there really is another one behind the rubble heap, and assuming it's about the same size as the others, we'll only have to go in about five to six metres. We don't need to dig a tunnel to take a metro train – a simple corridor will be enough, and we can sort out the details afterwards."

"Cédric, I'll leave the honours to you," Karl laughed. "We'll find you a pickaxe. Monsieur here will take away the spoil while you dig, and you can change over every two hours."

"While you twiddle your thumbs and do sod all?"

Lantois was beside himself with rage.

"No, I'll be overseeing you. It's a very important job."

"Karl, we haven't got time to sit around making jokes. We need to act fast. We'll pitch in too for half an hour from time to time so they can have a recovery period. Now go and find a shovel, a pick and a barrow. There's no time to lose. Angèle, you can keep an eye on the gendarmette every quarter of an hour."

He spoke in such a peremptory manner that no-one dared make any protest.

Work with the pickaxe began shortly afterwards. Cédric groaned with every stroke he made, while the shovel grated at his feet as it took away the debris that fell in a heap around him. They'd spotted a wide fissure in the rock wall of one of the underground passages, not far from its entrance. The tuffeau was more fragile here, which made their task easier. Lantois was doing real work for the first time in his life. Constrained as he was to undertake forced labour, he took neither pleasure nor pride in it. Sweat began to gather on his brow and to sting his eyes. His T-shirt was becoming wet, outlining the ridge of his spine and then spreading across his back. He was hot all the time that he was striking with the pick and putting his back into it, but as soon as he slowed down, his own perspiration and the natural chilly temperature of the cave made him feel frozen. An hour later, his hands were blistered and he had gone in about two metres, but he was on the edge of exhaustion.

Charles motioned to the proprietor to take over while Karl grabbed the shovel.

"Go and lie on the grass in the sun... I'll give you half an hour and then you can come and be the one to remove the debris."

"Thanks, boss," said Cedric sarcastically, only too pleased to have got off lightly.

He collapsed on to the grass.

A few minutes later, Angèle came over to him and handed him a bottle of cold water.

"Have you found anything?"

"No, but I've dug out about half of what's needed. In an hour's time at most, we'll try driving in a length of iron reinforcing rod. If there's only a metre or two left, it will penetrate the neighbouring cave and shoot off like an arrow. And if it doesn't…"

"I'll bring you a coffee in five minutes' time. I don't want Karl to see me spending too long talking to you. I'm watching his comings and goings with the barrow."

He fell asleep as soon as she'd gone.

"Your coffee!"

Cédric awoke with a start. He didn't quite know where he was. His T-shirt was already beginning to dry out in the sun, but his back was frozen.

"Thank you," he stammered. "I'll need another jersey, or I'll catch a cold."

"I'll get you one."

He watched tenderly as she departed. Water, coffee, dry clothing. Was she in love with him too?

The chateau proprietor was used to undertaking heavy work on his own and was more effective with the pickaxe than Cédric, who made a better torturer than a quarryman. Progress was spectacular after he had taken over, making Karl's trips with the barrow more frequent. At about four o'clock, Charles decided that their excavation was deep enough to try the test with the iron rod. It was also a way of sparing his right-hand man, not to mention himself, a painful spell with the pickaxe. Cédric was told to take the long metal bar and hold it horizontally at the end of the excavation, while the proprietor struck the end of it with a sledgehammer. To avoid being affected by the vibration of the bar, Cédric needed to hold it near the point where it was being struck. It was an additional trial for the torturer as his arms absorbed part of the shock. The rod went in painfully slowly, almost bending several times. Eventually, there was only about a fifty-centimetre length of it sticking out.

"We should have waited until we'd gone another metre in," said Karl dejectedly.

"Possibly, but it was worth trying."

The blow that was struck at that very moment saw the rod suddenly disappear into the rock wall.

"That's good, there has to be a cavity or underground passage behind it," said Charles in a self-congratulatory way. "We've only got another two metres to dig, so we'll take a break for a quarter of an hour. I've found an old Chinon behind the fagotts in our chateau master's cellar. I'm sure it will be perfect to toast our success before our two specialists get back to work."

CHAPTER 34

A phone call from the Gendarmerie in Melun interrupted Georges' meditations. He was unsure what to do next. Mounting a full-scale PSPG operation without being at all certain was likely to cause more problems than it solved. In any case, would their commander agree to set up an armed intervention without being given precise details of the reasons and circumstances? And sending a reconnaissance team there might alert the criminals, putting Patricia and possibly other people into danger.

"Lieutenant Georges," he announced as he picked up the phone.

"Adjudant Pierrard again. We've finished searching the archivist's home. There's not much to tell you. We've taken his cheque books and bank statements, but there's nothing there of any interest to us. Apart, that is, from a few old documents, one of which dates from January 1945. It's a report of an investigation in Chinon."

"Nothing from 1940?"

"No."

"Pity," Georges sighed. "Send me everything you've mentioned, urgently. Thanks for what you've done and let me know if you find out any more."

He motioned to Gendron to come in.

"Have you unearthed anything else?" he asked as he hung up.

"I've just been trying something," the Adjudant replied, looking uncomfortable.

"What?" said Georges in alarm.

"The chateau has holiday lettings. They're managed through the Gites de France agency."

"So?"

"I had the idea that they might ring up on the pretext that a mistake had been made with the rental charges, and say they were sending an inspector round at the end of the afternoon. We might then perhaps find out if there was a problem."

"You're mad! A stunt like that would be guaranteed to end in disaster!"

"No, because it would be their reservations office calling from a verifiable number: there'd be no danger."

"So why the long face?"

"Gites de France have informed me that all bookings for the next two weeks have been cancelled as from yesterday, because the proprietor of La Vauguyon has a family bereavement. His phone isn't answering."

"Have they tried his mobile?"

"They've only got his landline number. It seems he's a rather odd character who doesn't like people bothering him."

"Strange coincidence. He may have been bothered more than he'd bargained for since yesterday," said the Lieutenant sarcastically. "We desperately need to find out what's going on over there. And without attracting any attention. Have we got any plans, drawings, anything?"

A few minutes later, they were poring over a large-scale map of the area.

* * *

At the chateau, work had started again with a vengeance. Harried by Charles and his sidekick, the two serfs were making rapid progress with their forced labour despite their fatigue.

The rock wall suddenly gave way as the proprietor struck it, causing the point of his pickaxe to arc round in a circle and hit him in the shin. Cédric, who had just come back with the wheelbarrow, looked on uncomprehendingly as the two other men rushed to pick him up.

Karl made a rapid diagnosis as he tried to lift the victim up:

"Broken leg. It's bleeding, but it's a superficial injury. No open fracture."

"It's time we stopped anyway! Carry him back to the room and give him whatever you can find, anti-inflammatory medication, and don't stint on the dose. Get the gendarmette to do it. She must be trained for things like this, she can clean his wound and nurse him."

Karl ignored the screams of the suffering man as he grabbed hold of him by his clothing, picked him up and dumped him unceremoniously in the empty barrow.

"Take him over there," he said to Cédric, pointing towards the chateau.

"Take him yourself," Charles corrected. "Lantois, come over here and make this hole bigger. It's time to wind things up and get out of here."

A few minutes later, they emerged into a tunnel parallel to the one they'd started from. All they could see were a few old tools, rusty shovels and rakes that had been lying there at rest since the time the retaining wall had come down. The gallery extended under the hill and ended in an almost circular cave. There was nothing unusual about the wall opposite them, no possible crevice to hide anything. The floor of the cave was smooth, with no sign of any back-filled excavation. The two men were distraught. All that effort for nothing!

Charles turned round and swept the light of his torch along the wall from the corridor where they'd just entered. A stone had come loose from an area about three metres up from the ground, where a small section of what was obviously masonry could be seen. Masonry that was covered in a mixture of earth and powdered tuffeau to make it look the same colour as the rest of the gallery.

"It's here!" he said, trying to hide his emotion. "We'll need a couple of ladders."

Cédric shone his own lamp on the same spot, silently

exploring it for himself.

"Is that it? Have you found it?"

"Is it there?"

The voices of Karl and Angèle came at almost the same time. The young woman had stopped near the opening they'd just made, while the shadows on the ground made by the henchman's lamp showed that he was striding rapidly towards them.

"Possibly," said Charles, not committing himself.

The hiding place turned out to be bigger than they'd expected. A narrow passage gave onto a cavity that could easily have contained five or six people. They could see fifty or so gold bars as well as bundles of banknotes, many of them affected by damp.

"All denominated in francs and no longer legal tender," said Karl regretfully.

"Yes, but there are dollars as well, look at that pile. I think they'll still be valid."

There was a large decomposing cardboard box containing rolls of coins, gold napoleons, which had mostly gravitated to the bottom of the cavity.

"What does all that lot come to?" asked Karl.

"At first glance, between two and three million Euros. Nearer three, I think. To be shared between us."

"Are you including our two hangers-on?"

"Of course not!"

For her part, aware of the danger hanging over her as well

as her lover since the discovery of the hoard, Angèle had just retrieved the young gendarme's mobile phone. Wearing a balaclava, she entered the room where the two detainees were being held. Patricia was fastened hand and foot with shackles and was still tending the injured man. The dog had no idea what was going on and was lying alongside his master, vigorously licking his hand.

"I'm as much their hostage as you are, I just have some freedom of movement up to the point that they decide to get rid of me," Angèle explained. "I've picked up your phone and I can have it working again if you give me the PIN code. Your colleagues will be able to trace us and get here before it's too late."

Patricia hesitated for a long moment, wondering whether this was a trap to put her team mates off the scent. However, given that she had a fellow prisoner who was seriously injured and unable to move, she didn't have any other option.

"You don't need a PIN number," she said at last. "Just switch it on and the geolocation software will work automatically."

"That's too much of a gamble. You know as well as I do that it could take some time – it will only work if a tracking request has already been made. It would be much better to alert your colleagues by making a call."

The way she spoke, together with the way the two others had reacted towards her at Charles' house, when they were proposing to ditch her, militated in her favour. Patricia had already been hoping to find a way of getting the woman on her side, and now she was doing it of her own accord. How could she turn down this one last chance?

"You must have worked out by now that they don't trust me," said Angèle. "They wouldn't even let me come near you. There isn't much time, but I could save all three of us," she continued.

Patricia gave in and said Gendron would be the best person to call, as he'd do everything in his power to come and find her. Angèle thanked her for that precious piece of information. She switched the phone on and raised her thumb as a sign of success as she left the room.

Having hidden the precious object in a safe place, the young woman went back to join the group. The three men had started transferring the hoard from the back of the cave to the van, which had been parked inside the entrance to one of the tunnels.

"Nearly finished?" she asked innocently.

"We'll need another half hour," Charles growled. "Your friend isn't very quick and we can't get the barrow through the entrance. We shan't be leaving here before nightfall, at any rate."

"What do we do with the two prisoners?"

"We get rid of them. At the point we've reached, the fewer witnesses the better. I've already warned the big boss organising this operation. We've got a safe house a long way from here. All we need to do is lie low for a while. And then, off to Italy, Greece, and a boat to Turkey."

"A plane would be quicker!"

"That's a very good idea, assuming you want to be arrested before you even get on board," he sneered. "They've got our fingerprints, DNA and all that crap, or they soon will have. If this goes wrong, we'll already have been identified."

"I'm going to see what the workers are doing," she interrupted, heading towards the tunnel.

"You seem less claustrophobic all of sudden, now you know where the goods are."

She shrugged but didn't turn round.

CHAPTER 35

The gendarme burst into the office, sending flying papers that had already been pushed aside by the maps Georges and Gendron had spread out.

"Lieutenant, Patricia's phone is back on, and it's been traced."

"Where? How long ago?"

"Has she called us? It's worrying if she hasn't," Gendron said with a frown.

"It was about ten minutes ago, and you're right, she hasn't phoned. Her mobile is at the Chateau de la Vauguyon. We're sure of that because the nearest houses are over a hundred metres away."

The two gendarmes hesitated. It wasn't an easy matter to pull together all the information and reach a conclusion in a few seconds, especially in a case as complex as this. The phone's location confirmed what they'd been thinking as well as what they feared, but what did its sudden reappearance on the network signify? Was it a trap set by the criminals, or a desperate attempt by their colleague to contact them?

It seemed clear that Patricia wasn't free to act, or not

completely so, otherwise she'd have phoned them or at least sent a text message. Making a call to her could possibly alert her captors. It was a delicate situation.

"We need to decide on something," Gendron snapped.

His phone started to vibrate, heralding the reception of a text message.

"Patricia", he whispered as he looked at the screen.

"*La Vauguyon. Can't call,*" he read out.

Georges made an instant decision:

"I'm going to contact the PSPG. It's becoming too dangerous – we're going to bring in the big guns."

* * *

The boss looked at his watch, as if aware of the impending danger. He was becoming impatient.

The transfer was taking longer than he'd expected. Cédric was exhausted and was bringing the contents of the hoard ever more slowly down the ladder. He then had to carry it along the galleries and the narrow passage they'd just dug before taking it to the vehicle hidden in the tunnel entrance. He cursed Charles and, particularly, his guard dog Karl: he was the only one doing any work, while they'd spared their own efforts right from the start. And he cursed them even more because they were making it impossible for him to think and act to protect Angèle.

All his thoughts were directed towards her. She'd tried to

comfort and protect him when he'd collapsed with fatigue in the middle of the lawn. He was fortunate in being able to rely on this extraordinary woman, but how could he return her affection and protect her in turn?

For the first time in his life, the torturer was feeling concern for someone other than himself. Was it the beginning of the path to redemption? Or merely the result of exhaustion?

Angèle was waiting for him by the van with a bottle of water and a towel. She really was an angel.

Cédric rubbed himself down as Charles looked on, sneering at this exhibition of human frailty: the nun giving succour to the afflicted, and the cretin she'd seduced. How touching!

As she took the bottle back, the young woman slipped a piece of paper into her lover's hand. The look on her face told him that he shouldn't give anything away. He controlled his emotions, curled his fist round it and went to fetch the next load.

When he was half way along the narrow passage, he read what was on the paper by the light of his head lamp:

"Be ready to open the big gate leading to the woods when I give you the sign this evening. Don't worry."

Heartened, he continued walking with steps that were now less heavy.

Angèle want back to the chateau and settled herself

comfortably in a garden chair to enjoy the sunshine. Almost immediately, she jumped up again.

"I'm going to have a look out from the top of the pigeon loft," she told Charles. "I'm getting nervous."

"You've no reason to be. We've got the upper hand, and they're not ready to take any action."

The pigeon loft was surmounted by an octagonal slate-roofed turret, which was difficult to get to. It had a series of glass skylights which provided a panoramic view of the area around the chateau, and was high enough to let her see over the retaining wall into the deer enclosure. There was no unusual movement to attract her attention. She checked her watch. It was nearly two hours now since she'd sent the first text message. The absence of any reaction made her anxious and put her plan in jeopardy. She grabbed the phone and composed a second message:

"Worried. When U getting here? Just 1 txt msg."

The response was not long in coming. Gendron was distraught and couldn't wait to reassure his protégée:

"PSPG. 1 hr."

The reply brought a smile to the young woman's lips. Perfect. They'd be making their assault after the goods had been transferred, at the point when everybody was starting to relax. And the gendarmes would be sure to strike in daylight, just before nightfall. She went back down and resettled herself in the courtyard.

The loading of the van was eventually completed some thirty minutes later, to the great relief of Angèle and, especially, of Cédric.

"It will be dark in just over an hour," Charles pointed out. "We'll take it in turns to have a shower and change and then we'll have a drink and a snack. In two hours' time, we'll go out through the big porch gate and get away from here."

"I'll shower first," said Cédric.

"You'll do..."

"Stop!" Angèle shouted angrily. "He's done all the work, and if you want him to go on being any use to us, you need to let him shower and have some rest."

"Get on with it, then, and hurry up," said the boss, giving way. "You've got three minutes, no more."

Three minutes, which would turn into five. The timing was becoming acute.

"I'm going back up the pigeon loft," she announced.

"You've really got the jitters," laughed Charles.

"I'm feeling under pressure, and I'd rather be overly cautious than not cautious enough. I'm involved in all this too."

The young woman climbed rapidly up the stairs and looked all round the horizon before sending another text message:

"2 got away. 2 still in chateau. Am hidden in underground passage, pigeon loft. Battery 0."

She took out the battery as soon as she'd sent the text and went back down to the courtyard.

Charles had just gone into the bathroom when she arrived.

"I think something's going on all round the chateau, away in the distance," she said to Karl, putting on a worried look. "I'm possibly getting worked up for nothing, but I think you ought to go and take a look for yourself."

Karl's face went white. He raced over to the pigeon loft and hurled himself inside. This was exactly the moment Angèle had been waiting to tell her lover to open the gate leading into the woods. She went back into the chateau, took the handcuffs off the gendarme and showed her the way out, whispering to the injured man not to move and to await help.

The two women rushed outside and got into the van. Angèle drove off, tyres spinning, and went through the gateway just seconds after Cédric had opened it.

"Shut it again` she screamed, even before the van had come to a halt. "Help us," she said to Patricia, jumping out with the ignition key in her hand.

The three of them managed to close the large gates just as Charles, hearing the sound of the engine starting up, came running out naked into the courtyard.

"We need to block the gateway," Angèle shouted hysterically. She pointed to a huge wooden beam that could be slid across the two gates. "I've already locked the pedestrian gate, they can't get through that way."

"It won't hold longer then fifteen or twenty minutes," Cédric said.

"That'll be long enough."

They piled into the vehicle to the sound of the shouting coming from the courtyard. Angèle set off like a tornado and hurled the vehicle along the track, just as Karl came up with an axe. The sound of heavy blows began to echo round the courtyard, covering up Charles' cries of rage. Two hundred metres further on, the fleeing vehicle penetrated the undergrowth that Angèle had reconnoitred earlier and stopped next to the pick-up truck. They were on the far side of a low hill and couldn't be seen from the chateau. Dusk was already starting to fall across the centuries-old trees, and in under an hour they'd be in total darkness.

In the distance, the gate to the courtyard was beginning to give way. Charles had taken over from Karl and was striking even harder blows with all the venom of someone who knows he's just been double-crossed.

"What the hell did you think you were doing? You've totally screwed this up," he yelled, turning towards Karl.

"That bitch has taken all the loot and two of the guns. She's going to pay for this! And how!"

His stooge merely gritted his teeth and made no reply. He was swearing to himself that he would disembowel that slut with his own hands, after using her in front of her accomplice, the so-called torturer – who would very soon find out there were others far worse than him. That squeamish wimp who watched kids' movies!

Two planks gave way, and Karl immediately slipped through to release the wooden beam that was holding everything in place. The two men opened the gates.

And just at that moment, a heavy sound caught their attention. A very characteristic chopping noise in the air…

"It's a helicopter," Charles bawled. "Move!"

They ran for shelter in the chateau and rushed to look out of the windows, staying glued to the wall. They still couldn't see anything, but the sound was approaching.

The helicopter came over the crest of the hill, level with the treetops; it then flew very low over the deer park, unseen from the courtyard, scattering the terrified animals in all directions. The aircraft landed some fifty metres behind the retaining wall, disgorging heavily-equipped men who jumped out and, keeping their heads down, moved swiftly to the positions they'd been assigned. It immediately took off again and hovered at an angle to the chateau. A sniper was leaning out of one of the doors, able to see across the whole of the courtyard and buildings and provide covering fire for his colleagues.

This unexpected assault had taken the two criminals totally by surprise and they were at a loss what to do. Karl appeared to make up his mind more quickly: he had already seized his gun and was about to leave through the porch gateway when Charles grabbed him by the arm.

"No! These aren't ordinary cops, we've got the GIGN or some such on to us. If you leave here, they'll have you before you know it. They'll be all round us by now. Our only chance is the hostage."

"The hostages, plural! They don't know that our girl cop has already gone – as far as they're concerned, we've got two of them."

They rushed over to the chateau owner, who was still stretched out on the ground. The dog had run outside barking, as if happy to welcome even more visitors to his domain. A hypodermic dart had an instant calming effect on him.

"I'm getting some infrared images," one of the gendarmes reported to the HQ, which had been set up five hundred metres from the chateau. "One lying down, and two next to him. Unfortunately, the thickness of the walls is causing a problem and I keep losing them. I can't locate anyone else, but the underground passages are very deep and cold."

"That fits with our information. There are only two of them left, plus the owner who's clearly their hostage. Can Team 2 get in there without exposing themselves to danger?"

"Yes."

"I'm picking up sound on the window panes," reported a second gendarme, who was a little further away and at an angle to the front of the building. "But it's practically inaudible. The room is too big, it's got double or triple glazing, and the walls are much too thick."

The HQ gave the signal and the PSPG gendarmes who had been concealed in the grounds of a house near the pigeon loft came swarming over the wall into the area behind the chateau, keeping close to the building. Others came round via the track that that led into the woods. They had total control of the perimeter of the property, and their targets had been identified. The hostage negotiations could now begin.

While this was happening, other men had gone into the underground passages and started to check them out. Two more crawled along the front of the chateau towards the window of the room where the two hostage takers had barricaded themselves. One of them stood up cautiously, his back to the wall, holding a small electronics box.

"OK, everyone's in place and ready to go, you can proceed with caution," said a tinny voice in his earpiece.

A hand reached round the corner of the stonework and slowly felt for the window casing. Two fingers got a hold on the wooden frame next to the upright.

"You're nearly there. Go slowly and fasten your receiver without pressing on it."

Inside, increasingly nervous and racked with uncertainty, the two men had placed themselves opposite each other to give mutual cover. As a precaution, they'd left the separating doors open so they had a view into the adjoining rooms while keeping out of sight. They had their backs to the wall, watching the windows without going near them; Charles took those facing north and Karl those of the southern side.

"I can't see anything," Karl remarked. "They're well hidden."

"Those bastards will have thermal imaging goggles. Luckily for us, the walls are very thick and they'll have to come looking for us. Make sure you don't place yourself between two opposite windows

"OK, I know how the music goes," Karl growled. "It's a bugger we can't get at the aluminium foil in the kitchen. If we could have wrapped ourselves up in it…"

"The main worry now is if they slip a fibre optic cable with a camera attached to it through one of the window frames."

Charles instinctively looked over to the south side of the

building. He stood up suddenly. He had just noticed a shadow in the corner of a window pane and raised his pistol ready to shoot. Karl was quicker off the mark and opened fire at the same instant: it shattered the glass, which exploded with a loud noise.

The gendarme rolled down to the foot of the wall, still holding the receiver and protecting himself from glass that was falling as hard as a March hailstorm. He knew that if there was any danger he'd be covered by two snipers, one on the ground and the other in the helicopter, but nevertheless he quickly flattened himself against the stonework to be as little visible as possible. Karl for his part had immediately thrown himself to the floor and crawled over to the injured proprietor, while Charles, still standing and ready for anything, watched each of the windowed façades in turn.

"I've got two hostages," he shouted. "If you move, or if you try anything, I'll start by executing your little lady colleague."

"Let them know you're here," Karl bawled at their injured captive, "otherwise you're dead meat!"

Furious and impatient, he struck the unfortunate man's shinbone with the back of his hand. He was answered with a scream of pain.

"Hostage's life in danger," was the immediate response from HQ. "Go, go, go."

Two windows exploded simultaneously, letting two demons in balaclavas into the room. Two other gendarmes rushed in behind them. Surprised by their noise and speed, the ex-legionnaires began firing at random. A bullet hissed a couple of centimetres above the head of the man who had gone for Karl. Taken by surprise, he rolled onto his side without taking his eyes off the hand holding the gun, which he managed to block just in time. Another bullet lodged itself in the door opposite. Hand-to-hand fighting ensued, then Charles was grabbed by the ankles and fell heavily, dropping his weapon. A second man charged at Karl to give assistance to his colleague, who was in some difficulty. Eventually, and not without considerable effort, they managed to wrestle their opponent to the floor and made him drop his gun, which was in fact already empty.

"A ferocious bastard, this one," said the man who had been the first to jump on him. "He could easily have topped one of us!"

"HQ? Hostage freed, no wounded," said the squad commander into his microphone.

The whole operation had lasted less than ten minutes. A few moments later, Gendarmerie vehicles drove up to the porch gate, all sirens sounding.

"It's OK, guys," said the PSPG major when he saw Georges and Gendron. "We're going to start searching everywhere. There's one injured man who looks really messed up, and we're taking him off by helicopter.

However, we haven't located your colleague yet. It's clear that the other two accomplices have got away, as you told us."

"We need to look for an underground passage near the pigeon loft. It seems she hid in there, but her phone's gone dead."

"My men are going to finish making sure the chateau is secure, as well as the tunnels under the hill. I'll leave two of them with you to help you search."

"Can the forensic team start their investigations?"

"In ten minutes time, provided we don't find anything suspicious."

CHAPTER 36

Hidden in the wood, the three escapees had heard the helicopter arrive and could well imagine what was going on just a few hundred metres from their refuge.

When the Gendarmerie sirens started up, Patricia knew the end was imminent.

"No shots being fired, that's odd," she said turning to Angèle.

"No. I think your colleagues have brought in the special force. Bound to be the PSPG, given that you were taken hostage."

"The PSPG? You seem to know our organisation extremely well," said the gendarme in astonishment.

"I thought I might join them one day, but now that's totally screwed."

A dozen minutes later, just before nightfall, they heard the helicopter leave with the injured man and knew the operation was over. They got out of the vehicle.

"We can go back down now," said Patricia.

"Wait."

Patricia turned towards her liberator. She felt the blow without seeing it coming. A violent kick in the solar plexus made her fall heavily, her eyes wide open in surprise.

Oblivion descended. The handcuffs were put back in place in a matter of seconds, while Cédric gagged her and then placed her on the back seat of the van.

"Listen to me carefully," said Angèle, as her lover tried to take her in his arms. "You need to keep a cool head, otherwise this whole thing will fail."

"I'm listening."

"We'll be leaving here in a few minutes, at more or less the same time as the chopper lands at the hospital. The gendarmes down below won't hear the vehicles until we reach the gateway. You'll take the pick-up and follow me as far as the exit. I'll stop there, and you'll set off to the left. Afterwards, go up the lane on the right, then take the first road on the left."

"What about you?"

"I'll go in the other direction, to the right. We'll split up to confuse the pursuit. In any case, by the time they react and get to their cars parked in front of the chateau, we'll be a long way away."

"How will we meet up?"

"There's a phone in the pick-up. It's the one Charles had as a spare, it isn't being tracked. Switch it on in half an hour's time, and not before. I'll call you to tell you where to meet me. You've got the PIN number on a piece of paper. But make sure you're a long way from here before switching it on."

"Perfect. I'm still amazed."

"We'll soon be rich, and that's the most important thing."

He hugged her to him. God, how he wanted her now, despite his extreme fatigue.

A long, languorous kiss sealed their complicity. Cédric was lost in admiration. She'd thought of everything, planned for everything, even the chopper leaving for the hospital. Now they'd have time to get away and put the cops off the scent before the aircraft could get back. And it would soon be dark.

As he was about to let go of her, he took her in his arms again. He stroked her face, gazed at her for a long while, admiring her clear eyes which were a luminous green even in the semi-darkness.

"I love the colour of your eyes," he told to her. "They look emerald in the moonlight."

She kissed him tenderly once more, then gently removed his arm from her.

"Come on," she said. "We need to go now."

* * *

In the meantime, and despite the assistance of the PSPG, the gendarmes under Georges' direction still couldn't locate any underground passage in the area of the pigeon loft.

"We'll have to call the chateau owner," the Lieutenant conceded at last.

Despite his size and heavy build, Gendron immediately set

off like a rocket to find the major, which he did very quickly.

"Commandant Hugo, we need to call the chopper, it's urgent!"
Within a few minutes he was in contact with the injured man.

"Near the pigeon loft?" said the latter in astonishment. "No, there isn't one there. But if you go into the woods, there's a tunnel with a stonework entrance just below a half-ruined dovecot. Perhaps your colleague hid in there."
A group of them ran up to the spot he'd described, only to discover to their horror that the tunnel had collapsed.

"Quickly!" said Gendron, taking off his weapons harness.
He rushed in and started pulling off enormous blocks of stone with his bare hands, and was very soon helped by others. The girl he looked upon as his own daughter was in there, and in great danger – nothing else mattered at all.
Three hundred metres further on, concealed by the slope and the trees, the two vehicles started up. The noise was deadened by the hillside and the distance, and none of the gendarmes busy with unblocking the tunnel noticed it.
Angèle brought the van loaded with loot to a halt. She blew a kiss to her lover and signed to him to move off as quickly as possible. She watched as he drove round the bend, waited a few seconds, then put the vehicle into reverse and gave a few blips on the accelerator. She let the van roll backwards down the slope, made a perilous

half-turn and came to rest silently in the same concealed position that she'd been in a few moments earlier.

The men unblocking the tunnel stopped work when they heard the pick-up start off along the road above them. When the sound of the second engine reached them, they reacted.

"The two accomplices are getting away," Georges yelled, running up to the top of the hill.

"I certainly heard two vehicles," said a gendarme running alongside him.

Gendron didn't even lift his head.

"They can go to hell."

He continued removing the pile of stones with rage in his belly, a worried and furious man.

He'd just reached a bend in the tunnel that had stopped the rock fall when the gendarmes who'd gone after the vehicles returned, out of breath.

"Too late, they've gone," Georges confirmed. "Let the PSPG commander know," he said to one of his team. "We'll need the chopper back. And set up road blocks all over the area, within a radius of twenty kilometres."

He detailed off four of his men:

"Get in your cars and drive round all the country lanes and tracks round here."

"She isn't in there! They've taken her with them!"

Gendron had just reappeared from the tunnel, which had

at last been cleared, and his voice conveyed all the misery in the world.

"We need to grill our two suspects – urgently," the Lieutenant replied.

CHAPTER 37

The two criminals were refusing to talk, but they were plotting their revenge. They didn't yet know how Angèle and Cédric had worked out that the Gendarmerie assault was about to take place, unless they'd connived with the young gendarme. Or had they actually betrayed them? Had they been set up by their accomplices?

Vengeance is a dish best eaten cold and it should be wreaked personally, not via intermediaries, so there was no question of telling the investigation team anything. They'd wash their own dirty linen, and in their own way: not by putting those two degenerates behind bars, but guaranteeing that they'd regret ever having tried to mess with former members of the Foreign Legion, followed by a bullet between the eyes. The interesting thing about being held in custody is that you are not obliged to answer any questions. And so...

"They drove off in a vehicle," Charles said at last, exploding with rage. "They double-crossed us, how the hell should we know where they've gone?"

Further questioning failed to elicit any further information whatsoever. Karl was the more stubborn of the two. He just sat there with a fixed stare and his jaw clenched, as if hearing or seeing nothing.

Georges was furious, and wouldn't allow Gendron to take part in the questioning. He'd foreseen how the two suspects might behave and was worried that the big man would turn violent.

The door opened suddenly and Gendron appeared, mad with excitement.

"Her phone's come on again! It's in a stationary position and we've got two vehicles very near to it, they'll be there in two or three minutes' time."

"No blues and twos!"

"They know that."

The ten minutes that followed seemed like an eternity. The gendarmes spent the time pacing up and down, watched contemptuously by the two gangsters.

"They've crashed into a ditch," said Charles sarcastically.

"You can belt up, otherwise I'll make absolutely sure you'll want to shut yourself away for a few years," Gendron threatened, moving towards him.

The telephone rang at last, diverting his attention from the murderous feelings that had come over him. The Lieutenant took the call, switching to loudspeaker mode. He went out of the room accompanied by Gendron.

"Georges here. Have you found her?"

"No. It's getting very convoluted. We've just apprehended the third man in the gang. He's got Patricia's phone, but he's on his own. He seems about to have a nervous breakdown, we can hardly understand a word he's saying."

"Be more precise," Georges shouted.

"It seems he left the chateau followed by his accomplice, who was in another vehicle with Patricia and the loot. They went in different directions. His confederate was supposed to call him to say where the rendezvous would be, but she hasn't done so."

"That doesn't make any sense! Nobody's going to call him, or get him to come to them, when he's using a phone that we're tracking. It's more likely she set him up so we'd go after him while she got away…"

"I think he's just come to the same conclusion. He's crying like a kid – he looks all in and unable to take any more. A right gangster we've got here!"

"He's got to tell us what vehicle she's using and where she was headed. Find out which way he went, perhaps we can work out the woman's own direction from that. There's only a very limited number of possible routes from that chateau exit."

A quarter of an hour later, the PSPG commander informed Georges that the entire chateau area was secure, including the caves and the pigeon loft, and no-one else was on the premises.

"The chopper and our vehicles will be here shortly, and then we'll be off. Unless you find your colleague and still need our help with the escapees?"

"Thanks, but I think that from here on in we're back to old-fashioned policing methods. Unless I can trace the other vehicle and know what it is, we can't do very much. Especially at night. Anyway, well done on your little show."

"It was a good training exercise for my lads! We're at your disposal if you need us, especially if you locate Patricia."

"I hope we shall, very soon."

They touched fists and went their separate ways.

The two gendarmes had just returned to the room where the suspects were when Georges' mobile started to vibrate again. It was Jacques, in charge of the forensic team.

"Yes, Jacques – anything new?"

"Didn't you see my text message this afternoon?"

"No. Was it important?"

"Fairly important, yes! The trace evidence we found at Charles' house shows the fingerprints of Angèle Courtois: she's a former women's champion in Thai kick-boxing, as well as a few other extreme sports. She's had a few run-ins with the law. She seemed to have gone straight after setting up her own security firm about three years ago. Her business partner claims that he hasn't seen her for nearly three weeks. She may be dangerous. She's the one who trains their top-level guards."

"Shit!" said Gendron. "And she's at large with Patricia Blancard as hostage. We don't even know what vehicle she's using. Is her company based in this area?"

"No, it's at Savigny-le-Temple. That's near Melun."

"No! And they wouldn't by any chance happen to provide security services for the Ministry of Finance Archives Centre?"

"Yes, among other places. How did you know?"

"Just a lucky guess. And I didn't even need a crystal ball or any coffee grounds."

Georges ended the call in a black rage. Pascal Aupetit had concealed his hand very well, but now the game was up. The birds were going to sing. All of them!

CHAPTER 38

The Beauceron was attached by a long leash and yelping like a soul in torment. Not only had his master gone away but he'd lost his new friend, Charles, who'd given him a hefty kick when the animal had licked his cheek as if to console him while he was being handcuffed.

Angèle was standing on a low wall, propping herself against a tree growing out of it so she could hide in its dark shadows as she observed the preparations the gendarmes were making to leave the scene. The dog had been rescued by a neighbour and she was relieved to see that it was tied up, so it couldn't come out if she went near the courtyard.

Georges had his men close and padlock the external gate to the park, then gave the order for the return to the Gendarmerie barracks.

"We'll leave several vehicles on watch – one down here, and two up near the gateway. They'll be relieved every two hours."

Shortly afterwards, one of the cars stationed itself in the chateau entrance facing the large porch gate, which had been wedged open.

These monitoring vehicles were positioned where Angèle had anticipated they would be, but the one down below was parked in the middle of a sort of open-air corridor flanked by two walls. From there, the gendarmes sitting in it had an uninterrupted view as far as the foot of the hill. Behind them was a wrought iron gate that had not been closed for decades and was now solid with rust. There was no way of getting to the car unseen without climbing over one of the walls. It was an awkward situation.

Angèle decided to wait for the duty change-over. She told herself that in two hours' time, three hours after her supposed escape, the vice might not grip so tightly. It was a card worth playing, even if there was an element of danger. She stayed watching for a few moments after the gendarmes had gone, then went back to the van. She felt she could do with some water and one of the sandwiches she'd made earlier.

* * *

Georges settled himself at his desk to try to put his thoughts in order. Everything had happened so fast during the course of the day that he definitely needed to make a summary.

So – Pascal Aupetit had been aware of the existence of the documents. He was also acquainted with Charles and the formidable Angèle Courtois. Everything had begun some six or eight months previously, when Charles had come to Chinon to ingratiate himself with people there and get the last surviving protagonists to tell a story that was over sixty years old. He had three accomplices who'd arrived later and he'd been double-crossed by one of them, this Angèle, who was extremely devious and very well trained. She now had the loot in her possession, as well as a hostage. A very special hostage!

He decided to make another phone call to his opposite number in Melun. Since Aupetit was still being held in custody, he might be persuaded to talk if he was told about the current situation and the fact that the loot had been hijacked. Unless, of course, he had absolute confidence in Angèle.

"Lieutenant Georges in Chinon. Sorry to bother you, but I need your help."

"No problem."

He summarised the essential points as quickly as possible and finished by setting out the situation and what he was hoping to achieve.

"What you're telling me sounds more like a whodunit novel! Are you sure you didn't read about this somewhere before you fell asleep?" his colleague joked.

"Unfortunately not, I know it's true."

"Let me get this straight: you want me to tell him he's just been double-crossed, and he'll receive the maximum sentence because this affair involves the abduction of a female gendarme. It could be worth a try. I'll call you back when I can."

"OK, thanks."

"No, hang on. He asked to me to notify his head of service, somebody called Laure Pellegrin, to say he wouldn't be in on Monday. She immediately went ape –

told us he was a model employee, he couldn't be accused like this, and so on and so forth."

"Yes, I can well imagine."

"The problem is, she's decided to engage a lawyer to represent him, so there might some delay before I can get back to you."

"And has he agreed to accept legal assistance?"

"He seemed surprised, but he didn't raise any objection. I'm not sure he quite understands the seriousness of it all."

"But on the other hand he was intending to take early retirement in a few weeks' or months' time."

They ended the call. A thoughtful Georges went off to find Gendron.

"I'm making some progress," the latter said to him as he came out of the room. "I'm treading on eggshells while I wait for the judge to arrive."

The idea of this giant of a man nearly two metres tall and built like a mountain being able to tread on eggshells brought a smile to the Lieutenant's face, but he let him continue.

"Cédric Lantois is beginning to crack. I've asked for a doctor to come and look at him, by the way, he looks as if he's about to have a breakdown. He's confirmed that the person who gave him his instructions was called Pascal Aupetit. He's never met him and everything was arranged over the phone."

"Have we got any trace of those calls?"

"No, they used mobile phones that they got rid of on a regular basis. I changed the script a bit with the two others – I told them that Lantois and Angèle had double-crossed them on the orders of the archivist, Aupetit. There was no reaction from the fair-haired character, he's a really stubborn type. Charles was different and started spewing out a stream of invective. He was recruited by phone as well, and by the same person. Again, there's no trace of the calls."

"But they must have been able to communicate with each other somehow or other," the Lieutenant insisted.

"Yes, but I still don't know exactly how."

"We'll find out. But in the meantime, I think all the things that have happened since Patricia disappeared have made me overlook one very important point: Charles doesn't come from around here, so how did he manage to find those two houses linked by a tunnel that allowed the whole gang to escape?"

"I'll question them."

"He won't say anything. I'm going to look into the land registry records and the title deeds of the properties. We might find something important there. Shall I fetch some sandwiches?"

"For the others, yes. I'm giving up for the time being, I've got some thinking to do," said Gendron, walking away.

CHAPTER 39

Patricia regained consciousness in the back of the van. She'd had no idea what was going on while Angèle was staging her fake departure before returning to her hiding place. A gleam of hope had lit up at that moment. Angèle was clearly being forced to act by Cédric Lantois, but she'd just managed to get rid of him. She would now set her prisoner free and seek the protection of the Gendarmerie.

She was quickly disabused. Her handcuffs and gag remained in place and her captor's attitude gave her no hope whatsoever. She'd been left on her own in the van for over half an hour and had become very stiff. She wriggled over onto her stomach and, as she pushed against the seat so she could sit up and change position, her foot struck against a metallic object.

The bolt cutters!

They'd been thrown carelessly onto the passenger seat, but the jerking of the van and the violent half-turn it had made had caused them to slide down past the handbrake and end up on the floor of the vehicle. This was an unexpected chance – provided she could work out how to manipulate them with her hands still fastened behind her back!

The snapping of a few dead twigs signalled the return of Angèle and put an end to her preliminary attempts.

Do nothing, don't move, stay lying down in a faint.

It was an automatic response as might be made by a teenager used to watching television serials. But what else could she do? Patricia needed at all costs not to be separated from the precious implement she now had to hand. So, don't give the mixed-race woman any reason to make her leave the vehicle.

Angèle sat herself behind the wheel and closed the door carefully so as not to make a sound.

There must be gendarmes around, and not very far away. She wouldn't take the risk of getting her out of the van.

"Would you like a sandwich and some water?"

The question took the prisoner by surprise. Since she was gagged, she couldn't answer in any case. And if the gag was taken off, she'd be able to call for help!

"Don't pretend to be asleep, that's an old trick and it's worn out by now. And don't go getting any ideas either, the windows are fastened and the childproof lock is activated."

"Mmmm."

"I advise you not to try anything, you haven't got the build for it. That kick I gave you is nothing to what you might get now. Understood?"

"Mmmm."

"I'll take that as a yes. Sit up behind the passenger seat."

After a few efforts, Patricia managed to get herself into position. Angèle immediately slid the front seat back to wedge in her knees, then made it recline to its maximum extent to do the same to her chest.

"Now, slowly, I'm going to free one of your hands and take off your gag. If you call out, I'll put you back to sleep in my own special way!"

A few minutes later, the young gendarme's left wrist was handcuffed to one of the headrest mountings and she was able to drink thirstily from the half-bottle of water she'd been given. Any attempt at escape was impossible while her captor remained where she was.

Meanwhile, the young woman was finalising her plan. The gendarmes guarding the site were too far away to hear the sound of the engine when she started it up. Once she'd got back onto the track, she could switch it off and coast down the slope as far as the gateway into the area behind the chateau. The gendarmes hadn't bothered to close the wooden gate that Charles and his accomplice had managed to open and, placed where they were, the two who were now on duty wouldn't be able to see anything.

All she had to do after that was to neutralise the next team when they arrived, and then take their car. If she got a move on, the transfer of the loot shouldn't take more than five minutes and there would then be a good two hours before the next relief car could sound the alert. Sufficient time to go to ground – particularly as she would have access to the gendarmes' radio frequencies!

CHAPTER 40

Georges was in his office, convinced he wouldn't be able to extract anything worthwhile from the three detainees for the time being. He decided instead to go through all the details that he and his team hadn't yet had time to take into account. The two houses used by Charles hadn't been selected at random, but none of the four gangsters could have had previous knowledge of them in that detail. There must therefore be another, local, accomplice involved. But who?

Gendron was meanwhile mulling over the few pieces of information he'd managed to get out of Cédric Lantois about his escape with Angèle.

Something there didn't seem right, but what? How could he use these meagre details with no apparent link between them to get back on Patricia's trail?

The torturer, tricked by his lover, had been the first to leave the chateau grounds. The mobile phone she'd given him was intended to lead the gendarmes to him. And the idiot didn't even know which direction she'd taken, when the vehicles had been following one another. But the road… He paused, not believing what he was thinking. Could it be possible?

It was impossible. Nobody would attempt a bluff like that. And yet, if she had….

He wondered whether to alert the others, then decided it would just make him look stupid. But failing to check out this possibility could well seal Patricia's fate.

His heart skipped a beat as he sprang up from his seat and ran to get the pool car, picking up his phone to let the Lieutenant know.

Line busy. He'd call him later. Anyway, the two lads on duty were there.

He set off at enormous speed, activated the blues and siren despite the lateness of the hour and the absence of traffic, and only switched them off after he'd crossed the Vienne. His face was lined with worry.

* * *

Angèle emerged cautiously from the van, now parked at the entrance to the courtyard, and she spent some time studying her surroundings. Pale moonlight was causing endless shadows to be cast from every prominent feature and provided a frame for all the recesses along the side of the chateau, while the silhouette of the trees was projected like a Chinese shadow play. A light breeze played over this strange setting, stirring the treetops. Seeing there was a pool of darkness at the foot of the retaining wall, the young woman slipped into it and made her way over to the pigeon loft on the other side of the courtyard. She knew that next to it was a door she'd noticed the previous day which gave access to an external kitchen garden and, thirty metres beyond that, the wall bordering the chateau driveway would keep her out of sight of the Gendarmerie car. She could hide behind it and patiently await the arrival of the relief vehicle.

Left on her own in the van, Patricia had managed to lift up the bolt cutters with her feet and wedge one of the handles between the door and the rear seat. It was an awkward and unstable arrangement. She now had to move the other handle and turn around to be able to place the chain of the handcuffs between the jaws. Half lying on the seat, she used her feet and part of her shin to prevent the cutters from falling over, then moved her other foot as far as she could. It wasn't enough. She raised her hips to get nearer, pushing with the upper part of her shoulders and twisting her knee and ankles round to open the jaws sufficiently. She could barely get any purchase on the cutters, but at last they yielded and rewarded the young woman for her efforts, to her great relief.

Now came the delicate part: placing the second handle on the floor of the vehicle without letting it fall, and turning round to slip the chain down to the right spot. After that, she had to push her legs backwards and make the handles close again to release her from her fetters. Leaving aside the contortions needed for the manoeuvre, she wasn't sure she could exert enough force to make it work when she was like this.

Her first attempt failed. She pushed the cutters at an angle, and they wobbled. She just managed to keep them from falling over with the lower part of her back and succeeded in putting them back in place. She was now sweating copiously, partly because of her efforts and partly because she was afraid she might be surprised by her captor.

At her second attempt, the jaws merely slid along the handcuff chain. Patricia swore in anger as she felt the tool swaying about, but she made a desperate lunge with her left foot and held it in place just in time. The violence of this reflex action and the way she had to twist her body were beginning to exhaust her. She started to feel cramp coming on and knew she wouldn't be able to hold out for much longer. The handcuffs were biting cruelly into her wrists, making her cry out in pain.

Fortunately for her, she succeeded at the third attempt. Patricia was getting the hang of her rudimentary set-up and, making a supreme effort, she gave a sigh of satisfaction as she at last managed to separate her two hands. Her forearms were aching and she was drenched in sweat, but time was of the essence and she couldn't relax yet. She pulled out the gag and freed her legs in under a minute, slid over to the passenger seat, picked up a bottle of water and took off into the park without further ado. Going towards the chateau and the gendarmes presented too many risks: she'd seen Angèle make her way down there and didn't know where she'd got to by now. Calling out was a waste of time at this distance, and would only attract the attention of the treacherous young woman.

The first thing was to get right away from the van and the chateau, then conceal herself and think about what to do next.

* * *

Hidden by the kitchen garden wall, Angèle watched the relief car arrive. The new team took over in more or less the same way as the previous one had done. The young woman climbed over the wall and slipped behind a tree in the vehicle's blind spot. This was becoming dangerous. The men were sitting in their car with their seat belts unfastened, too far apart for her to take them both out in the same assault.

She needed to make one of them leave the vehicle so it would be unlocked. She was thinking over the two options she'd planned when the gendarme on the right placed his hand on the door catch and leaned over to his colleague to speak to him.

This was an unexpected opportunity. She readied herself to spring out from her hiding place, all her senses on alert and her muscles tensed.

"I'll take a look round and then I'll be straight back," said the man, half-opening the car door.

He had barely got out when she suddenly jumped on him, twisting his fingers. Disorientated, the gendarme stumbled over onto his side, unable to take in what was happening. She took advantage of this to pull him violently towards her, striking his head with her knee and laying him out cold on the ground. She entered the vehicle in the same movement and struck the second gendarme on the temple with her left fist just as he was reaching for his side arm.

He slumped senseless. She was like a Greek Fury as, out of breath, she checked that her two victims were unconscious, found their handcuffs and set to work fastening them. Not feeling strong enough to lift the men up, she contented herself with dragging them under the trees by the wall.

All that was left now was to drive the car into the courtyard and transfer the loot with Patricia's help. A Gendarmerie vehicle would enable her to look the part and slip through any security cordon the PSPG might have set up in the area, a precaution that they normally took. A general alert in two hours' time would be useless as by then she'd already be in a place of safety.

The young woman parked her new car next to the van and got out to unfasten her prisoner and put her to work. It was only then that she noticed the half-open door and rushed over to find that Patricia had fled the scene.

Angèle was undecided. Should she waste time going after her, or else take the risk that she could alert her colleagues in the security cordon?

She didn't spend very long thinking about it. Her plan was too detailed to allow a single minute to be wasted. At night, with a Gendarmerie car and Patricia's documents, she still had a chance of getting through.

Angèle starting transferring her booty.

She was carrying four gold bars, one in each hand and one under each arm, when a violent blow to her back hurled her forward and made her trip over. All her senses were aroused as she let go of her load, extending her fall into a kind of forward roll to end up in a standing position facing her opponent.

It was Patricia.

CHAPTER 41

Patricia had returned and was now trying to stop her!

Angèle laughed contemptuously. This pathetic young girl didn't have the wherewithal to take her on. She could make her shriek with pain without even striking a blow, just by knocking against the cuffs that were still round her hands and feet, especially as her wrists were already inflamed by the efforts she'd made to free herself.

"So, you've come back! You should have run away while you still could."

"After what you did? What you did to me?"

Patricia was cautiously holding a length of wood that she'd found in one of the garages a few moments earlier, and she kept her distance from her adversary. All her senses were on alert and her mind was as ready for action as her muscles, concentrating on the basics: don't leave yourself open, let your opponent make the moves, then counter them. She had a confused notion that time was running out for Angèle and she would soon have to react in some way.

"I needed you," said her adversary. "And I would have left you alone, and alive. I did after all rescue you from the clutches of those two bastards. They wouldn't have given you any chance at all."

She was now just two metres away from her. Patricia expected she would jump at any moment.

"Help me, or else run away, and nothing will happen to you," she repeated. "If not, you're going to get hurt. Badly hurt."

"No way."

Angèle had been waiting for that moment of distraction when her adversary, almost within reach, would start talking and lose some of her wariness. She threw herself at the gendarme's legs and knocked her over, avoiding the length of wood that came whirling towards her. Although she'd been ready for action, Patricia wasn't able to get out of the way quickly enough. She fell on her side, immediately freed herself with a few violent kicks and stood up, still holding her improvised cudgel.

The two women confronted each other once more. The pale moonlight revealed the anger on the face of Angèle. She hurled herself forward, not giving her opponent the time to raise her wooden weapon. She seized her by the two wrists, violently twisting the handcuffs and at the same time raking her right foot across her opponent's legs. Patricia screamed with pain, dropped her weapon and collapsed in a heap. Angèle immediately leapt on her, immobilising her arms and legs. Her nose and a bleeding lip showed that Patricia's kicks had struck home, but it was an unequal struggle from then on. Beside herself with rage, Angèle looked down at her victim lying on the ground. There was a large stone next to her head.

"You're making me lose time," she screamed. "I'll smash your head in! Is that what you wanted? Is that what you came for?"

She could no longer contain herself. Full of menace, she swiftly snatched up the stone, ready to bring it down on her prisoner's head. As she raised her arm to strike, it was suddenly dragged backwards, making her squeal with pain. The sharp and unexpected twisting of her shoulders meant she had to swivel backwards to free herself. She had been trained how to react to such attacks and rolled onto her back in a pure reflex action before springing at the attacker who had just caught her by surprise.

Gendron parried her blow with his left arm. Although he was trained in judo combat, he was taken aback by this woman's reaction and agility – an agility that he himself had lost a good few years previously. Angèle was on her feet again, facing him and ready to bring him down despite his imposing size. Standing in a defensive posture, she give a sudden kick with her left foot towards the big man's pelvis. He partly avoided it by stepping backwards, but the force of the blow made him grimace. Angèle was immediately ready to continue the action and her right foot lashed out with surprising rapidity and violence at her new antagonist's knee. However, the reflexes of Gendron's youth were now coming back to him and he managed to block the kick, using its force to twist her foot as he caught it, making the young woman topple over. He fell on her immediately to immobilise her on the ground. Blows were exchanged for the next few minutes, during which time Angèle gradually became exhausted and it was only her raging anger that kept her going. Once Patricia had regained her strength and stood up, it was definitely game over for Charles' last accomplice.

"It seems I got here just in time," Gendron said calmly. "Put my cuffs on her."

CHAPTER 42

SUNDAY

Pushing open the door to his office, Georges was immediately struck by the light flooding into it. The windows had been abandoned long ago to the vagaries of the weather and indifferent cleaning, but they couldn't prevent the summer sun from penetrating into the furthest corners of the room. It was a radiant sun, harbinger of a fine day and the end of a week of doubts and tensions. He was thinking about the twins and his wife who'd just called – Jeanne, now relaxed, proudly telling him that she'd finished filling all the packing cases and boxes. Or at least those she'd been unwilling to entrust to the removal men, she'd carefully added. He hadn't sought to enquire further, afraid of asking a question she might perhaps have already answered a few days earlier, afraid of spoiling through his own clumsiness a conversation that had been much less tense than those of the previous few days. All the same, while he hadn't detected any sign of reproachfulness or unspoken blame in his wife's manner, Georges had hung up with a troubled heart and a sharp sense of separation, of his lack of availability and of being prevented from taking part in the everyday life of his little family. The laughter of the twins, happy to be able to speak to their Daddy, had also affected him.

He came to a halt in front of the window and looked out at the square, which was already being invaded by cars. He watched in amusement as they appeared to wander around cautiously like mechanical beasts looking for a lair or some unoccupied shelter. He turned away at last and picked up the case file he'd prepared a few hours earlier. The night had been so eventful and so full of new information that he needed to put his ideas into some sort of order, especially in view of the latest intelligence from his colleagues in Melun.

He walked into the briefing room some twenty minutes later. By the end of the morning, the whole of the brigade had arrived: they were now welded together more strongly than ever as a team. Patricia was looking anxious. She was standing next to Gendron, solid as a rock; he had the delighted grin of a man who'd just discovered that his female team mate was alive and well. Or perhaps he was simply pleased to have regained the sensations of his sporting youth that he'd thought he'd lost for ever.

"I've received information this morning from the Section de Recherches in Orleans and our colleagues in Melun, which has brought our investigation to an end," Georges began. "But before going into detail, I'd like to thank Gendron and congratulate him on his intuition. It certainly saved Patricia's life and prevented Angèle Courtois and her accomplices from getting away."

"Her accomplices were already in custody," commented one of the team.

"Only some of them," the Lieutenant continued. "One of the big fish could have slipped through the net – namely, Laure Pellegrin, the Director of Archives."

"So the archivist and his boss were in cahoots?"

Georges remained silent for a few seconds, smiling at the surprised look on the faces of those who had not yet been brought up to date with the latest twists in this affair. Then he went on:

"Seven or eight months ago, our archivist discovers a document concerning the robbery in June 1940: this provides some details, such as the names of the thieves and of the German officers who recovered the loot. Being conscientious, he goes to his Director, who is more interested in her career prospects than this ancient file. However, she eventually reads it and then summons her subordinate to give him a dressing down. In reality, she realises what it could lead to and instigates other enquiries, from which she learns that the stolen goods must still be somewhere in Chinon – that was from the 1945 document found in Aupetit's house. Laure Pellegrin sees this as a tempting opportunity and takes it to the director of a security firm, chosen by herself, whom she rates very highly – Angèle. Angèle manages to convince her that she can set up an operation to get the last two survivors to talk. She offers to find a gang to do it, to put it in place and to take control of it."

"So Angèle, Aupetit and his boss make the arrangements for the job and the three criminals carry it out?"

"That's more or less it. Laure Pellegrin takes part in what she believes to be a straightforward theft, but of an amount large enough to justify the risks involved. She finances the operation by signing false invoices for fictitious extensions to the security firm's contract. But the two women's main concern is to conceal Angèle's role from her accomplices so she can keep an eye on them and then double-cross them after the job has been carried out successfully. Unluckily for them, things start to go wrong. Charles feels that insufficient progress is being made for his liking and believes the two witnesses are hiding facts from him. He eventually takes things too far with the murders of the Doyen and of Laurent. He doesn't find out very much else and has to go after Derouchy's son, who he thinks might have some rather more specific information obtained from his father."

"Which was in fact the case," Gendron interposed.

"Exactly so. Putting the new information with all the rest, Charles identifies the location as the Chateau de la Vauguyon, as we did too later on. But the two murders are making this operation increasingly dangerous for Angèle, who now needs an ally to help her get out of the hornet's nest she's been thrust into because of Charles' impatience. That ally will be Cédric Lantois, as she's already noticed his weakness and his infatuation for her. From then on, her aim will be to use Lantois to double-cross the other two and then set him up as bait for the Gendarmerie. An excellent way for her to stay in the background and then get away with the goods. You know all the rest and, if it hadn't been for the interventions of Patricia and subsequently of Gendron, her plan would have succeeded."

"And so we have three people standing to benefit from the operation – Angèle, Laure Pellegrin and her archivist – and three to be sacrificed by them: Charles, Cédric and Karl?"

"That was their intention, if everything had gone to plan. Except, that is, for Aupetit: he was also included on the list of sacrificial lambs. And in any case, he didn't have a clue as to what was going on: Angèle's accomplice had impersonated him when they recruited the gang.

"I can see," Patricia ventured, "that Laure Pellegrin knew we'd be all over the wretched archivist – he was the one who discovered the dossier that started everything off, and he went to the same sports centre as Charles did. So she gave us a big bundle of clues to put us off the scent."

"And she added to them when she spoke to me about Aupetit's supposed premature retirement," Georges finished off.

"If he really had been innocent, he'd have told you everything the first time you went over there."

"The man has no self-confidence, and he'd become demotivated at work. He preferred to remain silent rather than talk about the file and create new problems for himself. Laure Pellegrin was playing a game when she took on a lawyer to defend him: she made him think she was supporting him. From then on, he wouldn't say anything that might place her in a compromising position. At least, up until the point where I was able to explain matters to our colleagues in Melun. Angèle's accomplice had planted that 1945 document in his house to incriminate him – after he'd already been arrested, by the way, which was a mistake."

"I see… And there's something else. Charles was a newcomer to the town, so I don't understand how he was able to find those two houses which let him get away from us that first time."

"For quite a while, I thought that somebody local must be helping him. In fact, it's because of that very issue that we were finally able to put everything together. During the course of my enquiries, I discovered that the two properties belonged to a very old lady living in a retirement home. Power of attorney was held by her niece… Laure Pellegrin. She'd stayed there many times as a child and knew all the secrets."

He let silence descend once more. A silence that was quickly broken by a question that everyone present was thinking without daring to say it outright:

"And where does Patricia stand in all this?"

Before responding, Georges stared for some time at Gendron, then at his young colleague. His brow was furrowed as he replied:

"Patricia was on leave. She was passing Charles' house when she noticed two vehicles, one of which looked like a van that had been stolen the previous day in Saumur. Our colleague is still young. Through inexperience, she made the mistake of stopping to identify it. I think the lesson has been learned. Mistakes often prove more instructive than successes."

The young woman simply nodded her head in agreement. Her reconciliation with Paul, the support of her teammates, the events she had lived through, all conspired to burst the bubble of anguish that had been surrounding her. Her eyes were running with tears, then she burst out sobbing.

"Thank you, everyone, for your support. You're my friends, my family," she stammered, as Gendron tried to comfort her.

She was caught between tears and laughter in a strange emotional state of mind where overflowing joy and optimism were mingled with terror as she looked back on the events that had happened so recently.

EPILOGUE

Georges rested his hand on the handle of the half-open door as he stared at the less attractive part of his job lying on his desk: an impressive heap of files, reports and forms which he had to re-read and authorise. He gave a thin-lipped smile as he looked at them. Doing one's job, reacting in the thick of the action, making instant decisions in sometimes tricky situations – all this was part and parcel of the life of a detective. As was getting lost following up false trails. Bringing a case to a successful conclusion was wonderful compensation, and gave a sense of satisfaction in having carried out one's duty.

But afterwards…

Afterwards, unfortunately, came the tedious paperwork and the questions, the points raised by lawyers and judges, the finicky arguments made by those who experienced events only after they were over, in the calm and comfort of their office. Those who read reports as one would a novel, revisiting the past and making value judgements on decisions taken in the heat of the moment, when they already knew the end of the story and all its details.

Reports. Which were nevertheless the only way to record everything and limit the subsequent questioning… but which did no more than limit it.

He closed the door without going in and went instead to the office that Gendron shared with three of his colleagues. He found him in there alone, his countenance dazed in the face of all this paper, the usefulness of which he could not even guess at.

"Are you here by yourself? Has Patricia gone?"

"Yes." The big man was hesitant. "I sent her away to find something to make her feel better."

"Is she that bad?"

"What will make her feel better is being with Paul, her 'partner' as they say nowadays. That's what I think will be most beneficial to her."

"Excellent idea. I came to suggest we go for a beer and then have something to eat. Are you still on your own this weekend?"

"Yes, I'm with you. We could both do with a bit of fresh air and some sun. And thanks for what you did for Patricia – that was very good of you."

"Why? Did you have anything to add to what I said?"

They walked out in silence.

The square was bathed in sunlight, and Joan of Arc was still charging at an invisible enemy, fixedly pointing with her bronze sword as she had done for more than a hundred years. A few tourists braved the heat as they took photos next to her. English tourists. Georges stopped for a moment to look at them, amazed at their phlegmatic response to someone who had tried to throw them out of

France. Five centuries had passed since then, transforming a prolonged tragedy into a mere historical anecdote.

He cast a glance over the area, admiring the plane trees along the banks of the river Vienne. Before him stood the fortress, partly in ruins but still proud of its rich past, and of its future. And then there was the hillside, crowning the town with a series of magnificent slate-roofed dwellings built of tuffeau that stretched as far the chapel of Saint Radegonde, wife of Clotaire, who had taken refuge here with Saint Jean of Chinon.

He stopped suddenly, frowning.

"What's that monument? Is this Rio?"

"That's the statue of the Sacré-Coeur de Chinon", said a man passing by. "It does look rather like the one in Rio but it hasn't got the same stance, and the fold of the robe is different."

The man had a round, friendly face surmounted with white hair and he looked with some amusement at the Lieutenant's astonished expression.

"It was erected at the beginning of the war to protect the town and its inhabitants", he went on, "and it was dedicated during the Occupation, in 1942."

"That's odd, I've never noticed it before."

"You can't see it properly from very many places – it's not as high up as the one in Rio. Look at the position of the head. The German authorities wanted it like that, apparently. There was a saying that most people have now forgotten, which goes:

> 'In Rio, the Corcovado welcomes you.
>
> In Paris, it blesses you.
>
> In Chinon, it shows a way for you'.

"A nice story. The way to where?"

"The Chateau de la Vauguyon."

SOME DETAILS ABOUT THE EVENTS AND PLACES IN THIS BOOK

1939-1940

The decision to transfer the Ministry of Finance to Chinon in the event of the outbreak of war had been taken early on, probably at the end of 1938. Various public and private buildings had been requisitioned in the town and the surrounding area. The National Lottery, which came under the Ministry, had been installed in the Château de Coudray-Montpensier a few kilometres away. Several places in the locality were used as storage sites, probably for archives, but not exclusively. The decision to leave Chinon and to evacuate all the ministries from southern Touraine was taken on the evening of 13th June 1940 and ministers were informed of this during the night of 13th - 14th. The intended destination was no longer Quimper as originally planned but Bordeaux, because of the German advances. The situation must have caused an enormous upheaval, on which I have relied to write this fiction.

On the other hand, the Bank of France was still a private institution at this period. It held the 2,200 tons of the country's gold reserves (and also those of Belgium, which had made over its own reserves.) All of this was successfully evacuated to our colonies and to the United States before the Germans arrived. It was the second-largest gold reserve in the world after that of the USA.

The Statue Of The Sacré-Coeur Of Chinon

The construction of the statue was proposed in 1939 by arch-priest Vivien, curé of the church of Saint-Etienne, to protect the town and its inhabitants. It was erected after the transfer of the Ministry of Finance to Chinon. Work was begun in September 1940 and seems to have been completed in June 1941, but the dedication ceremony did not take place until 28th March 1943. Several pilgrimages took place after the end of the war, but without great success. The foot of the statue is surrounded by private land holdings and is virtually inaccessible.

The Chateau de la Vauguyon

My description of this chateau, or at least of its exterior, is almost exactly in accordance with reality. The pigeon loft, the deer park, the gates and the underground passages do all actually exist, as does the part of the wall and adjoining caves that has collapsed. My thanks to my friend Célian, the real owner, for having allowed me to find out about these. I hope he will forgive me for having him supplanted by a character who bears little resemblance to him, and for letting criminals take over his home.

The tunnel linking the two houses

I have based this on the cellar under my own house, which

dates from 1830, probably replacing an earlier construction. The cellar is in a sort of underground passage built of dressed stone and walled off at one end because of building works that took place in 1950. At the other end, there is stonework at the boundary with the neighbouring property. The axis of this passage, now a cellar, points towards the fortress some two or three hundred metres away. Tunnels of this kind were intended to facilitate the escape of the inhabitants of a castle in the event of some serious situation occurring.

Saint Radegonde and Saint Jean of Chinon

Local legend says that this troglodytic chapel was the refuge of Radegonde, the fugitive queen of Clotaire I, son of Clovis. It seems likely that she had simply presented herself to a hermit who lived there, the future Saint Jean of Chinon, whose feast day is 27th June. She then left for Saix in the Maine-et-Loire, where she founded an oratory and a hospice.

THANKS

My most sincere thanks are due to all those who, through their advice and suggestions, have helped me to give substance and credibility to this novel. I have in mind in particular the advice of Chef d'Escadron Dufour, of Captain Dorlin and of François Jousset, as well as Monsieur Duthu, the real-life owner of the Château de la Vauguyon. Also, of course, to my proof-readers and advisers Clarisse Poisson, Isabelle Jacquot, Annick Jourdan and Nathalie Vignal. Thanks also to Tamara Choy-Smith and Nicholas Plant for their advice.

And, last but not least, special thanks to my brilliant translator Michael Bayliss, who is a regular visitor to the Château de La Vauguyon and is well acquainted with the Loire Valley, including all the places and institutions described in this book.